Praise for the novels of

CAROLYN DAVIDSON

"Carolyn Davidson creates such vivid images, you'd think she was using paints instead of words."
—Bestselling author Pamela Morsi

"Davidson wonderfully captures gentleness in the midst of heart-wrenching challenges."
—*Publishers Weekly* on *Haven*

"Readers are in for a treat."
—*Romantic Times BOOKreviews* on *The Bride*

"For romance centering on the joys and sorrows of married life, readers can't do much better than Davidson....This is a sweet and sensitive novel that fulfills an evening's dreams."
—*Romantic Times BOOKreviews* on *Nightsong*

"[An] unflinching inquiry into the serious issues of the day."
—*Booklist* on *Redemption*

"Davidson's touching western romance delivers what readers expect from a writer who strives to understand the deepest feeling and dreams of our hearts."
—*Romantic Times BOOKreviews* on *Haven*

Also available from
CAROLYN DAVIDSON
and HQN Books

The Bride
Nightsong
Haven
Redemption

Other works include:

Harlequin Historical

*Edgewood, Texas
**Montana Mavericks
†Colorado Confidential

CAROLYN DAVIDSON

Eden

HQN™

Recycling programs
for this product may
not exist in your area.

ISBN-13: 978-0-373-77362-6
ISBN-10:   0-373-77362-5

EDEN

Copyright © 2009 by Carolyn Davidson

Dear Reader,

I love to write of days long ago when the world as we know it was a perfect place to live, filled with men and women of good character, children who thrived and flourished within the arms of family and friends, and homes where love and affection was widely disbursed among those who were fortunate enough to live there. Alas, there were also places, perhaps not too far from those happy families, where children were abused and sometimes brutalized, not given the opportunities to thrive as was their right.

Katie was such a child, and her story lived in my mind and heart for months before I sat down to write it. It made me look around me, perhaps seeking out children in my vicinity who face similar problems. For they are out there, and they are victims, as was Katie. My heroine was fortunate to find a man who would understand her and love her enough to face her fears with her. And so I offer you Eden, a place designated for love and happiness, with two lovers who deserve only the best that love can offer.

Carolyn Davidson

This story is dedicated to those victims of abuse by an adult in their lives. Such actions still remain as a painful memory in these men and women. Child abuse is not a thing of modern times, but has existed for centuries in our world. Today it is still an issue that must be faced and obliterated. May each of you find joy, as did Katie in my story.

And most of all, this book is dedicated, as is everything I accomplish, to the man in my life, Mr. Ed, who loves me.

Eden

CHAPTER ONE

Eden, The Dakota Territory
February, 1890

SURELY HER OWN MOTHER had not lived such a life.
Through the window of the Dogleg Saloon, Katie
watched the women who roamed the smoke-filled area,
seeking out men upon which to try their skills. Hair
upswept, makeup all too obvious and dresses too gaudy
to be believed all added to their allure.

Or so they apparently believed. "How sad." The
words were but a whisper as the young woman watched
the parade of females conduct their pursuit of the
cowhands who worked on outlying ranches and farms
and assorted married men from the town of Eden, in the
Dakota Territory. That she could ever live in such a
manner was something she would never have considered during the days of summer, when the warm
weather protected her slender body from the cold
winds. When she did not bear the shame of a mother
who had once worked in this place. Or so she'd been

told by the couple who'd raised her, reviling her with a tale of a woman gone bad, bearing an illegitimate child.

She'd found that the parents she'd thought were her own, were but unkind strangers who had taken her into their home as an act of charity. And if what they had done in the name of charity were known among the townspeople, they might not be able to hold up their heads in Eden.

But a young girl would not be believed when her word was placed next to an upstanding pair who posed as ideal parents of a girl who had turned out badly. And Katie was that girl, if her foster parents were to be believed.

In that same home dwelt a second child, a younger female, the abandoned daughter of a relative of Agnes Schrader, who had been given the privilege of schooling at the town's one-room schoolhouse. But Katie was not so fortunate, for with a background so filled with disgrace and shame, she wasn't considered worth the trouble to educate.

She had been whipped and treated as a slave for twelve years, was now approaching her eighteenth birthday, yet had done the work of a woman while still a child. Taking her courage in both hands, she'd left the farm where she'd lived in servitude and set out to find shelter. Shelter for a weary body and sanctuary for a mind confused by the perils life had dealt her. Most of them derived from the man who had become a threat to her on another level over the past weeks, for Jacob

Schrader had attempted to crawl beneath her quilt on three occasions. She feared him more than she had thought possible.

Tonight, his words of sly entreaty had brought chills to her flesh, his looks of dark anger and the flashes of masculine power he'd brought to bear upon her were enough to find her running for her very life. The thought of his hands on her body was enough to force her to flee.

She'd walked for three miles, shivering in the ragged clothing she wore, wrapped in a shawl she'd taken without permission from a hook by the back door of the farmhouse, desperate for a safe place in which to hide. Any rude shelter would do, so long as it provided surcease from the north winds that promised snow, sweeping across the plains of Canada down to the fields of the Dakota Territory.

Summer had been bad enough, with long days spent in the fields, evenings in the farmhouse, where her work was never done. Now, in February, things were changed, the sun an infrequent visitor to the sky, replaced by snow clouds that threatened to spill their weight upon the surrounding countryside. The oncoming weather would be her worst enemy, unless she included that house she had just left.

She peered again into the saloon, its smoke-filled interior teeming with men seeking enjoyment, many of them half-drunk, the other half well on their way to that state. The smoke from their cigars and hand-rolled cigarettes rose to the ceiling and formed a haze guaranteed to make her cough and choke, should she linger long in its presence.

But, it seemed she might have no choice, for the saloon might indeed be the only haven available to a young woman without a job, or a place to live. Surely she could bring herself to serve drinks to men, smile at them and return their remarks. Even dance with one or two if the necessity arose, if she could but learn to sway to the music as did the other females in this place, curving their bodies closely to the men who held them.

For even now, two of the women inside the place were swaying to the raucous sounds of the piano, their chosen partners holding them close, moving between the tables in a parody of a dance. It didn't hold a candle to the square dancing she'd seen on one never-to-be-forgotten evening, when she'd slipped away and observed couples dancing at the Grange Hall in Mason's Creek, just two miles from the Schrader farm.

But then, those dances were attended by a different breed of men and women, and the dancing was a far cry from the suggestive gyrations that were taking place in the Dogleg Saloon this night.

The swinging door was pushed open and a drunken cowhand staggered out, his hat cockeyed upon his head, his shirttail free of his trousers, and bearing a disreputable appearance. His bleary eyes scanned the wooden sidewalk and he staggered to where an upright post provided a spot for him to halt, leaning his weight against it as he looked over the assortment of horses that lined the hitching rail.

Katie moved back a bit, into the shadows, lest he see her. But the motion of her feet apparently caught his eye for he lifted his head and turned his gaze in her direction.

"Well, looky here," he muttered, attempting to move from his leaning post, his body not cooperating with his aim, as he began to move toward her. "You lookin' for a man, sweetie?" His laugh was harsh, a raw sound that pierced her ears, and she turned from his reaching hands.

There was nowhere to go, for she was caught against the outer wall. As his dirty hand touched her arm, she stiffened, then spun in place and almost fell against the swinging door.

It gave way obligingly with her weight and she was inside the saloon. The door swung behind her, its weight nudging her farther into the room, and she cast a quick look around, seeking she knew not what. Perhaps a friendly face.

Of those there were a handful, most of them whiskered, several of them belonging to men who sat alone at tables meant for three or four. One rose, taking a step closer to her, his hands outstretched to touch her and she twitched to one side, lest his grimy hands leave their stain on her person.

"What's the matter, honey? Ain't I purty enough for you?" His drunken drawl brought a shudder of dread to her slender form, and she sidestepped away from him, only to brush against another man.

A long arm circled her waist and she was drawn close to another table. The man who held her sat on a chair, his hat tilted back, his head tipped upward as he took a survey of her form. His gaze rested for a long moment on the dark bruises apparent on her arms and face.

"You don't belong in here," he said, his words low and to the point. "Does your mother know you're out on the town?" His lips twisted, lifting one corner of his mouth, as if he were unused to smiling and this was his best attempt.

"My mother?" Katie shook her head, fear touching her with chilly tendrils that brought gooseflesh to her arms. The man was another sort entirely than the two she'd already encountered in the past few minutes; his features were more finely sculpted, his hand at her waist was clean, and he wore dark clothing, with a holster against his leg.

Yet Katie exerted her strength against him, fearful of his hand trespassing beyond the place it had chosen to rest. But he would not relax his hold and she looked down at him, her tongue dampening sudden dry lips as she whispered pleading words. "Don't touch me. Let me go…please."

As if her polite words amused him, his mouth lifted into a genuine smile, whether his amusement was for her benefit, or he was merely entertained by her helplessness she could not discern, for she could not release herself from his hand. And he knew it. Knew that his grip was solid and firm, that she was helpless to move away from him.

"Sit down. Here." He reached with his other hand, an awkward movement, and pulled another chair close to the one he occupied, and then pushed her onto its surface.

She blinked, aware that the attention of several other men had moved in her direction, and her head lowered quickly, not wanting to see their expressions as they evaluated the stranger in their midst. A mist appeared before her eyes and she fought back the tears that threatened to fall.

"Don't be afraid," her companion said quickly. "Lift your head and look at me. Nowhere else, just into my face."

Surprised by the direct order, schooled to obey, she did as he told her, swallowing the bile that threatened to spill from her throat. His eyes were dark, his features harsh, but not unkind, and she felt a flare of relief as his hand left her body to grasp the cold fingers that lay in her lap.

She was obviously terrified, and John felt a jolt of sympathy as he watched the girl before him. And then he spoke, his voice stern, his words direct. "Sit up straight and act as if you've recognized me. The rest of them will leave you alone if they think I'm an acquaintance of yours." He leaned back a bit in his chair, drawing her hand to his knee in a gesture he knew would send a message to the men watching. A message of familiarity, a gesture she was obviously accustomed to. She looked uncertain, as if she'd only just realized that she was the target of men's looks, those lustful glances that were now being cast in her direction.

"I didn't mean to come in here," she said quietly, in an attempt to explain her abrupt entrance to the saloon.

"I didn't think so. It's no place for a young girl," he agreed, reaching to scoot her chair closer to his own, loosening his grip on her hand to do so.

She retrieved her fingers and hugged them to her waist, meshing them with those of her other hand. "I'm not that young. I'm almost eighteen," she said, speaking the word with dignity.

"Almost eighteen." He smiled, his teeth white and even, and his face softening with the movement. "You're a child. You don't belong in a place like this. Where are your parents?"

She lifted her chin. "I don't know. I take care of myself. I don't need anyone else."

"Well, you've apparently taken a wrong turn tonight, honey," he said in a low whisper, leaning toward her a bit. "You're shivering and you look like you haven't had a good meal in a week. This is no place for you."

Her glance was angry. "It's warmer in here than out in front."

He smiled again, in admiration for her spirit. "Well,

there is that. But you'll find there's a price to pay for whatever warmth you find here."

"A price?" Katie wondered at his words. Surely they wouldn't charge her to sit in a chair and get warm, would they? And yet, from the corner of her eye, she saw the bartender giving her long looks of inquiry, as if wondering what her purpose was.

The man beside her spoke again in an undertone. "Do you need a bed for the night? They've got a whole hallway upstairs, lined with bedrooms. I'm sure there'd be any number of men willing to rent one for you, so long as you let them occupy it with you." The words rolled off his tongue and settled around her ears, burning them with the threat he suggested might be her lot.

"I couldn't sell myself, mister," she said quickly, for she had heard of such a thing. "I just need to get warm." And wasn't that the truth, for her body felt like a chunk of ice in the midst of the creek in midwinter. A long shiver ran the length of her spine, and she felt the first thawing of her fingers as they knit together at her waist.

He lifted his other hand, the one not occupied with the back of her chair and one of the scantily dressed *ladies* approached, smiling at him, glancing with pity at Katie.

"Sadie, bring us a glass of whiskey, with lots of water."

The woman laughed, sauntering to the bar. Then, within minutes, she reappeared with a glass containing a golden liquid and scooped up the coin the man offered in payment.

He picked it up and held it to his mouth, tasting the contents and frowning, then offered it to Katie. "Take a drink. It'll warm you up, honey."

She shook her head, unwilling to put the foul-smelling stuff in her mouth, and his jaw hardened and he leaned closer, offering the glass, holding it to her lips.

"Take a swallow. Don't argue with me or give me that high-toned look, honey. When it comes to booze, I know what a swallow of it will do for a gal like you. Your stomach could use a belt, and in a few minutes your system will lap it up and you'll generate a little heat."

"Please—" Katie turned to look him full in the face "—I don't want to throw up, and if I taste that, I think I will. My stomach is hurting already, and putting whiskey into it isn't going to help any."

His gaze narrowed on her trembling lips and he bent closer, his voice a low whisper. "Are you hungry, girl?"

She swallowed her pride and nodded, just once, but it seemed to be enough to answer his query to his satisfaction, for he shot her a look of understanding, picked up the glass and downed the contents with two swallows.

"Come on." He lifted her bodily from the chair and walked with her, his long arm circling her waist, to the back of the saloon, flicking a quick look at the bartender as they passed that stalwart gentleman. He opened a door that stood beneath the stairway, almost hidden in the gloom.

His hand on her back gave her no choice and she kept up with his long stride, almost skipping to keep up, fearful of the contact he forced upon her, yet thankful for the warmth of his body. Beyond the open door was a kitchen, and he ushered her over the threshold, closing the wooden portal behind them.

If the temperature had been close to freezing in the bar, it was nearer to the fires of Hades here in the kitchen, she decided, shivering at the blast of warm air that the big cookstove aimed in her direction. The woman who stood before it had opened the oven, and the heat from within made her back away from its intensity, but to Katie, it was a welcome shot of comfort and she did not evade it.

In fact, she took another step closer to the huge stove, warming the front of her body and shivering in reaction. The man next to her spoke, catching her attention and that of the woman who was dealing with the food atop the cooking range.

"Hey there, Molly. Anything left from supper? This little gal's hungry."

Why that should make Katie bristle so, she didn't know. Perhaps it was because the man acted as though she were a child to be fed. Or maybe because he looked at her from his greater height with a look of amusement, as though she were someone to be mocked.

"I'm not starving," Katie said defensively. "I can wait till tomorrow to eat."

"And where will you find breakfast?" the man asked, even as the woman he'd called Molly turned from the stove to shoot her a long assessing look.

"Land sakes, John Roper. Leave that little girl alone. Quit your pickin' at her."

With a swift step, she approached Katie, lifting a warm hand to touch her shoulder. "Come on over here, honey. That cowboy don't know which end is up. Just ignore him, why don't you. I've got a kettle of beans and spuds here that's probably gonna be food for the pigs by morning if I can't push it off on some hungry soul."

Katie caught the glimpse of tenderness the woman tried to hide, her words almost curt, but her eyes warm with another emotion entirely. It was enough to coax her from her stiff resistance, and she stepped closer to the stove, to where a kettle sat on the back burner, steam rising from its depths.

"I'd eat some beans and potatoes, ma'am," she said quietly. "I'm probably hungrier than the pigs, anyway." Her mouth twisted in a smile, and as if she had gained a friend, Molly grinned back, drawing Katie nearer with a quick touch on her hand. A touch Katie fought to accept, sensing that Molly meant her no harm.

"Sit yourself down, honey. I'll fetch a bowl and fix you something to warm your belly." And if the invitation was not couched in genteel terms, Katie found it didn't matter, for the look of kindness Molly wore more than made up for her blunt speech.

A chair appeared from beneath the edge of the table, and the man—hadn't Molly called him John?—stood to one side, offering her a seat. Katie took it with a nod and then thought twice about the condition of her hands.

"Ma'am? Could I bother you for a dab of soap and some water to wash my hands?" She looked toward the back of the kitchen where a sink held a pitcher pump and a large basin beneath it, and Molly nodded.

"Of course. Come on over here and I'll fix you up. I might have known a girl like you would need to tend to herself before she sat down to eat." The plump form bustled across the room, one rounded arm reaching for the pump handle. Ensuring that a gush of water poured into the basin, she reached beneath the sink for a container of soap.

"Here you go, honey. Not French-milled, but good old lye soap, like I use for the dishes." Molly looked quickly at the mottled flesh on Katie's arms and her eyes sought those of the man who watched. A barely imperceptible nod caught Katie's eye and she felt confusion overtake her.

Her voice quavered as she recognized that she was the object of an unspoken discussion. "That'll do just fine," she told Molly, thankful for the freely given offer. For the first time during the long hours of this evening, she began to breathe more easily, sensing a kindred soul in her vicinity. Not that the help of the man called John had gone unappreciated, but finding another woman who offered her a bit of sustenance was a bonus she had not looked for. And Katie was not one to look a gift horse in the mouth.

The steaming offering of green beans swimming in a thick broth laced with bits of ham and braced by the addition of three small potatoes was mouthwatering and she bent over it, inhaling the aroma as she picked up the fork Molly offered. Her mouth burned from the first bite, but she was so hungry she barely noticed, shifting the bit of potato from one side of her cheek to the other as it cooled.

"How about a glass of milk, girl?" Molly made the offer even as she poured the glass full from a pitcher in the icebox.

Katie looked up and met her gaze, basking in the friendly smile she was given as if it were her due. "Thank you, ma'am. I'll have to admit I'm a little hungry." And then proved her words by devouring the bowlful of food as if it might be removed from her presence at any time.

"Take your time there, girl. Molly won't rush you any," the man told her quietly.

She looked at the man named John now, a quiet figure who watched her from dark eyes and then darted a look at Molly as if asking for direction.

"Why don't you stay with me tonight?" Molly asked her, surprising her with the kind offer. "I've got a big bed upstairs and a spare nightgown you can use."

Katie shivered, huddling in the chair, aware that her trembling was from a source within herself, not a result of the temperature in the room, for the stove gave off a comforting heat she was only too aware of. But the relief of finding sanctuary in this place threatened to bring quick tears to her eyes, and though she had long since abandoned tears as a form of expression, she found now that they burned just behind her eyelids.

"Thank you, ma'am. I'd be pleased to take you up on your offer," she said quietly, scraping the bottom of the bowl and eating the last morsel. A fluffy biscuit appeared on a small plate beside her bowl and a container of butter was moved close to her glass of milk, accompanied by a table knife.

Such largesse was more than she had ever expected to find here, and Katie looked up at the woman and felt a tear fall from her eye, trailing slowly down her cheek and falling to her bodice.

"Come now, girl. Don't waste time on cryin'. Just eat up and we'll worry about everything else tomorrow." With a quick look at John, she gave orders swiftly. "It might be good if no one knew that the girl was here with me, John. I'll put her to bed and lock the door so she won't be disturbed. There's men in there—" she nodded at the saloon just beyond the kitchen door "—who'd be tickled to get their hands on her tonight, but I'll see to it she's safe and sound."

"I'd appreciate it, Molly. And I'll be back in the morning to settle with you, and take her off your hands."

Molly snorted. There was no other word for it, Katie decided, for the inelegant sound was a combination of laughter and disdain. "And what will you do with a bit of a girl like this, John Roper? You gonna put her in the bunkhouse out there at the ranch with those cowhands you work with?"

He shook his head, his mind working rapidly. "No, I'll put her in the cabin the boss gave me when he made me foreman of the ranch. He said it was for a married man, but he suspected I'd be taking on a wife before long, so he said I'd might as well move into it now. He's got four or five cabins for his married hands. There's room for this little gal in mine."

"And then what will you do with her?" Molly pushed the issue with a harsh look that asked his intentions. "You got marriage on your mind?"

He shook his head. "No, I'll just take care of her till she gets back on her feet. If the bruises I can see on her arms and her face are any indication of what she's wearing under that dress, I'll do a better job than whoever's been looking after her."

Molly nodded. "I wouldn't be surprised, but your boss is gonna be asking questions if you bring a woman there and move her in and she's not your wife."

John was silent for a moment and his gaze touched Katie with kindness. Then he spoke again and she knew that her future had been decided for her and she would not argue with the man, for he was far and away the best prospect for shelter she saw in her future.

"I need someone to keep things up for me, Molly. Let's call her my new housekeeper and cook. I'll bet she can do better on that cookstove than I can, and it'll mean I won't have to go to the big house for my meals if this little gal cooks for me." He shot Katie a long look. "Can you put a meal together, girl?"

She nodded quickly. "I've been cookin' and cleanin' for a lot of years. The folks at the place I lived wasn't much on keepin' stuff up to par, but I learned how to cook a long time ago. I can make biscuits and bread and fix a meal from most anything."

"You want a job working for me?" John asked bluntly. "Not much pay, but a place to hang your hat and a warm pallet in front of the stove at night, or else on my sofa. It's not very long, but you're not very tall, so it might work."

"What kind of an offer is that for a young woman?" Molly asked sharply. "This girl don't need to be in those sort of circumstances. She'll have the folks around here talking a mile a minute about her, and you, too, John."

"Sounds better to me than where she's been living. And I'll guarantee you I won't be leaving any bruises on her like those she's wearing tonight." As if that were the final word on the subject, he looked directly at Katie and asked the question that would offer her a choice as to what might lie in her future.

"You interested in a job, girl? No strings attached, just cooking and cleaning and keeping my clothes up to snuff."

Katie thought but a moment, measuring what little she knew about the man before her with the certainty of the peril that awaited her should she be returned to Jacob and Agnes Schrader. Her reply was quick, for she knew she was able to run again should this man not be as honest as he appeared.

"I'll work for you, mister. Just give me a place to sleep and a warm spot to roost during the day. I can cook and clean all right, and I don't need any money from you. Just food and a place to live."

CHAPTER TWO

"SOUNDS LIKE I'VE GOT a new housekeeper," John said to Molly, "if you'll keep her for the night. I'll come back in the morning to get her. I'll need to talk to Bill Stanley before I bring her out to his ranch, make sure he understands the circumstances. I won't make a move that will jeopardize my standing with him."

Molly cast him a measuring look and then as if she found his words to be all that was truth and honesty on his part, she nodded. "I'll keep her here tonight, safe in my bed, with my door locked. But you'd better be on the up and up, John Roper, or I'll skin you. Understand?"

John nodded, meeting her gaze. He'd not put it past the woman to do just as she threatened. Molly was as honest as the day was long, even given that she worked in the kitchen of a saloon, she was known as a woman to be respected. That he bore the same reputation was knowledge he prized, for his honor was not questioned by any who knew him.

The girl would be safe with him, for he had no need of a woman in his bed, his masculine instincts long since subdued by the memory of the woman who had forever left him with anger as his companion. The wife he'd buried six years ago had been unfaithful, her acts of immorality documented by the men who had received her favors. Then she'd left him to run off with another man, and the disease she'd gained from her acquaintance with him had brought her to an early grave.

He'd taken care of her needs during the days of her illness, hiring a widowed lady to nurse her, a woman who had lived in the same room with Sadie, tending her until the day she breathed her last. And then, with her burial, a solitary moment he'd shared with no other person but the local undertaker, he'd cut his ties and traveled from home. Two years of wandering had brought him to the north country, and here in the Dakota Territory, he'd found work and a place in which to bury his past.

No, an attachment to any women was the last thing he wanted, and only the basic goodness of his upbringing had prompted him to offer this fragile child a place to live. His mama would roll over in her grave if she thought that a son of hers would turn his back on someone in need.

John Roper was known as an honest man, a good man with a horse and handy with a gun. There was little about him that could be considered soft, for he stood tall, broad-shouldered and yet lean. With dark hair and eyes, he knew he presented a picture of masculinity that appealed to women, and yet he felt little need of them, only an occasional visit to a widow who had been more than welcoming when he deigned to visit her.

So now he settled his hat on his head and made ready to take his leave from the kitchen where Molly reigned, cook and general overseer of the women who lived and worked under the roof of Tom Loftin's saloon. A woman who watched him now with eyes that questioned his motives.

"You'll be back in the morning? And you'll guarantee this girl a safe place to live?"

"That's what I said, Molly. You'd ought to know enough about me to know that I don't tell lies or make promises I can't keep. I've been around these parts for a while, and you won't find anybody to point a finger at me."

She shrugged. "You're right there, John. And it don't look to me like this child has much choice. Not for now anyway."

His gaze scanned Katie's face once more and his words were kindly. "Do I need to know anything more about you, Katie? Is there anything that would stand in the way of you working for me. I don't even know where you're from, now that I think about it. I'm not about to do anything illegal here, so if there's anybody with any ties on you, speak up."

"I can tell you where she's from," Molly said. "I knew when I saw her that she was familiar, and after watching her for a few minutes, I figured it out. She's been livin' at the Schrader place outside of town for a dozen years or so. Ain't that right, girl?"

Katie nodded, her eyes wide as Molly spoke words that amazed her. How the woman knew anything about her was some sort of miracle, she thought, and she waited silently to hear more.

"She looks like her mama," Molly said. And Katie closed her eyes, her mind turning back to the days before she had gone to live with the Schraders. In just such a kitchen as this she had eaten meals and spoken with women around a table such as this one.

"Have I been here before?" she asked, her voice soft, her heart pounding in a rhythm that threatened to choke her.

"Just think about it a minute and you'll remember. You'll know you have, girl," Molly said. "You're old enough to remember the days when you lived upstairs with your mama."

Her mind flooded with almost-forgotten thoughts, Katie sat at the table, stunned by the words Molly spoke. "I was a little girl, wasn't I? Surely not more than five or six. But I remember you, I think." And the vision of a younger Molly filled her mind, a kindly woman who had fed her and held her in her ample lap.

"Why would she have lived here?" John asked, his tone dubious, his look skeptical. "And why was she sent to live elsewhere?"

"This was no place for a young'un, and when her mama died, the boss looked for a couple to take her and give her a home." Molly was silent a moment and her eyes touched Katie's face, perhaps noting the swelling on one cheek, the bruise that bloomed in purple splendor on her jaw. "It looks to me like he chose the wrong place for a child."

The door leading into the saloon opened and the bartender stood in the entry. "What's goin' on back here, Molly? John? What's this gal doing here? Is she lookin' for a job? We don't take on kids, Molly and well you know it."

"She's not lookin' for a job, Tom. Just a place to sleep for the night, and I've already offered the other half of my bed. She's just hungry and John brought her back for a meal."

The man, Tom, looked at Katie with awareness dawning in his eyes. "Who is she?" His tone was strident, his words harsh.

"Just who do you think she is?" Molly asked, her chin tilted up as if she offered it as a target. "You know damn well who she is. One look at that face oughta tell you."

"What's she doing here?" Tom's face reddened, his eyes sparking fire as he stepped into the kitchen and closed the door behind himself. "She don't belong here."

"I already told you," Molly said. "She was hungry and John brought her in for a meal."

"You know what I mean," Tom said harshly. "She don't belong here," he repeated, more sternly this time. "Where's your folks, girl?"

"I don't have any folks," Katie told him staunchly.

"I lived with the Schraders outside of town for a lot of years, but they're not my folks."

"Well, they're all the folks you've got," Tom said, stalking across the kitchen, his eyes never leaving Katie's bruised face. "How'd you get here?"

"I walked. I didn't intend to come in here, but a man frightened me out in front and I got pushed through the door into the saloon and this gentleman offered me a chair."

The gentleman in question shot a grin at Tom. "She looked hungry and frightened, and you know what a *gentleman* I am, don't you, Tom?"

"You're a cowhand, is what you are, John. And what are you plannin' to do with a young girl like this?"

"Maybe you'd better sit down while I tell you about that," Molly said with a look of warning. "You'd might as well know, Tom."

"All right. I'm sitting." Tom pulled out a chair and sat in it, his eyes never leaving the girl across the table from him. "Now tell me what's going on."

"This little gal is gonna go to work for John Roper tomorrow. John here said he's got a cabin out at the Bar-S ranch. Bill Stanley gave it to him as part of his wages out there. So he's gonna take Katie home with him tomorrow morning and make her his cook and housekeeper."

"Katie? Are you sure this is what you want to do?" Tom examined her minutely, her face and slender form, the rough, tattered homespun of her dress, the dark hair that hung down her back in a ragged braid. And then he turned to John with a shake of his head and words that growled with anger. "She don't look old enough to know much about keeping house, John. You sure you know what you're doin'?"

"No." John laughed softly. "I probably don't, but I'm gonna do it anyway. I can't see sending her back to where she came from, Tom. It don't look like the folks who were responsible for her have taken very good care of their obligation, does it?"

"No, I can't say that it does," Tom agreed, his eyes dark. And then he eyed John again. "What will Bill Stanley say when you bring her home with you and put her in your cabin? Won't he wonder—"

"Maybe," John said quickly, before Tom could finish his query. "But I'll explain things to him. There won't be a problem."

Katie felt her head swimming, her attention splintered between the three people who seemed to be settling her future for her, her eyelids drooping as the heat of the cookstove penetrated her clothing and the food she had eaten weighed heavy in her stomach. She drank the last of her milk and set the glass down on the table.

"Could I go to bed now, ma'am?" she asked Molly quietly. "I'm pretty tired."

"I'll take her up," Molly said, motioning toward the open staircase that led upward to the rooms overhead. "I'll see you in the morning, John. Unless you change your mind."

He shook his head, lifting Katie from her chair, his eyes widening at her flinch as his fingers clasped her wrist. One big hand under her elbow, his head bent to speak softly into her ear. "I won't change my mind, little girl. I'll be here in the morning. I promise you won't be abused again, by anyone. Can you trust me? Will you go with me?"

She looked up at him, at the strong features, the dark hair, the sharp eyes that seemed to see within her, that offered kindness she had not thought to find here tonight.

"I'll go with you," she said quietly. "I'll do anything you want me to."

How he'd gotten into this fix was a conundrum, John thought, his mind filled with plans for the morning to come. But there was no way in hell he'd leave that bit of a child in the hands of whoever had dealt her blows that left bruises. No one deserved treatment of that sort, and certainly not a young woman. And for a moment he wondered at what her clothing must conceal. No doubt more of the same, and that thought only served to make him even more certain that he'd decided to do the right thing.

His mama would roll over in her wooden casket should he turn his back on a woman in peril, especially one so vulnerable and in need of the simplest of human care.

And if he found that the Schrader fella had abused her in another way, he'd be looking him up and handling it for himself. The memory of her reaction to the touch of his hand on her arm thinned his mouth, and he wondered what sort of peril she had faced in her years with that family.

If it took putting his life on the line, he'd see to it that she was tended to and cared for as a young woman should be. He didn't know much about girls of her age, only the memory of his younger sister, a much-cherished and loved child. More than once he'd been cast in the position of protecting her from harm, whether from a balky horse or young boys intent on teasing, as boys would.

His scant knowledge of women had come later on, when as a husband he'd faced the knowledge that the woman he trusted had abused that trust and found pleasure with other men. Perhaps he'd been molded by that, for he'd held himself aloof from females, from those who cast their eyes upon him and offered themselves. He wasn't husband material, apparently, if his past could be relied on as a record of his skills in the art of marriage.

But he'd guarantee he could do a better job of looking after this female, this small waif without anyone to look after her and protect her, than her erstwhile guardians had done. And there was something about her that had hit him hard, right where a man was most vulnerable.

She was frightened, her face bruised, her body no doubt skinny from lack of a decent diet, and yet she had a beauty that appealed to him. Maybe not just her beauty, but the valiant effort she had made not to cry, not to show how frightened she was. He'd caught a glimpse of his younger sister in Katie, had experienced a backward look at the girl he'd once felt deserved his protection. He'd known in those first few moments that Katie was worth his attention, as his own sister had been, and now he was in this over his head, for he'd committed himself to looking after her.

And that, he decided with a grin, wasn't all bad. For he suspected that she held the ingredients of a housekeeper within that slender form. And that was what he needed. And when she was healed and whole again, she might be willing to consider something other than what he could offer, perhaps a marriage with one of the other men who worked the ranch, or a position in town with a decent family.

Now he rode up to the small cabin Bill Stanley had allotted him as a part of his salary and looked at it in the moonlight with eyes that saw the sagging porch, the bare windows. He knew that the interior wasn't much better than what anyone passing by could see. The front door swung open beneath his hand and he stood in the darkness, smelling the musty scent of field mice and the odor of wood smoke from the fireplace.

He'd might as well settle in for the night, he decided, ignoring his own empty stomach as he found his bed in the back room. The blankets that covered his bed were warm, the mattress was wide and the room was as clean as a broom and mop could make it under his hands. He wasn't much of a housekeeper, but he'd quickly managed to clean it up enough to take possession of it as a resting place at night. Preferable to the bunkhouse where an assortment of cowhands slept and ate.

Now he thought of bringing a girl here, a woman really, for most females her age were either already married or planning a wedding. Marriage had probably not entered her head, for she had not likely seen much of an example of happiness between a man and wife out there on the Schrader farm.

Maybe, someday, when she had healed, both in body and soul, and felt ready to be on her own, he'd talk to her about the years to come, help her to face a future that would in all certainty be better than the past she'd left behind.

His eyes closed as he tugged the blanket over his shoulder, and he wondered if his little waif was asleep yet. He tried to imagine her in Molly's bed, and laughed aloud as he visualized her in the cook's nightgown. She'd swim in it, her slender form lost in the enveloping folds. He'd have to buy the child a nightgown of her own tomorrow, he thought sleepily as the weariness of hard work claimed him for the night.

"I'LL BE BRINGING BACK a woman today, Bill, and moving her into the cabin. I'm thinking I need a cook and housekeeper, and I've found a girl who needs a place to live and a warm spot to land for a while." As news went, it was an eye-opener, he thought, as Bill Stanley shot him a look of doubt.

"What are you talking about, John? You can hire one of the men's wives to keep your place clean. There's always one or another looking for bit of income if that's what you need. I can't imagine you getting a woman to move into your place, doesn't sound like something you'd do."

John laughed shortly. "It's not, come to think of it. But this girl is down on her luck, and she's been abused by the folks she was living with. Once I get her something decent to wear, I'm gonna bring her back here and turn her into a housekeeper."

"Who is she?" Bill asked, obviously dubious of the proposal John had made.

"Her name's Katie. Don't know if she has a last name or not, but she ran off from the Schrader place outside of town, to tell you the truth. From what I understand from Molly down at the saloon and what the girl herself told me, she was given to the Schraders a dozen or so years ago, and they've been using her as a servant ever since. She showed up at the Dogleg saloon last night. Molly, the cook there is taking care of her for me until I can get into town this morning and pick her up. I'm gonna bring her here to live in the cabin you gave me."

His jaw firmed as he faced his employer, aware that Bill was a man of principle, and the plan for Katie's welfare might not hit him well. As if he expected a harsh rebuttal, John stiffened his neck and waited for what Bill Stanley had to say. The man was fair, a good man with a prosperous ranch, and his choice of John as his new foreman had been a surprise. John was only thirty years old, but most men would have thought twice before taking a chance on a man so young to run his operation.

But Bill Stanley had a reputation for being smart, and apparently he'd found something in the man standing before him that merited his approval, for he'd not hesitated when the last foreman left to buy his own place and set up business in the next county. Now he tucked his hands into his trouser pockets.

"If you're sure of your ground you're welcome to bring her here, John. It's time and past for you to settle down."

John laughed and shook his head. "I'm not marrying the girl, Bill. I'm hiring her. Don't get the wrong idea here. I've got no need for a wife, but having somebody to keep my place clean and cooking decent meals for me sounds like an idea I can handle."

Bill nodded, but his look was still cautious. "Well, if you're sure this is a good idea, we'll just have to see how it works out. And it sounds to me like she'd be tickled to death to have a spot of her own to claim."

John nodded his agreement. "I just wanted you to know what's going on, Bill. I didn't want you surprised when I show up later on today with a woman. This way you know right up front what my plans are. I hadn't planned on moving anyone into the cabin with me right off, but maybe Katie can make it more of a home than it is now. I'll have to think about adding on a room, though. I'll need to give her a place of her own."

"There's plenty of lumber in the barn, and I'd think the men could lend a hand if you start with a building project. We'll see how it goes," Bill said. "I've never known you to be devious, John, so I'll trust you on this."

John turned and mounted his gelding, taking up the reins and swinging his mount in a half circle. "I need to be in town early on. Molly will be thinking I've abandoned the girl if I don't move along." he said, tipping his hat brim in a small salute as he rode from the ranch house.

He wondered at his own actions as he rode, thinking back to the night before, the sight of the small female who had burst through the saloon door with fear lighting her features. He knew that his intentions were at least aboveboard, and not those of the men who looked for a fast and furious joining with a woman there in the Dogleg Saloon.

As he thought of the young girl who awaited him in town this morning, John nudged his gelding into a faster pace. It was past breakfast time already, and Katie would begin to wonder if he was a man of his word, or perhaps she'd hope for the opposite. Maybe she'd changed her mind by this morning, and wouldn't be willing to fulfill her part of the bargain they'd made.

John Roper had lived a lot of years with only his own

company, and now he was about to change all that and take on the responsibility of a woman in his house. The thought was a bit daunting, he thought, but not without merit. It would be good to come in at night from the range and find a hot meal waiting for him.

He pushed aside the memory of big eyes, of long hair and a slender form. "I'm looking for a housekeeper," he reminded himself. "I'll treat her as I would my little sister."

CHAPTER THREE

THE SALOON WAS QUIET when he approached the front door and he heard only the tinny sound of the piano as the man who tickled the ivories, as he called it, practiced for the night to come. John pushed his way into the barroom and nodded at the man behind the long bar.

"Tom." It was a single word of greeting, and Tom's brief nod was all the reply he had expected. His long strides brought him to the kitchen door and he pushed his way within the room, his nose pleased at the fresh aroma of coffee and of bacon frying on the stove.

"Morning, Molly," he said by way of greeting, and was not surprised at the smile he was offered by the cook. "Is my new housekeeper up and ready to travel?"

"She's washing up now. I gave her something else to wear. That dress she had on wasn't fit for wearin'. It was clean, but that was about all you could say for it. And what she had on underneath it was pretty pathetic. Especially the bruises that had her all colors." Her gaze was sad as she faced John. "She's just a girl, John. She's been abused and misused, and it hurts me to see such a thing. I'm hoping your good sense will recognize that she needs help, not the attentions of a man."

His lips thinned and he clenched his hands as she spoke. Knowing that he had been right in his estimation of facts didn't do much to improve his mood. He'd like to take Schrader out behind a barn and show him how it felt to wear bruises. There was nothing meaner than a man who'd hit a woman, and if he ever got the chance, he'd show the man how it felt to get back a little of his own.

"I'm not looking for a woman thataway, Molly. She'll be safe with me."

A look that might have been relief touched Molly's countenance. "Sit yourself down and have some coffee while you wait, John," she said, pouring him a cup from the big pot on the stove. "You have breakfast already? Or did you skedaddle out of there before the cook fed you?"

"I was in a hurry, Molly. I haven't eaten."

"Well, neither has Katie, so you can take a few minutes and eat with her. The ladies have all finished their breakfast, but I'd thought to share mine with the girl. I don't mind including you."

"Thanks." He sat and picked up the cup she'd placed before him. It steamed and the scent was pure ambrosia to his senses. Nothing like a cup of coffee in the morning to get a man ready for the day. And then he heard footsteps on the back stairway and his gaze shot to where Katie's slender form descended the steps, heading in his direction, her steps hesitant, her limp not pronounced, but apparent.

She looked at him, a flush touching her cheeks, as if she had been thinking of him, and now the reality of his presence had startled her. "Good morning," she said, crossing to the table where he waited. The dress she wore was clean, but ill-fitting, and he hid a grin at the sight of her slim form wrapped in an old dress from Molly's closet.

"Sit yourself down," Molly said, and Katie did as she was told. Probably used to being given orders, John thought.

"Haven't changed your mind, have you?" he asked her quietly, and was almost relieved when her head shook once, back and forth, letting him know that she was still of a mind to go home with him. "I'll take you to the general store and find you some clothes before we go out to the ranch," he said and was stunned at the tears that appeared in her eyes.

"What did I say? I didn't mean to make you upset," he said quickly.

"No. It's not that," she said, wiping at her cheeks with a bit of white fabric she had apparently been given to use as a kerchief. "I just didn't expect to have anything new to wear. Molly gave me this dress and I'd thought it would be fine, long as I can find a needle and thread to take it up so's it'll fit me better."

Molly snorted. "That dress is about ready to use for dust cloths and scrubbing rags," she said firmly. "Once you take it off, you'd as well rip it up and make better use of it, child."

John nodded his agreement, for surely he could buy her something that would fit her. "You're gonna be working in my house, Katie. You'll wear decent clothing and shoes, not heavy boots. You can pick out what you need at the store and I'll buy it for you."

"I knew you had a good heart, John." Molly turned from the stove and nodded at him approvingly, carrying a plate to place it before him as she spoke. "This little gal hasn't got much of anything to her name it seems. A new coat will be little enough to pay for somebody keeping your place up, and fixing meals for you. I'm gonna let her use mine this morning, but she'll need one of her own."

John sent Molly a grateful look, and added another black mark to the Schrader family name as he looked back at the girl he'd decided to take home with him. "Just be thinking of what you need, Katie, and we'll take care of it right after breakfast," he told her and she only nodded, as if she could not find words to speak.

Another plate of food was settled in front of her and with an admonition from Molly to get busy and eat, Katie picked up a fork and dug into the steaming food. From the corner of his eye John watched her, watched the furtive looks she cast toward the door as if she feared someone would enter the room and take her plate from her.

"It's all yours, Katie girl," he said quietly. "No one's gonna take your food away from you. Just take your time and finish your breakfast. It's gonna be a long time till dinner, and we've got a lot to accomplish this morning."

With a grateful look in his direction, she did as he said and tackled the eggs and bacon Molly had prepared. A thick slice of bread, buttered and spread with jam was placed on another plate and pushed in her direction as Molly sat down across the table.

"You need some weight on those bones, Katie. I'll warrant that John here will make sure you have enough to eat from now on."

"You're right, Molly." He agreed with her, his nod determined, thinking that the child looked as though she hadn't had a decent meal in months. Her arms were thin, her cheeks hollow and she wore the frightened look of a baby bird, just being shoved out of the nest for the first time.

"You won't be overworked, Katie. There's just me to look after, and Berta, the cook at the big house, will lend a hand if you need anything."

"Thank you, John. I could hardly sleep last night, thinking about what will happen today, what with you taking me home with you. I'm not sure just what you expect of me, but whatever it is and wherever you take me, I want you to know that I'll do the best I can."

"That's easy enough, Katie. Like I told you last night, I'll give you a place to stay and something decent to wear and you'll keep up my place and tend to my clothes and keeping me fed." He frowned then and his thoughts became words. "You said you know how to cook, didn't you?"

She nodded quickly. "I did most of the cooking at the Schrader house. I learned a long time ago how to bake and churn butter and make biscuits. I can tend a garden and can the vegetables and cut up the meat when it's been butchered."

She was not yet eighteen years old and already had done the work of a woman full grown. John shook his head, unable to believe that she had been so used, that the family who should have cared for her as a child had instead made a servant of her.

"Well, just cooking for me won't be too big a load for you then," he said cheerfully, not willing to let her see his shock at her former circumstances. "Can you keep my clothes clean for me? Do you know how to wash and iron?"

She laughed. Joyously and without restraint, as if she had been given permission to express her happiness. "If you have sad irons, I can use them. If you don't, you'll have to buy a pair of them and a handle. I can iron on a kitchen table if need be. I'll keep your house clean and when spring comes I'll plant a garden."

"Looks like you've got things all lined up, John," Molly said with a laugh. "This little gal will make your life a whole lot easier, I'd say. You mind my words."

"I have to agree with you, Molly." He met the woman's look with a nod of approval. "I'm happy with my decision. Katie will be safe at Bill Stanley's place."

"I never thought such a thing would happen to me," Katie said softly, her hands in her lap, her eyes wide as she considered the future ahead. "I'd thought to spend my whole life out there on that farm, just working and trying to please the Schraders. And there wasn't any pleasing them, let me tell you. They're a pair of nasty folk, they are."

"You won't have to worry about them anymore," John said forcefully. "I'll be sure you're taken care of from now on." Molly's coat hung on a hook by the back door of the saloon's kitchen and in moments it was wrapped around Katie's slender form, covering her from neck to toe in warmth.

THE GENERAL STORE WAS LIKE a wonderland to the girl who walked in the door beside John Roper fifteen minutes later. She stood behind him as he approached the long counter and only his long arm reaching for her brought her in sight of the proprietor, Shandy Peterson. That gentleman cast her a long glance, then looked back at John.

"You got yourself a girl, John?" he asked quietly.

"I've got myself a housekeeper and cook here, Shandy. Katie's gonna keep house for me. Just as soon as she picks out some things to wear. She needs a new dress or two and whatever else you think is appropriate. Molly said she needs a warm coat, too."

"Molly? The woman over at the saloon? What's she got to do with this?" He looked over his glasses at Katie and his brow furrowed. "I don't believe I know the young lady. You from around these parts, honey?"

"Yes sir," she said politely.

Apparently she had decided not to elaborate on her background, and John spoke for her. "Katie needs a place to live and Bill Stanley gave me a good-sized cabin to live in when he made me his new foreman. I figured there was room for her in it with me. I'm needing a housekeeper and she looks to be qualified for the job. We'll head out there as soon as we find some things for Katie to wear."

"Well, John, looks to me like you've made up your mind. Hope it all goes well for you." And if Shandy Peterson wondered at the woman John had chosen to move into his home, and had any questions as to her background, he kept them to himself. It didn't pay to be too inquisitive, was the general consensus in this part of the country.

Katie looked over the counter at the glass bins of clothing that lined the wall, her eyes widening as she considered the varicolored bits and pieces therein. Her eyes opened even wider as Shandy brought two bins to rest in front of her.

"These are dresses, miss. Let's see what we have in your size."

John lifted Molly's coat from Katie's shoulders, readying her for the shopping ahead, then waited for Shandy to show them his wares. With a long look at the girl before him, Shandy picked up several of the dresses

from the glass bin, held them up and then refolded them
and placed them aside as being the wrong choices,
whether by size or by John's discerning eye, Katie
couldn't tell.

And then, with a flourish, the shopkeeper lifted a
blue flowered dress from the bin before him and shook
it out, holding it up for her approval.

"That's a pretty one, Katie," John said softly. "Do
you like it? It looks like it would about fit you, doesn't
it?"

She nodded, reaching to touch the fine percale
fabric. "It's lovely, John. Prettier than anything I've
ever had. And with the sash to tie in back, it ought to
fit me."

"If it does we'll take that one, Shandy, and Katie can
go into your stockroom if she needs to, to make sure it
fits," John decided. "Now find something else for her.
She'll need another dress and she can choose what she
needs to wear under them."

"I don't know…" Katie looked up at the man beside
her, confusion at the thought of decision making
causing her stomach to churn. "I've never picked out
anything for myself before, just wore whatever they
gave me. I won't know what to get."

Shandy Peterson looked stunned by her words, but
recovered quickly. "My girl, Jessica, is right here in the
back room. Let's have her come out and help this little
gal choose what she needs. All right, miss?"

"Yes, of course." Katie was willing to do whatever

she was bid, and waited as the storekeeper called his daughter to come and lend a hand. The girl was pretty, slim and dark-haired, and had definite ideas about what Katie needed for undergarments. Quickly, she pulled bins down and sorted through the contents, piling an assortment of petticoats and drawers, along with two filmy chemises on the counter. Then several pairs of stockings were added to the chosen items, and Jessica Peterson nodded in approval of her choices.

"That ought to do it, Papa. Except for a coat that fits, and maybe she'll need new shoes, but I don't know. I can't see them from here."

"She needs shoes," John said firmly. "Pick out something for her, Jessica."

With a quick grin, the girl walked across the store to where boxes of shoes were on display, choosing several pairs and bringing them back. "Come sit down and try these on. One of them should fit you," she said coaxingly. "If not, I'll pick out some more."

Katie was overwhelmed. Never had she been offered such choices, and the shoes that Jessica held ready for her approval were light and made of soft leather. Unlike the heavy boots she was used to wearing, they felt like feathers on her feet. Between them, the two girls decided on the pair she held now, her fingers touching the black leather as if she could not imagine owning such footwear.

While Katie was still swimming in a sea of uncertainty at the clothing that was to be hers, John approached her, holding a black cloak in his hands.

"Let's see how this looks, Katie," he said and draped it over her shoulders, then lifted the attached hood and settled it on her hair. He took out his leather wallet and led her back to the counter.

Katie was sent to the storeroom in the back of the store, Jessica carrying the clothing she would try on, and the rest of their choices were bundled up, a night-gown being added to the pile at the last minute.

His purchases were wrapped in brown paper tied firmly with a length of cord. John reeled off a list of foodstuffs that he wanted and Shandy Peterson sought and found all he'd listed in a matter of minutes. Jessica appeared then, leading Katie back to the man who watched her closely.

Shandy's daughter spoke softly to John, then added a few things he hadn't thought of to the pile on the counter; tins of peaches and pears from the shelf, a round of yellow cheese from the big wheel on the counter and several other items that Katie peered at with wide eyes.

Overwhelmed by the bounty before her, Katie was silent, almost aghast at the amount of money John was spending, most of it on her behalf. Surely she was not worth so much to him, that he should lay out the contents of his wallet on the counter without hesitation, only smiling at her when she tugged at his sleeve and whispered her words of doubt.

"It's too much, John. I don't need all of that. I won't know how to act with all these things to wear. And that cloak must cost a fortune."

He grinned widely and his hand touched her shoulder lightly. "You'll get used to it, Katie girl. I want you to have enough clothing to wear."

His method of thinking was beyond her, but she only smiled and stood beside him, relishing the warmth of his hands as he spread her new cloak across her shoulders, feeling as though Heaven had opened, showering her with more blessings than she could contain.

In but a few minutes, John had arranged with Shandy for a wagon to be used to transport his purchases back to the ranch.

"I'll get all this stuff loaded up for you, John," Shandy said easily, obviously pleased at the size of the order John had paid for. "You can tie your gelding on the rear of the wagon. Bring it back when you come into town next. I don't use it much anyway, and I don't mind lending it to you for a few days."

With his assurances ringing in their ears, John and Katie left the store and walked to where Shandy's wagon stood in the open area behind the store.

Jessica came out the back door and watched as John lifted Katie to the wagon seat. "Come back to see me again," she said brightly. "Maybe I can drive out to the Stanley ranch and visit some day."

"I'd like that," Katie told her, hoping she might have made a friend today.

With a hasty farewell, they left, John's hand firm on the reins. After a quick stop to return Molly's coat to her, he guided the team of horses to the main road leading out of town. Beside him, Katie wrapped her new cloak about herself, her hand brushing the fabric carefully.

"Are you ready to go home?" he asked with a grin. He thought she looked frightened and he would not have it. His hand touched hers briefly, and then he took up the reins and snapped them briskly over the team's backs, and the wagon rolled down the road. They went past the bank and post office, the wheels turning more rapidly as they neared the hotel and the barbershop. Then finally the team broke into a trot as they traveled past the boardinghouses that edged the town on the west.

"We're on our way home, Katie," he said, looking down at the girl who was rigid on the seat beside him. "Are you all right? You look kinda peaked, like you're not feeling up to snuff." And little wonder, he thought, what with the enormous changes in her life over the past hours.

"I'm just feeling like I'm in the midst of a dream," she told him, and he thought her words were almost like poetry, so softly did they fall on his ear. "The air is so clear, the sun is so bright and the birds are singing. It's a beautiful day, and I'm beginning a new life, John. I don't know what to say to you. You've changed everything for me, and I haven't been able to figure out why you should care what happens to me. I don't even know you, and you've made my best dreams come true."

"If this is all it takes to make you happy, I'm a lucky

man, Katie girl. I'm getting a cook and a washer lady and a housekeeper all in one, and all it cost me was a couple of dollars for your clothes. What more could I ask?" His laughter rang out and Katie responded with a soft giggle that pleased him.

He'd not heard her laugh, and this bit of girlish glee touched him as nothing else could have. For the first time, she had responded as a young girl might and he was pleased. At eighteen, she was far too young for him to consider in any other way than as a younger sister, perhaps. For at thirty, a man who had known love and found it to be wanting, he was not in the market for anything other than exactly what he had promised Katie.

If there were looks of doubt from the men on the ranch, if they cast aspersions on her virtue, he would defend the girl. Somehow, some way, he would make up for the cruel life she had fled. He would provide her with a home, and perhaps offer to her the opportunity for a new beginning.

CHAPTER FOUR

THE CABIN LOOKED LIKE a dream come true as the horses pulled the wagon up in front of it. Katie knew her eyes were wide and her mouth couldn't seem to close properly as she climbed down hastily from the seat to walk to the narrow porch. She ran a hand over the railing and jolted when John admonished her.

"Be careful, Katie. That thing isn't too sturdy. I haven't had much of a chance to work on things yet, and I need to nail it in place a bit better. This cabin needs a lot of fixing to make it fit for you to live in, I'm afraid."

"It's wonderful, just as it is," she said determinedly. "It's beautiful, John. I can't believe you're apologizing for it. Not to me, anyway. If you could see where I come from you'd know what I'm talking about."

"I've heard that those folks weren't anything to brag about, Katie. I didn't know about you living there, but they don't have much of a reputation for good. Leastways not that I've heard. I think you're well rid of them."

She nodded, agreeing with his words, then turned

and opened the door. Stepping inside the room, she halted, hugging herself as she looked around the four walls. A fireplace built of stone filled the back wall, with a wide hearth that invited her to come nearer. She stepped across the room, her hand touching the back of a chair beside the hearth, as if she could feel the warmth of John's head there. For surely he must have sat in that very place of an evening, watching the fire.

She paused, then stooped beside the open fire pit, reaching to place several logs inside from the pile he'd left on the edge of the hearth, and looked back at him.

"Can we have a fire here tonight? Will it be cool enough outdoors to warrant wasting the wood?"

He grinned at her, delighted that she approved of the home he had offered. "We can do anything you want, Katie. If a fire will make you happy, I'll be sure there's enough wood to build a dandy blaze."

She rose and her cheeks turned rosy, as if she were embarrassed, and he stepped closer. "What is it, Katie? Is something wrong?"

She shook her head. "No. I'm just having a hard time believing that this is all real. That I'm truly here, and I'm going to work for you, John. I don't deserve this and I can't tell you how grateful I am to you for being so good to me."

He walked across the room toward her and thought she shrank from him as he neared. He halted a few feet from her and softened his voice as he spoke words of comfort and assurance. "Don't ever be afraid of me,

Katie. I don't ever want you to worry that I'll hurt you in any way. I'm not angry with you, not now, not ever. Don't forget that. Don't ever feel that you have anything to fear from me."

She nodded, her eyes wide, her stance uneasy as he took her hand in his. "You're a woman, almost full grown, Katie. You have my respect and my consideration in all things. Can you understand that?"

She nodded slowly. "I think so, John. It's just so hard to know what to expect. When you turned so quick like and came toward me, it made me think you had cause to be angry with me. I didn't know if I'd done something to make you upset with me. Sometimes it didn't take much for those folks I lived with to get mad and sail into me."

Sensing she needed reassurance, he spoke quietly, his heart aching as he felt the pain of her fear of him. "I won't hurt you, Katie. I promise not to cause you harm in any way. If we have differences and if you get angry with me, you can speak your mind and I'll do the same, but we won't ever be mean or hurt each other. Is that agreed? I want us to be friends, not just a boss and his housekeeper. I may be bigger than you, and yes, stronger, but I'll not use my strength against you, Katie."

She sat quietly, then looked up to where he stood, and he recognized the trembling of her body as something instilled by her experiences in the past. He knew that she feared him.

He crouched down before her. "Your heart is pounding

so hard, it's a wonder it doesn't thump right out of your chest," he said quietly. "I can't stand it for you to be afraid of me."

She looked past him, at the wall behind him, and he recognized that she was unable to meet his gaze. He stood then, stepping back, unwilling to make her feel trapped by his greater build, by the size and shape of him, and his mind sought for a way to bring peace to dwell between them.

"Do you suppose we can sort out the foodstuffs we bought now? Maybe put together a meal of some sort?" His words were calm and slow, his intent being to steady her and make her more comfortable with him.

And in that he succeeded, for she rose from the chair with haste, turning to open the packages they'd brought in, sorting through the boxes of groceries and finding places to put all the supplies he'd ordered. Her hands were quick as she stacked the canned goods in the pantry and made order from the assortment of dry goods he'd purchased.

"I'm going out to tend to the wagon and put the horses in the barn," he told her, watching as she worked.

She nodded, turning to watch him leave the cabin, then went on with the work that was familiar to her. The small pantry just next to the cookstove held most everything, with shelves on either side of the door. It was about six feet deep, and had four shelves on either wall, enough room to hold canned goods and anything they might need from town with which to prepare meals.

The lower shelf held an odd assortment of kettles, with iron skillets stacked neatly. Katie stooped before the clutter of pots and pans and pulled forth a medium sized kettle, then the smallest of the iron skillets. "These will work for dinner," she murmured to herself, carrying them out to the kitchen and across to the sink, where she pumped water into a dishpan there.

The reservoir yielded hot water from the stove and she added soap to the pan from a bottle beneath the sink, then set about washing the kettle in preparation for cooking his meal. As she was wiping out the skillet with a piece of brown paper, John came back in the cabin and hung up his outdoor clothing, taking off his boots by the door.

Katie dabbed a bit of paper into the lard from the pail in the pantry and returned to the skillet she'd wiped clean, using the lard to coat it. "You don't wash your iron skillets, do you, John? You're not supposed to, you know, only wipe them out. Water's not good for them."

John thought she sounded worried and in response, he only nodded his agreement, unwilling to confess that he had washed that very skillet only yesterday after frying eggs in it.

She put the vessels on the stove and found a small slab of bacon in the store of supplies John already had in the pantry, located a knife and sliced through it, forming six thick pieces for their meal. The remaining bacon was wrapped in cheesecloth and put away for another time and the skillet was placed on the stove, where the remains of last night's fire kept the stovetop warm.

"I'll have to build up the fire a bit before you can cook anything much," he told her and she stepped back, giving him room.

"I can do it, John, if you have chores to tend to. I know how to make a fire."

He grinned up at her, as he crouched before the wood box. "I'm sure you do, but for tonight you don't have to. Bill gave me the day off, and the men don't expect to see me till morning."

In less than ten minutes, he had a fire worthy of its name glowing in the depths of the stove, and she was busily turning bacon and thinking of what next she could do to make a meal.

"There's beans and such in the cupboard beside the sink," he told her. "Berta works in the big house and she brought out a supply of canned good for you to use. She heard from Bill that you'd be here, and she said she'd leave some stuff for you in that white cabinet."

He opened the doors and revealed rows of home-canned produce on the three shelves, both pints and quarts, all of them full of colorful vegetables and fruits.

"My word," Katie murmured. "I never saw so much good food in one place."

"Didn't the Schraders have a kitchen garden?" he asked.

"Oh, yes. But we had to sell a good bit of it to make money. Mr. Schrader took it to town to sell at the general store, and we canned the leftovers. I made applesauce from the windfalls, and he picked the good apples to sell. He didn't believe in wasting the best of the crops on his family."

John merely shook his head, aghast at yet another example of the stinginess she had lived with for so long. "You don't have to worry about such a thing here, Katie," he told her. And meant the words with every bit of his heart, for she had lived a life of frugality such as he had not thought possible. Yet had survived with her spirit intact. She was a bright shining flame of womanhood, glowing with a beauty he had seldom seen in his life.

Pushing that thought to the back of his mind, he settled instead on the plans he had set in motion. And decided that he needed to make his thoughts clear to the girl who would be living in his house.

"Katie, I need to tell you something, and I don't know how you're going to take this."

She turned her head and her eyes were calm, as if she were ready to be agreeable, no matter what he had to say.

"I'm not a marrying man, Katie. I just want you to know that there isn't much of a chance that I'll ever be bringing a bride home to this house. You don't have to worry about me pushing you out the door to make room for another woman. So long as we can get along and things go well here, I'm planning on you staying here until you decide on something else for your life. I've already talked to Bill about you and—"

"I don't plan on making any changes in a hurry, John," she said quickly . "I've barely had time to settle in here. Don't be planning on me moving on any time soon."

He laughed. "Just so we understand each other, Katie. I don't want you to think that I'll be pushing you to sleep in my bed or be anything other than an employee here."

"I can sleep right here on the floor in front of the cookstove, John," she said quickly. "It'll be warm and if you've got a quilt I can wrap up in, I'll be happy. I used to sleep with my sister, Jane, when we were young'uns. But lately…"

What she was thinking as her gaze sought the floor was not apparent, and John did not poke into her silence, but watched, even as he wondered at the mention of Katie having a sister. Something he'd not heard of before.

And so he spoke of what was more important right now. "I'll be making a room for you in the near future, Katie. For I have but one bed, and one bedroom. You can sleep on the floor if you like, but there's a sofa there in front of the fireplace, and it should be long enough for you. I want you to be secure here, and know that nothing will harm you, least of all me."

Her eyes darkened at his words, and she drew in a shuddering breath. "John, I'm fearful of a man's hands on me. I don't know any other way to say it than that, but I'm hoping you'll know what I mean. Jacob Schrader seemed bent on slidin' into my bed more than once, and he gave me the shivers, just lookin' at him, let alone how I'd have felt if he'd laid his hand on my—" Her voice broke off as she groped for words, and

John knew a moment of pure rage as he thought of the man who had so frightened this girl.

He considered all he had to say to her and wondered if it might be better to call a halt to his ramblings, lest he frighten her off. There was no point in upsetting the girl.

She swallowed, a visible effort and her eyes veered from contact with his, as if she had not the courage to look into his gaze. "I appreciate you being kind to me, John. I just feel sort of uneasy right now." She threw up her hands as an expression of frustration, unable to verbalize her thoughts and he took pity.

He took her hands in his, feeling her draw away, but determined to make this small contact. Holding her before himself, he grinned. "Don't worry about it, Katie girl. It will all work out and we'll do well together. For tonight, just cook us a meal and we'll eat and talk about what has to be done to make this place more comfortable for you."

She looked about her, her eyes touching the curtainless windows, the bare floor and the table without the adornment of any covering, and then she smiled. "This is perfect, John. I can't ask for anything more. Everything I need is right here. I'll have a place of my own and I can fix it up as I go along. But for now, I'm happy to be here, in your home, with you."

An emotion he hadn't expected flooded his heart as he looked down at the girl he'd brought home with him. An impulsive move on his part, but perhaps the smartest thing he'd ever done. If anyone had told him just yesterday that he would have a housekeeper here, he'd not have believed it. But it was true, and for some strange reason he felt that he might have made a good choice, that his life would be easier from now on.

THEY ATE AT THE SMALL table, their knees almost touching beneath, their eyes tangling several times, as if words should be said between them, but for some reason the silence that filled the room did not lend itself to small talk. Katie was edgy, her hands trembling as she dealt with her knife and fork, her plate seeming heavy as she lifted it to carry it to the sink. It slid from her fingers into the dishwater she had prepared. She turned back to the table to retrieve John's plate as he cleaned up the final bite of his beans, scooping them onto his biscuit and carrying the bite to his mouth.

His hand covered hers as she fit her fingers around his silverware, the warmth of his skin comforting, and she looked into his eyes, wishing she didn't feel such a dolt, so unable to speak. But it seemed her words were like dust in her mouth, and she could not form them upon her lips.

Hot tears sprang to her eyes and she turned quickly from him, carrying his eating utensils and plate to the sink where she added them to the dishpan.

"Katie." He spoke her name softly and waited. Apparently he expected her to turn around and face him and she couldn't find the strength in her legs to do that simple thing. Added to which, the tears that slid down her cheeks made her feel foolish and she would not allow him to know the fear that lay just beneath the surface of her mind.

"Katie, come here. Please."

Had it not been for his final word, the simple plea he uttered, she might have remained apart from him. But she could not resist his softness. Perhaps she could have tilted her head and walked from the room had he simply ordered her to obey his whim, but John Roper apparently was wiser than that.

She bowed her head and shook it carefully, not willing to turn toward him, yet unable to ignore him. His chair scraped across the wooden floor and she sensed his presence behind her as he moved to where she stood, her hands clutching the edge of the sink.

His wide palm covered her shoulder and she knew a moment of fear, for he was more than capable of forcing her to his will and she was only too aware of the power of a man's hands. That John would raise his to her in anger seemed not to be an issue, for she had sensed a careful control that reinforced his promise to her. That he would not harm her, that she would suffer no injury at his hand.

"Look at me, Katie." He could have forced her to turn on her heel and face him, and indeed, she expected him to. But instead he only waited. And then his second hand touched her arm, a presence so gentle she could not move from it. She released the hold she had on the sink and moved to obey him.

"Relax, Katie," he whispered. "I only want to talk to you about our living arrangements. And since I seem to be in charge tonight, I'll make the decisions and tomorrow you can let me know if you see things differently than I. Will that suit you?"

She blinked furiously in an attempt to halt the tears that ran unimpeded down her cheeks and he smiled, then bent and pressed his lips against her forehead. A relief she had not thought to feel swept over her then and she recognized that he was being most patient with her emotional state. Her forehead felt the impression of his mouth, there where his lips had touched her so briefly, and she searched her memory for such a thing happening in her life.

"No one's ever kissed me before, John. Like you just did, I mean. Maybe when I was little, for I think I remember a lady who held me on her lap, but not in a lot of years."

His mouth opened as if he searched for words to speak and then he shook his head, telling her of what would happen. "I've taken your new clothes in the bedroom, Katie. The bundle is on the floor, but I put your nightgown on the end of the bed. I want you to get undressed and wrap yourself in the quilt that's on my bed, and then come back out here. All right?" He waited then, his patience seemingly unending and his lips curved again, his eyes kind as he watched her for her response.

"Yes, all right." It was all she could manage, but it seemed to satisfy him. He nodded and released her,

turning her toward the other room, where the bed lay
in shadow. She stepped over the threshold slowly, and
then stiffened her spine. John had been clear on this
matter, and all she must do was as he asked. Get undressed and wrapped in the quilt he'd offered.

The man had told her the lay of the land and she
might as well do as she'd been told. After all, she didn't
see that she had much choice anyway. And if he'd
wanted to hurt her, he could have already done so. For
there was within her a fear of anything masculine, and
if nothing else, John Roper was just that. A man. A man
who was capable of bringing harm to her if he so chose.

Her chin lifted, her pride coming to the forefront and
she sat on the edge of the bed, easing her heavy shoes
from her feet. Then she bent and slid her stockings off,
unwilling to wear the heavy things another minute.
Tomorrow would be time enough to wash her under-
clothing. Perhaps the man had a washtub and some
soap. And it would be none too soon, for her undercloth-
ing was the same she had put on three days ago, the
Schrader family not being much on clean clothes or
bodies.

Her mind traveled rapidly to the new clothing he'd
bought for her and she smiled with a quick lightening of
her spirits. She'd have new underthings to wear tomorrow,
those soft leather shoes and even brand-new stockings.
Her old things could be washed up and put aside for an
emergency, but tomorrow she would wear soft new undergarments next to her body and dress as a lady.

It had been a bone of contention during the years of her life that Katie had taken every opportunity to wash herself and her belongings, and had taken much abuse because of her high-falutin' ways, as Mrs. Schrader had said. Now, perhaps she would have hot water and soap available on a regular basis and her body would be as clean as a scrub rag could make it. That thought alone was enough to cheer her and she smiled.

Glancing up at the kitchen as she rose from the mattress she caught sight of John as he locked the back door, then turned down the oil lamp over the table. The glow from the wood-burning stove gave substance to his form as he crossed to the bedroom door.

"Shall I light a candle? Or can you make out what you're doing in there?" He halted, hesitating in the doorway and she paused in the unbuttoning she had begun, her dress open down the front, her chemise exposed.

"I've undressed in the dark my whole life, John Roper. There's enough light from the window and that fireplace out there to see what I'm doing, and I suspect there's a slop jar in the corner where the washstand is."

"You're right on both counts, Katie. There's towels and washrags over there in the drawer beneath the bowl and pitcher. Help yourself." He went to the kitchen sink then, pumping water easily, filling a cup and drinking from it as he waited for her to make ready for the night.

The washrag smelled clean and she poured some water into the bowl provided and sloshed the rag in it, then rubbed his bar of soap on it, wrung it out and used it on her face and reaching beneath the bodice of her dress, used it beneath her arms, not willing to carry the scent of her perspiration into bed with her. A matter of pride she supposed, but she'd smelled the odor of unwashed bodies for years and if it was in her power, she would not allow her own to be of that ilk.

In moments, she had rinsed the cloth in the water and repeated the journey it had taken over her face and arms, removing the soap readily. The towel was rough, but she was used to such things and it took only moments to prepare for bed. Using the slop jar was beyond her right now, for there was no screen or any way to hide her doings from him and she could not bring herself to be so familiar.

"Can I use the outhouse?" It was the most difficult thing she'd ever had to request, but he didn't appear to be shocked, only murmured a different solution.

"I'll stay out in the kitchen a little longer and close the bedroom door. You can use the facilities over in the corner. I'd just as soon not send you outside again tonight, but you're welcome to your privacy, Katie."

He was as good as his word and did as he'd suggested, leaving her to tend to her duties hastily before he should return, the few minutes long enough for her to don the nightgown he'd bought for her. She'd barely pulled it down over her body, admiring the soft fabric and the small pearl buttons marching down the front placket, when he rapped on the door and then opened it, making a small production of entering the room, as if he would give her warning of his coming.

She grasped the quilt he'd offered and wrapped it around herself, then walked past him into the other room, heading for the couch he'd offered for her use. She slid quickly atop the firm surface, forming a cocoon of the quilt.

"All set?" He stood in the doorway between the two rooms, and asked the question softly. "There's a pillow here for you to use, Katie," he offered and approached carefully, tossing the pillow to where she lay.

"Thank you. I appreciate that," she told him, watching as he went back into his bedroom, listening as she heard the bed creak beneath his weight. Whether he undressed or not, she did not know, for she turned her face to the back of the couch, her head on the pillow he'd given her, and closed her eyes.

"I've never had so nice a pillow." The words came from her lips before she thought twice and she grimaced as she thought of how foolish she must sound. As if a pillow was a thing of great importance. Yet it was true. The feathers that filled the pillow beneath her head provided a luxurious place to rest and she was grateful.

From the bedroom, John's laugh was soft, and she was aghast at her own words. He must think her foolish.

But apparently he was not surprised by her words for he spoke readily. "Berta, the housekeeper in the big house made me the set when I moved into this cabin, just the other day," he said. "She dug up the towels and quilts for me, too, and the canned things you saw in the kitchen cabinet."

His voice carried to her and she turned over on the couch, forming an answer. "She must be a nice lady."

John chuckled. "She is, but no one would dare to call her nice to her face. She puts on a big front, snapping and snarling at the men when they come in for meals. Her biggest gripe is dirt on the floor, and woe betide the man who comes to the table with his hat on. She's a great one for manners, Berta is, for all that she's gruff and picky."

"She sounds like someone I could like," Katie said, realizing that her words were slurring just a bit. Her eyes were fighting to stay open and she felt the weariness in her bones sweep through her whole body.

"Go to sleep, Katie," John said from his bed. And then, almost as an afterthought, he spoke again. "Are you comfortable?"

She nodded, aware that he couldn't see from his bed, with her in the dark, the only light in the room the faint glow of the fireplace. She was sleepy, and strangely, felt safe here in this place, even though a man would sleep only a few feet from her. "I'm fine," she said softly, and realized that the words were true, that she felt safe and secure for the first time in longer than she could remember.

WHEN KATIE AWOKE IT WAS with a start as she heard a rooster crowing outside the cabin. And then she inhaled sharply as she sensed eyes upon her, and sat up quickly, unable to think for a moment where she was.

"You awake, Katie?" John's voice sounded like a saw cutting through a length of wood, rough and rusty, but she knew no fear, only a sense of rightness that she could not explain.

"I'm awake." She opened her eyes, saw John at the sink, watched as he bent his head and doused it with water and then picked up the towel there and roughly dried his hair, then his hands. He looked over at her and grinned.

"How was your first night as a housekeeper?"

"I don't know. I don't feel much like one yet," she told him. "Ask me tomorrow."

As she spoke the sound of men's voices came to her from outdoors, through the cabin's walls, laughter pealing forth as one of them apparently found something humorous to brighten his morning.

John crossed to the front door and opened it, then looked back at her. "I'll be back in a short while. I'm just going to talk to the men and get things sorted out. Will you make breakfast, or shall I go to the big house to eat this morning?"

Her stomach growled as he spoke, as if the thought of food had brought hunger to the surface. "I'll cook you breakfast," she said quickly, sitting up and swinging her legs over the side of the couch, careful to keep the quilt around herself.

He was gone then, the door closing behind him and

she went into the bedroom, seeking out the clothing she'd taken off the night before, and then changed her mind, recalling the new things John had purchased. The thought of the items inside the plain wrapping sent a quick thrill through her and she fought with her instincts that begged to wear new clothing.

Cooking breakfast for John did not require wearing a new dress, and she'd do well to locate her old things and get busy. But a quick look around assured her that the things she had discarded last evening in this room were here no longer. As though they had never existed, the worn, shabby dress Molly had given her and the dingy petticoat she'd stripped from before she donned her new nightgown were nowhere in sight.

It was there that John found her, just moments later, sitting on the edge of his bed, looking around her in dismay, wrapped tightly in the quilt. She looked up as he stood in the doorway.

"I don't know where my things are from yesterday. I wanted to get dressed but—" She spread her hands in a gesture of defeat, and chagrin reigned on her mobile features.

John spoke softly, aware of her confusion and unwilling to upset her further. "You don't need those old things, Katie. You've got a whole bundle of new clothes to wear."

All Katie saw, all she could take note of was the expression on his face. That and his rapid movements across the room to where she sat on the edge of the bed.

She moved quickly, attempting to rise even as she spoke an apology. "I'm sorry, John. I should have already started your breakfast, but I thought to get dressed first and—"

"Not to worry," he cut in swiftly. "Just get dressed and come out to the kitchen." He stood before her and his hand lifted, his index fingers pointing to the stacks of clothing on the dresser, where he'd placed them early this morning. He turned then to face her and his voice took on a teasing growl.

"I'm hungry, girl. It's past time for breakfast. There's work to be done, and time's a'wastin'."

CHAPTER FIVE

THE SIGHT OF THAT WIDE palm extended to her sent a chill of unwarranted fear through Katie and she hovered, drawing her legs up, bending her head to shelter it on her knees, making herself as small a target as possible. Even as she heard his exclamation of consternation, the words that resounded from the walls, she knew that she had cowered for no reason. She knew in her heart that he had only offered kindness, yet his voice sounded harsh in her ears.

"What is wrong with you, girl? You act like you're scared to death of me. I just brought you a cup of coffee from Berta's kitchen to give you a head start on the morning. I left it on the table." The look he bent on her was full of concern and when he knelt before her, his hands trembled as he held them aloft. "I wouldn't strike you, Katie. I told you last night—"

"I know, John. I just…" She could not speak the words that would tell him of the fear she carried within her soul, that the sight of a man's big hands struck her to the core with panic, that she had thought, just for a moment, that he would use his fists against her softer flesh.

"Ah…damn, Katie." He touched her knee, then her hand where it lay, fisted tightly there on her thigh. With gentle care, his fingertips touching the flesh as if he handled something precious, he looked into her face. "I'm sorry I scared you thataway, sweetheart. I didn't mean to come at you so quick. I was just going to suggest that you might wear a flannel shirt of mine so's you'd be warm enough to come out to the table and drink the coffee I brought. I'm sorry, Katie."

Hot tears could not be held back and she shed them without any attempt at hiding the evidence of her shame. "Don't feel you need to say that to me, John. I was still half-asleep, and I was already scolding myself because I hadn't gotten up early, when I told you I'd cook for you and keep your house. And then I got in here and couldn't find my things and I was—"

"There's time enough to eat, Katie. I didn't mean to frighten you," he said, his grin appearing as if he recognized that he must lighten her mood somehow.

He stepped back to the kitchen, retrieving the coffee cup from the table, then returned to where she sat and knelt at her feet, offering her the hot brew he'd brought for her.

"Take a sip, honey. Don't burn your tongue, now. Just sip it a little. That's the way," he said softly as she held the cup with her fingers enclosing his, tilting the cup toward her mouth and taking the hot coffee into her mouth.

"Thank you, John." She tried to smile, tried to reassure him, but her voice broke on the words and she felt shame that she had started off this day on such a sour note.

He waited until she had taken hold of the cup fully, then rose and reached for a hook on the wall where he'd hung a clean shirt, bringing it to her and holding it before her. "Stand up, Katie. I'll help you put this on to keep you warm."

She did as he asked, taking a last sip of coffee before she put the cup on the table and rose to stand before him. She dropped the quilt to the bed, feeling almost naked in the all-enveloping nightgown she wore and knew a moment of thanksgiving as he helped her don the shirt, as if he understood that she was not at ease before him with only her nightwear covering her.

He pulled the collar together, straightening the yoke over her shoulders, and his hands remained there at her throat, his gaze sweeping her length, from where her pink toes curled against the braided rug beside the bed, to the flush that rode her cheeks as she suffered his appraisal.

He bent a bit, touching his lips against her forehead. "There now. Let's go into the kitchen. Maybe you'll feel more comfortable there. I've built a good fire in the cookstove and it's nice and warm."

She walked beside him, her hands full with the coffee cup, unwilling to mention the casual gesture he'd made. She'd received two kisses from this man in less than a day, and her mind boggled at the thought.

His shirt hung to her knees and she was thankful for its protection, even though she wore a full-length gown beneath it. She pulled it together in the front before she sat in the kitchen chair, covering her legs with the fullness.

"You surely wear big shirts, John," she said, her fingers smoothing a wrinkle as she looked down at the plaid garment.

"I'm a big man. My mama said I'd have to be to grow into my feet when I was just a young'un. I always had the biggest shoes of all my brothers, and they teased me about it, till she told them that I'd be the tallest of the bunch when we were full grown."

"And are you? The tallest, I mean?"

"Yeah. And I've still got big feet, but so long as they make boots in my size, I figure I'll be all right." He looked down to where she had wound her feet around the chair legs. "Yours are bitty little things, girl. But then, you're not much bigger than a minute yourself. I guess it all works out, doesn't it?"

She had begun to relax, John realized, her smile brighter, almost as if she were comfortable with him, he thought, and for that he was grateful. That this girl feared him was not to be borne. He'd thought his assurances to her last night would be enough to soothe her fears, but perhaps the terror she'd suffered and the pain she feared ran too deep, and only time would give her the confidence she needed to deal with him. And God only knew what Schrader had done to put the fear in her eyes. Another question he would need to find an answer to.

"Drink your coffee, honey. I've got to go out to the

barn and get things under way for the day. Those men are working on the stalls and taking care of the livestock, but there's fencing to be mended and cattle to be checked on today. It's been pretty cold out there for well over a week. 'Bout time for another thaw, but we still had ice on the watering trough this morning.

"There's hay to deliver to the steers in the south pasture, and we need to be watching the cows that are getting ready to drop their calves soon. But I'll send the men out to handle that. I'll be working in the barn for today, close enough to hear you if you call me."

It was the longest speech he'd made in a month of Sundays, he thought as he fed her all the information he thought she might need to get her through the morning. He wanted her to know his routine, wanted to assure her that he would be nearby if she needed him.

She looked beyond him, out the window, where the morning sky was overcast, but the promise of sunshine hovered just beyond the clouds. "Looks like we're going to have a nice day anyway," she said, her mind working rapidly as she made her own plans. "I'll cook up some eggs for you right quick. And later on, at noontime, I'll have dinner ready for you. Will that be all right?"

"Sounds good to me. Get those eggs cooking. I'll be back in just a few minutes."

He let himself out the back door and she made haste to locate a skillet, then found a crock of eggs in the pantry. A bit of butter sizzled in the skillet and she whipped eggs to a froth in a small bowl, pouring them into the skillet quickly.

The room was quiet, his deep, masculine tones but a memory, and Katie went to the window to watch as he strode toward the barn. Two men stepped out from the wide, double doors and waved at him, calling words she couldn't hear, and then she caught the drift of their laughter as they slapped John on the back and went with him into the big building.

In just a few minutes, he was back and she slid his scrambled eggs onto a plate and found a loaf of bread in the pantry, slicing it quickly and locating the butter for his use. He ate quickly, intent on heading out to work, and she was silent, watching him and buttering a slice of bread for herself.

"I don't want you working too hard today, Katie," he admonished her as he rose from the table. "I think there's plenty to cook in the pantry, and I'd like you to just settle in this morning. All right?"

She nodded, watching as he left the cabin and then made tracks for the bedroom. Her own clothing wasn't nearly as warm as John's shirt, but she sought out the plainest of the new dresses he'd bought for her and slipped it over her head, carefully buttoning the bodice and sliding a new petticoat and a pair of drawers beneath it. Back in the kitchen once more, she washed in warm water from the reservoir on the stove, thankful for the fire he'd built for her comfort.

While getting dressed, she'd noted a basket in the

bedroom where he'd apparently tossed his soiled clothing for the past several days, and she sought out a container now to use as a washtub. In the small entryway hung a galvanized bucket, larger than a milk pail, not as big as a bathing tub, but a good size nevertheless.

In moments she had scooped warm water from the reservoir on the side of the big cookstove into it, then added soap from under the sink to make suds. His small clothes and shirts were readily doused in it, and she allowed them to soak while she made the bed and washed up the dishes.

The corner posts on the back porch were a handy place for a short line to hang clothes on, she decided, and searched out a length of rope from the pantry, stretching it from one end of the porch to the other, tying it as high as she could reach on the square posts that held up the porch roof.

Hanging on a nail in the pantry, she found a small scrub board, and she brought it to the washtub, using it to good purpose on his clothing. In an hour, the line she'd strung held John's clothing, his trousers and shirts and the bits and pieces of his underwear. Her own drawers she washed and hung behind the stove on the back of a chair, unwilling to allow them to flutter in the breeze where any passing ranch hand might see them.

A dresser stood against the outside wall in the bedroom and she sorted out the clothing she found there; John's supply of drawers and denim trousers were folded neatly and stacked closely. Emptying one drawer to make room for her own sparse assortment, she took time to brush all the wrinkles out of the things John had purchased yesterday at the general store, her hands careful as she handled the fine fabric of the chemises he'd chosen for her.

"I feel like a real housewife," she whispered softly to herself, aware that the sweeping and cleaning, scrubbing and folding that occupied her morning were enjoyable because of where she was, and who she was tending. John was a kind man, still a man, but with qualities she had not seen before in the one man who had made up her limited experience.

John would be easy to do for, and she sensed that he would appreciate her work on his behalf. Returning to the kitchen, she found a broom in the pantry and set to work on the dust that hid in the corners. A bit of cardboard served as a dustpan and she dumped the residue into the fireplace, noting that John had built up the fire for her comfort before he'd left the cabin.

A sharp rap from somewhere near the back door brought her out of her daydreams and she looked up to find a middle-aged lady watching her through the window. With a quick smile, Katie opened the door and faced her visitor.

"I'll bet you're Berta," she said quickly, opening the door wide, so that her welcome would be evident.

"I sure am, honey. And you're John Roper's hired help or I miss my guess."

"I'm Katie," she said, pulling a chair from the table

and offering Berta a seat. "I can make some coffee right quick, if you'd like, ma'am. After all, you sent me a cup this morning, early on."

"I figured you could use a bit of a lay-in your first day here," Berta said. "I make a big breakfast for those men, and there's always enough to go around." She'd carried in a burlap bag with her and now she bent to open it and began removing its contents. "Here's some potatoes and carrots for you and a sack of onions, too. I figured John might not think of getting them from the general store, and I've got bushels full in the fruit cellar under the house. I expect you've already found the food from the kitchen garden I put up last fall. I brought a few jars over and put them in the cupboard for you, along with that crock of eggs in the pantry.

"And here's a couple of jars of beef I cooked up and canned when we butchered last fall," she said, bending low to pull more from the burlap sack. "There's pork in the smokehouse and fresh ham in the lard barrel in the cellar, but beef don't keep good thataway. I just can it up every year, and in between butcherings I have plenty to cook with."

Katie was awed by the generosity before her. "I never saw so much good food in one place in my life," she said, her eyes lighting with glee. "I can fix John some dandy meals out of all that."

"He told me this morning that you could cook and clean, but I knew there wasn't much here in the way of stuff to fix for dinner today, so I raided the fruit cellar and brought a few things I figured you could use. There's always more eggs in the henhouse and milk in the pantry, or the milk house out back. Or else fresh from the barn if you know how to milk a cow. But the men keep the new Guernsey milked morning and night for the house, so you can just have them bring you some ever couple of days.

"Oh, and here's some butter, too," she said quickly, searching the bottom of the sack. "It got a little flattened, but it's wrapped up good. I must have set a jar of beef on it."

Katie looked at the bounty Berta had arranged on the kitchen table and felt her throat tighten, even as her head swam with the generosity of the woman who was prepared to welcome her without question. "I've never had anybody do for me this way," she said, fighting to hold back the tears that begged to be shed.

"Well, for goodness' sake, girl. Don't make a fuss about it, and sure enough, I don't want you to be crying. I came over to welcome you, not make you feel bad."

"Oh, I'm not feeling bad, just pleased that you're being so nice to me."

"Well, let's get this put away and set your kitchen to rights. I've probably got enough here to do you for a week or so anyway, along with whatever you can find in the smokehouse."

"John had a good piece of bacon in the pantry and I fried some up last night when we got in from town.

Made him a sandwich out of it and opened a can of beans, so he wouldn't starve to death before morning."

Berta dug in her apron pocket and found a small tin of tea leaves, announcing that a cup of tea was just the thing for midmorning, sending Katie to the stove where she slid the big covered teakettle over the hottest spot. In a few minutes they were sharing the tea, Berta declaring that next time she'd bring along some milk to put in it, Katie happy just to have the treat of tea, something that was a rare delight at the Schrader farmhouse.

Before long, Berta had taken her leave and looking up to where the sun hung behind a cloud, bringing its glow to the eastern sky a bit, Katie decided it was more than time to begin John's dinner. One of the Mason jars of beef made up the base of her preparations, and she added three potatoes from the bag Berta had brought, a big onion from the mesh bag, and then a handful of carrots that Berta had said were but a drop in the bucket when compared to the bushels in her fruit cellar.

When the dinner bell rang loudly from the back porch of the big house, Katie was on her hands and knees, washing up the final square of the kitchen floor, the rest of it drying rapidly in the heat from the stove. John came in the door, and she lifted herself to kneel upright as he stepped into the kitchen.

"Berta called the men in for dinner, Katie, so I thought I'd see if you were ready with mine."

"Watch the wet floor, John. Don't slip. It's not quite

dry over there by the door yet. Wait a minute and I'll wipe it with a towel and then I'll be done here."

"What are you up to, Katie?" He leaned past the table to see her, frowning as he caught sight of her kneeling near the stove. "It looks to me like you've been busy, girl. My trousers are almost dry out there on the line, and unless I'm dreaming, I can smell something mighty good on that stove."

She couldn't help the surge of pride that rose to the surface at his words. "It's your dinner, John. I made you beef stew."

His grin was wide and approving as he swept his gaze over her. "Well, doggone. This getting hired help is gonna work out just fine, Katie." He sat on a chair near the door and pulled his boots off, careful to set them to dry on a bit of carpet he kept there.

He hung his coat and hat on the hook and then headed for the sink to wash up. Katie carried her bucket of wash water to the back door and dumped it over the railing as he scrubbed his face and rolled his sleeves up to wash his arms. When she closed the door after hanging the bucket on a nail in the entryway, he was drying off with a towel, watching her as she moved across the floor to the stove.

"I don't want you working so hard, Katie. Doing the wash today was enough to wear you out, you didn't have to scrub the floor, too."

She stepped toward him and lifted her face to look at him squarely. "You don't need to worry about me,

John. I'm strong and well able to do anything that needs to be done in this house. What I do here is because I want to."

John would have put his hands on her, would have held her close, but she'd already turned in a half circle and was reaching for the cupboard, lifting down plates and then searching out silverware in the drawer that held it.

And he thought better of his first instinct, that of touching the girl who had worked on his behalf all morning. She was not ready yet for a man's hands to spread wide on her back, for a man's lips to touch hers. And might not be for a long time to come. He'd do well to stifle his instincts and let the girl alone.

On the stove sat the coffeepot, the tempting smell of the fresh brew wafting to his nostrils, and he reached over her head to snatch up two cups, depositing them on the table next to the plates.

Katie folded her hands and tilted her head, as if she judged her meal ready to be served. "All right, John. Just sit down and I'll fix your plate," she said, locating a large spoon she'd put atop the warming oven. She stretched up on her tiptoes to reach it, and John's breath caught as he watched her. Her arms lifted high, outlining her breasts against the bodice of her dress, the hem lifting to expose slim ankles and narrow feet.

He frowned as he caught sight of bare skin. "Where's your shoes, Katie? You'll catch cold that way. And you even went out on the porch barefoot. I don't want you coming down with pneumonia, girl."

She looked down quickly, as if she'd forgotten that her feet were bare of covering and then glanced at him, her reply coming quickly. "I took my shoes off when I washed the floor, and besides, I'm used to going barefoot. It saves on shoe leather."

"Well, you can go without shoes if you want to, but not because you have to save on shoe leather," he told her. "There's plenty more shoes where yours came from. When they wear out we'll get you new ones. In fact, they sell house shoes at the store, with soft soles you can slip on in the house." His look in her direction was one that expressed his feelings, a smile that warmed her.

"You can have anything you need, Katie. I don't want you ever going without food or clothing or whatever makes you happy. Understand?"

She nodded quickly. "I don't need things, John. I'm happy just as I am, with what I already have. I don't mean to argue with you, but—"

Her words broke off as he stepped closer and she lifted wide eyes to him, as if seeking out his thoughts. She was warm, smelling like soap and beef stew and woman, a combination he found irresistible. All of his good intentions fled as his head bent and his lips touched her cheek.

"Thanks for making my dinner and washing my clothes, honey. You're satisfied with so little, I forget sometimes that your needs are easily met. But, know one thing, sweetheart. You don't have to work so hard. I don't want to see calluses on those pretty little hands."

She watched his face as he spoke, and then drew her hands up between them to look at her palms, a frown on her face.

"I don't have pretty hands, John. I'm used to hard work, and I know my hands show it, but that's all right. I just want to do what I'm doing. I'm happy here with you."

He took her palms in his, moving her back from him so that he could better see the small fingers and the roughened flesh he held.

"You've worked too hard during your life, Katie. I can see that by looking at you. And that's all well and good, but it's in the past. From now on you don't have to work yourself to a frazzle. Just so long as you take good care of *me,* and keep my house clean and my meals cooked, I'll be one happy man," he said.

She looked puzzled at that and he relented, smiling a bit as he touched the end of her nose with his index fingertip. "You've got lots of years ahead of you to learn how to look after me, Katie. I'm planning on keeping you here for a long time, at least until you find yourself a good man and set up housekeeping in a place of your own."

She shivered, her skin pale and her words put a lie to his prediction. "I don't intend to ever get married, John. I didn't see anything in my years out there at the Schrader farm to make me yearn for that sort of life. I'll be happy to work for my keep and stay unmarried for the rest of my life."

He sat down at the table and watched her as she

readied his meal. "Haven't you ever thought of having a family of your own, Katie? Children, maybe, and a husband to take care of you?"

The look she shot his way was dark. "I can take care of myself. And from what I've heard, it takes a man to help make babies, and that doesn't seem like a good idea to me. I'll stay as I am, thank you."

If she wondered at the sassy grin he offered her, she did not question it or the words he uttered. "One day, you may change your mind."

And thus she missed the measuring look he aimed at her as he spoke and the laughter that he muffled for her benefit.

CHAPTER SIX

THE NEXT FOUR DAYS passed quickly for Katie, bound up in the discoveries she made in John's cabin. An extra sheet from his closet was cut up and hemmed to make curtains for the bedroom window, and she begged thread, a needle and pins from Berta to accomplish her goal. Her stitches were fine, her skills honed by years of darning stockings and mending trousers, not to mention the few items of clothing she'd made for herself to wear over the past couple of years.

Mrs. Schrader had not been enthused about the art of sewing and by dint of hard work and much stitching and then tearing out and redoing, Katie had learned how to put together two pieces of fabric and sew a fine seam. Curtains were a joy to make, she decided, especially when she knew John would be pleased with her efforts.

Berta contributed a dowel rod and together she and Katie tacked it into place over the window and the curtains were duly admired over a cup of tea, Berta's praise for Katie's skills falling on grateful ears.

John's thoughts on the subject were more than she'd

expected, for he told her that they would find a bolt of material in the general store that she could use for the kitchen, where curtains were sorely needed. She agreed with enthusiasm and made her plans accordingly, mentioning to John that a piece of oilcloth would look well on the kitchen table. A suggestion he agreed with, his pleasure in her plans for his cabin obvious.

She looked forward to the evenings spent before the fireplace, when John spoke to her of the cattle and horses, of the men who worked with him, and occasionally of his past. He came from a big family, his father still alive, although his mother had been buried several years ago. He had several brothers and a younger sister, he told her, all of them miles away, but close to his heart.

She envied him, a quiet sort of emotion that took nothing from his joy in his family, but a yearning for someone to call her own. John was fast becoming her friend, she thought, but she yearned to know that someone, somewhere might think of her as their family, perhaps the way John cared for his father and the brothers and sister he'd left behind. And yet, there was in her relationship with John, more than mere friendship, for she found herself yearning, on occasion, for a touch from him, perhaps his hand on her shoulder or his lips against her forehead, something he seemed to find pleasurable.

His touch was a comfort, his arm resting across her shoulders sometimes before he left the cabin in the morning to work in the barn or out in the pastures. But better yet were the infrequent times that he smiled at her and his gaze touched her with a heated warmth that went beyond his other gestures of tenderness. He'd placed his lips against her temple or cheek more than once, as a gesture of affection, and she cherished those small touches, aware that her presence in his home pleased him.

Today, after ironing his clothes and straightening his dresser drawers for the third time, she'd cooked a light meal for their supper, knowing he'd rather eat more heavily at noontime. And after the third trip to the window to look out into the twilight, she began to wonder where he could be. He'd told her he could usually be counted on to come in for his supper before darkness fell. And the sun had set already, making it necessary to light the lamp over the table.

She'd begun to fret, unable to think of what might have happened to make him so late, hearing the sounds of men walking to the house, their voices calling back and forth. And still, John was not to be seen.

Until, like a silent spirit in the night, he was behind her in the kitchen. She'd just turned back to the stove, rescuing the beans cooked with bits of ham before they burned, stirring the creamed potatoes one last time, deciding to give up and slide the whole meal into the oven to stay warm.

His hand was on her shoulder, his voice a whisper in her ear and she dropped her spoon on the floor with a clatter, turning to him, a cry of surprise and relief on her lips.

"John. Where have you been? I didn't hear you come in. I've been worried. When it got dark and you weren't home yet, I thought something had happened to you."

Her words spun a web of caring about him and John drew her into his arms, not caring that he might be pushing her in the wrong direction, unable to halt his movements as he lifted her chin with one forefinger and pressed his lips to hers. For the first time yielding to the temptation she so unwittingly offered. For up until now he'd eased his growing need for her with tender, brief kisses against her temple, her cheek.

And yet, there was a boundary over which he would not cross, would not make Katie think he thought of her as more than a friend. She was a woman, and though her behavior was that of an innocent, he knew only too well how a woman could lure a man into her web. And the thought of ever again being enthralled by a female was not one he harbored for a moment of time.

That Katie was of the same ilk as Sadie had been, he didn't believe, yet she was a female, a woman with the duplicity of her gender, no doubt. Hadn't she already brought him to a state of arousal on more than one occasion, merely by smiling at him, or by providing him with the comforts a man could expect from a woman. That she would no doubt withhold her kisses, should he venture to claim those lips was a given, for Katie harbored within her a fear he could sense.

She'd been abused, physically for sure, perhaps even in a sexual manner by the man who had raised her for the past years. For she cringed from his unexpected touch, although she allowed him to approach her if she had due warning of his intentions.

That he could put his hand on her arm or shoulder, even kiss her forehead or cheek was a part of their living together, but should he touch her without warning, she would bolt from him, her eyes wide with fear. And he could not stand to think that Katie feared him.

He'd caught her scent on occasion as they sat before the fire in the evenings and fought the demons that would have had him drawing her into his arms. And had congratulated himself on his self-control, even as he yearned for the warmth of her body. For John Roper had discovered that his liking for this woman who lived in his cabin had developed beyond the goals he'd set for himself, though he shunned the very thought of another wife, another woman who might betray him, as had the first female to whom he'd given his trust.

There was no woman worth the pain of betrayal, no creature on this earth who would ever touch his heart again and cause the pain he'd once suffered. And yet, his mind refused to center itself on his plans for Katie to marry one of the other hired hands. His high-flown notions of finding her a man to marry seemed to have fallen by the wayside.

For the image of Katie in the arms of one of the ranch hands made his skin crawl. The thought of her tender curves being touched by any man other than himself was enough to make him burn with anger.

Now, as he held her loosely against himself for the first time, his lips tasted hers and he cursed himself for his failure to avail himself of such a pleasure before this. She tasted of the beans she'd sampled just moments past, of the jam she'd licked from the spoon after opening a fresh jar for supper, and most of all exactly like Katie.

Like the woman who had tempted him for days and nights, whose eyes lured him with unknowing innocence, each time he saw her. He stepped back from her, releasing her in an abrupt movement that startled her, and she shuddered, crossing her arms across her breasts.

"I was worried about you, John. I don't know why." She caught her breath and stood before him, her eyes big and gleaming in the light from the lantern, suddenly accusing as if she had discovered an anger within that had not before been allowed to be let loose.

Her voice was harsh, almost shrill as she spoke. "Yes, I do know why. You should have been in before dark. You're always home by the time the milking's done and tonight the men left the barn with the buckets of milk and went into the house and you weren't here. It was past time and—"

His finger touched her lips and stilled the words that spewed upon him, the worry in her voice shaming him that she should be so concerned about him, when it would have taken little effort to have sent Shorty or one of the other men by to tell her he was on his way.

"Whit and I found a cow tryin' her best to birth her

calf, and she was having a hard time of it. When a couple of the men came by I sent them on to supper and waited it out with Whit, lest the mama have trouble and we lose them both. We brought the cow and calf back with us and they're in the barn now. Whit's going to keep an eye on her for a while, make sure she's all right."

Katie dropped her head, her breath coming in aching gasps, as if she had held back her fears too long, and they would not be contained a moment longer. "I was afraid, John. How can I be so afraid for you when I never worried about another soul in my whole life? Except maybe Jane."

He grinned, looking down into the eyes that had risen from their contemplation of the wide floorboards. "Maybe because you like me? Just a little, anyway?"

Her eyes darkened and her mouth firmed. "Don't laugh at me, you horrible man." She struck out at him, her fists impotent against the muscles he flexed to ward off her woman's strength. And yet, she was strong, he realized as he felt the rain of two blows from her small fists, and lifted his hands to capture hers.

"You're going to leave bruises on me, sweetheart," he murmured, doing his best not to laugh aloud at her fury.

"You know better," she said, subsiding as he gave her little room to wage her attack. As though her spate of anger had left her exhausted, she sank against him and he held her up, sensing that she had truly feared for him. No one had ever cared enough before to worry about him. Except maybe his mother, and that had been long years ago, when he was still young and vulnerable. And then there had been Sadie, who had promised much and given little. Who'd apparently been incapable of truth and had betrayed his trust. A trust he would not give lightly again.

He was still vulnerable. Perhaps in a different way, to a different sort of harm, but in a fashion that made him hesitate, lest he step wrong. For the ground beneath him was suddenly soft and he feared making the wrong move, one that might cause hurt or damage of some sort.

Not to John Roper, for he feared not for the man he'd become over the years, the man who held his heart encased in a coating of ice, lest he be prey to a female on the lookout for a man's protection. No, his thought was for the young woman who stood before him. She was still trembling, he realized, still shaky, as though her concern for him had taken the starch from her limbs, leaving her weak.

The thought of Katie without the energy he knew she possessed made him uneasy, for she was a girl of great strength. If not, she could not have endured growing up in the household where she'd been abused and mistreated. Could not have survived and escaped as she had, only beginning now to blossom into a woman any man would be proud to call his wife.

Any man but himself, he decided firmly, even as the lie resounded in his head. For he was not willing to allow her to be exposed to any other man yet. Maybe in a few weeks, when she'd come to be more able to stand alone. Then he might look around for a husband for her. And he laughed to himself as he considered that thought, for his feelings were in a tangle. He was a dog in the manger, unwilling to consider Katie as a woman who might be his wife in the future, yet unwilling to allow any other man near.

The girl stood before him, this female creature who tempted him so mightily. For now she was his responsibility, and even as his hands touched her waist, he was forced to face his own need. It was probably time to go visit the widow lady on the other side of town. It had been long months since he'd made the trip and being in such close proximity with Katie had turned his thoughts to forbidden subjects.

"Katie?" He spoke her name in a whisper and she sighed, stepping back from him.

He allowed it, not wanting to make her watchful of him, willing that she should set whatever limits she chose between them. "I'm hungry, sweetheart. If I wash up quick, can we eat? I swear I can smell ham."

"It's just green beans and onions cooked along with the last of the ham we had yesterday. It's ready whenever you are." She wiped at her eyes and he realized that she'd shed tears. Tears for him, for his safety. For just a moment, he reached for her again, holding her close to his long body, unwilling to relinquish all contact with the slender form that he recognized fit against him so well.

"John? Don't be touching me that way. It makes me feel funny, and I don't like it." She pushed him away, her questioning look shaming him as he turned her loose. She turned to the stove again, lifting the hot pads from atop the warming oven and opening the door of the wide oven below. Lifting the small kettle of beans out, she let it clang to the stovetop, then bent for the crock of potatoes that awaited her touch.

"There's applesauce that Berta brought over the other day," she said, turning with her hands full to begin setting the table. And as he washed up at the sink, she found plates and silverware in the cupboard. Two glasses followed and she opened the window to bring in a Mason jar of milk from the sill.

"I like the milk better when it's cold," she said by way of explanation. "And I thought if I could store it in the outside air it would taste better."

"Sounds good to me," he agreed, pulling his chair out from beneath the table and settling across from her as she poured their glasses full.

"Berta brought bread over today, and I churned butter this afternoon," she said, her chatter seemingly intended to cover the fear she'd tried to put into oblivion. She lifted the spoon and gave him a generous helping of meat and beans on his plate and then served herself. "You'll want potatoes, too, won't you?" she asked, her hands busy with the food she'd prepared.

"Sweetheart." He reached out and grasped her fingers, holding her hand in his for a moment until she looked up into his face. "I'm here, Katie, and I'm fine. I'm sorry I didn't think to send someone in to tell you I'd be late. But, next time I'll know better. I won't make you worry about me again."

"John…I need to tell you something, I think." As though the words were torn from her, as if she dreaded the telling, yet knew it was something she must do, she sat back in her chair and folded her hands in her lap.

"Whatever it is, it'll wait till you finish your supper, Katie," he said, willing her to eat and set loose the tension that gripped her.

"No, I need to say it now. I've been thinking bad thoughts and you need to know."

"You? Bad thoughts? Those two things don't go together, Katie," he said with a smile, spooning applesauce onto her plate and reaching to hand her the fork she'd abandoned by her plate.

"But I have," she insisted. "I've been thinking how lucky you are to have a family, people who love you and who you love in return. You've talked about your mother and father and the rest of them, and I know it's important to you—important that you have a family. And I, I have no one, John. And for just a little while, I was envious of you. Jealous that you have people who love you, and I've never had anyone to care about me."

She paused and he felt a pang of remorse that this lovely girl should feel so alone, so unaware that she was worthy of being loved, that there were those who cared about her. Berta, whose sharp tongue had only this morning told him how lucky he was to have found Katie, how wonderful that a girl so young should be so filled with goodness.

And how about you, John Roper? What about the yearning you have for the woman she's become since she's moved in?

He was silent for too long and Katie rose, taking her plate to the drainboard and leaving it there before she went to the bedroom. He eyed his food longingly, then rose and followed her.

"Katie. Listen to me." He caught up with her before she got to the bed and turned her into his arms. "I want you to listen to me, carefully." And then he inhaled, praying he would say the right words to heal her aching heart.

"You have so much to give to others, Katie girl. I don't think you know how appealing you are to everyone you meet. You're pretty…" And at the furious shaking of her head, he laughed aloud.

"Yes, you are," he insisted. "You have beautiful blue eyes, eyes the very color of a summer sky, and lovely hair, all dark and waving and full of midnight. You make me think of a doe sometimes, all big eyed and frightened. But, above all, I don't want you to ever be frightened of me or what I might do to you.

"For I have to admit that there are things I'd like to do that you might not like, Katie." He halted his words, fearful of her stepping out of his embrace, worried that she might not welcome his thoughts.

"I'll do anything you want me to, John. You know that."

"Yes, but I want you to feel the way I do, Katie, and you don't. You're young and you don't have any idea of the way things are."

She looked at him, this mite of a girl who had come very close to making a change in his vows of late, her fragile charm coming nigh unto stealing his heart, and he could not bring himself to obey his body's demands, his needs that fought to prevail over his good sense. And then she whispered words that almost sealed her fate, words that proclaimed her innocence, for she had no way of knowing the thoughts that had invaded his mind.

"I'll be whatever you want me to be, John. I know you wouldn't do anything to hurt me."

He ached for her. His body grew hard, his arousal prominent against his trousers and he pulled back from her lest she feel its presence. Unknowingly, she had given him permission to take her, to blend his body with hers and make her his—his what?

"Well, you're right there, Katie. I won't hurt you. I don't like to see the pain in your eyes that tells me you're unhappy. But I want you to know that you're not unloved, sweetheart. I think you're about the best thing that's ever happened to me, and I appreciate all you do for my comfort."

She sighed against his chest, her arms creeping

around his waist, holding him as close as her strength would allow, and he bent to kiss the fine wisps of hair that curled against her temple.

"Come on back in the kitchen and we'll eat, sweetheart," he said, coaxing her as best he could. She smiled up at him, apparently willing to be acquiescent and they went back to the kitchen. She carried the food back to the stove, dumped the beans and ham on their plates back into the kettle, stirred them together with the ones kept hot while they'd spoken in the bedroom, then filled their plates again.

"The potatoes need heating up, too," she said, eyeing the cooling milk gravy that covered them, and without pause, she gave them the same treatment she'd given the beans and ham. The plates steamed when she returned to the table and placed his in front of him. "Now, eat," she said, flashing him a smile that was only a bit frayed around the edges.

And so they did, John relishing each bite of the food she'd cooked for him, realizing that it had been a long time since anyone had taken care of him as Katie did, easing his weariness each day with hot meals, keeping his house clean, offering her smiles to brighten his days. Not since he'd left home long years ago had anyone paid him such mind, or spent their time and effort to insure his comfort. Not even Berta, who shared her bounty with six men around her table, unwilling or perhaps unable to allow her finer feelings to be shed on the men whose appetites she catered to.

The same Berta who had told him in careful, soft tones that his housekeeper was lovely, that she was worthy, that he was a man to be envied for his good sense in bringing Katie home with him, and taking care of her as he'd promised. That he'd do well to keep his hands to himself so far as Katie was concerned, unless he planned on making their situation legal. Unless he planned to observe the amenities.

Unless he had considered marriage.

CHAPTER SEVEN

THE KITCHEN IN THE back of the Dogleg Saloon was warm, redolent with the scent of food cooking and the woman before the stove turned as the door leading into the saloon opened, a man passing over the threshold.

He hesitated near the table and his words were hushed when he approached Molly, apparently chosen with care. "I didn't know, Molly. I'd thought I was doing the right thing for her, and when I saw her the other night…"

"Don't tell me you had no idea what monsters those folks were. You had to have some idea of what was going on with the girl. She was there for twelve years."

His shrug was one of male helplessness. "I was wrong. I admit it. But I honestly didn't know. What was I to do? I didn't have what it takes to take care of a kid. Not a girl, anyway. And when I heard of the Schraders wanting to adopt children, I thought she'd have a good home."

"And when you realized differently—why didn't you do something?"

"Why didn't *you* say something to me?"

She sniffed and rolled her sleeves up a notch higher. "Maybe it wasn't any of my business."

"You make everything else around here your business, Molly. I can't swallow that."

"Maybe I felt guilty that none of us had done anything to help. When Claire died, and the girl was left, I suppose I thought you might…"

"Might what? Buy a house somewhere and raise her myself? Or keep her here in a saloon with a bunch of whores for substitute mothers?" His laugh was harsh. "Not likely."

"She was abused," Molly said bitterly. "The girl had bruises all up and down her back when she took off her clothes and put that nightgown on in my room. The ones on her arms were just a drop in the bucket. They'd been beating on her for a long time, layer after layer."

"Then she's better off where she is, I'd say. John Roper has a good name. Bill Stanley gives him credit for a lot of intelligence, making him foreman up there at his spread."

"She still doesn't know who she is and she certainly doesn't have any idea that you even live and breathe."

"And she won't, Molly. She doesn't need to know about me."

"One day, Tom. One day, she'll need to know."

"No reason to fill her head with stuff that's dead and gone. And you'd be smart not to even think about it."

"No chance of me talking to her, and well you know

it. She's been gone from here for over a week, and I don't see much chance of John Roper bringing her around this place. He'll keep her as far from the saloon as he can, if I know anything about it."

"Just as well." Tom poured a cup of coffee from the blue enamel pot on the stove and carried it from the kitchen, his face a study, his steps slow.

IT WAS A WEEK LATER, and John had almost ridden from the barn, his horse already saddled, the newborn calf seen to and his routine set in his mind when Bill Stanley left the big house and headed for the barn. Close on his heels was the local law enforcement representative, Sheriff Len Carter, a man John had the utmost respect for. A man whose expression guaranteed he had not come this morning with small talk in mind.

"Morning, Sheriff. Hey there, Bill. What's going on?" He held the reins of his gelding, turning toward the front of the barn as the two men came through the open doorway.

"Sheriff needs to talk to you, John. Says there's a problem with your housekeeper."

"Katie? I just left her in the house. She's fine."

Len Carter cleared this throat and pushed his hands into his rear pockets, obviously uncomfortable with whatever he was stewing about.

"Spit it out, Sheriff," John said bluntly. And then waited while Len Carter looked at Bill and lifted an eyebrow.

"There's a problem with Katie. Her folks are looking for her and they're madder than a nest of hornets," Bill said shortly. "They've put it about that you took advantage of her and you've got her out here acting like a slave for you."

John laughed, shaking his head as though he'd heard the most absurd thing he could have dreamed of. And then he sobered, thinking of the girl he'd left in his kitchen, the girl who had curled on his sofa for the past week, and had lifted her face to kiss him of her own free will this morning when he left the house.

"Do you want to talk to her yourself, Sheriff?" he asked, knowing that Katie would be frightened almost out of her mind if she knew that the Schrader family was on her trail.

"Judge Henry wants her in court today. This afternoon, in fact, Roper. He sent me out here to get her."

"What's she charged with? I wasn't aware that you could treat someone like a criminal who hasn't done anything wrong."

"You're the one the judge wants to see, Roper. In fact, you're under arrest as of right now."

"What are the charges, sir?" John answered with all the respect he could dredge up, knowing that without his presence, Katie would not be able to handle this.

"Rape, for one," the sheriff said.

"I haven't touched her, at least not that way," John countered. "Katie's my cook and my housekeeper, Sheriff."

"I know that. I talked to Shandy Peterson over at the general store and he said you'd been in there with her,

buying her clothes and shoes. The Schraders are sayin'
you stole their girl away and they want her back."

"Well, why don't you ask Katie if she's here
under...what's the word? Duress?"

"I'll ask her." The sheriff shot a long look at Bill
Stanley. "What do you think, Bill? Do they have a case
against Roper, here?"

"Not up to me to say, but I'd bet my money on my
foreman. He's as honest as the day is long."

"Then you won't mind coming along and sitting in
on this?"

Bill shook his head. "Not a bit. I'd like to bring my
housekeeper, too. Berta has taken to Katie in a big way,
and the girl will need another woman to stick close."

Without hesitation, the sheriff nodded. "Sounds like
a plan to me." And then to John he issued an order he
was obviously uncomfortable with. "Go get the girl,
John. We need to be on our way inside of fifteen
minutes."

"It'll take that long to let her know what's going
on," John said, his anger rising as he thought of what
Katie's reaction would be. "She's gonna be scared half
out of her wits, Sheriff. She's terrified of the Schrader
bunch, and with good reason. She can tell you that
herself."

"She'd do better to save it for the judge." And with
that the lawman turned on his heel and mounted his
horse. "I'll give both of you fifteen minutes to be ready
to ride."

John nodded and headed back to the cabin, his horse ground-tied behind him. Bill went toward the house and John watched him walk away, then called out words he meant with his whole heart.

"Thanks, Bill. I appreciate you going along."

The big rancher only waved a hand and leaped over the two steps onto the porch, pushing open the door into his kitchen.

Inside the cabin, John found that Katie had been standing at the window and when he entered the kitchen, she turned to him with fright painting her features. "What happened, John? What does that man want? Is he the law?"

"That's what the silver star on his chest says, honey. He tells me we have to head for town to see the judge. It must be his week to hear cases in Eden, and the Schraders have laid claim to you. They're saying I stole you from them and I'm keeping you out here against your will."

"That's a lie, John. How can they say such a thing?"

"Anyone can say anything he pleases, honey. The problem rises when they speak falsehoods in court. Don't worry about it. We'll get this straightened out in no time. Now get yourself dressed in one of your new dresses and put on your new shoes. I want them to see how pretty you are when you get a chance to get all shined up."

"I'm afraid, John." The words were simple, from a

girl who could not tell a lie if her life depended on it, and John knew she spoke God's truth this time.

COURT WAS CALLED TO order in the sheriff's office, with his deputy at the door to keep out the curious townsfolk who had gathered in the street. Having the Circuit Judge come to town was a bimonthly affair, but usually his visit was uneventful, consisting of men who'd fought in the saloon or worse. Only on occasion did something happen that stirred the citizens of Eden, something like a horse being stolen or cattle rustling on an outlying ranch.

John walked into the Sheriff's office on his own hook, obviously not a prisoner, and the ladies who watched and were only too aware of the reputation of the family Katie had spent most of her life seemed relieved. Some of them appeared shamefaced, as if silently acknowledging their own guilt in not having interfered with the upbringing of the girl who existed in the Schraders' house outside of town. She'd not been allowed to attend school or church or spend time off the farm where she'd been kept since an early age.

Everyone was apparently aware that the Schrader family were an odd bunch, but if they were right in claiming that Katie had been hurt by John Roper, if their claim held true that the man had taken her to his home and kept her there against her will, John knew he would face the full penalty of the law.

Inside, Judge Homer Henry waited for the principals in this case, and from the look on his face, John knew he was not looking forward to his job today. When Mr. and Mrs. Schrader came in the door, their eyes swept across the room to where Katie stood between Bill Stanley and his housekeeper, Berta. John stood directly behind the girl and when she caught her breath and a small cry left her lips at the sight of the Schraders, he touched her shoulder and she looked back quickly to meet his gaze.

"It's all right," he said quietly. "Hang on, Katie girl."

"Quiet in the court," Judge Henry said sternly, looking down to where the principals in this hearing stood, the Schraders on one side of his desk, Katie and her protectors on the other.

The judge folded his hands before him on the desk and shot a look at the local lawman. "I'd like to hear the charges, Sheriff Carter."

Len Carter nodded and presented the judge with a piece of paper, then stood erect and spoke the words that the Schraders had spoken in his hearing early this morning. "This man and woman, Jacob and Agnes Schrader, claim that the girl they've had living in their home for twelve years was kidnapped by John Roper and forced to go with him to his cabin out on the Stanley ranch and has cohabitated with her."

The judge looked over his spectacles at John, his brows lifted in a question, even as he spoke it aloud. "What do you have to say about that, Mr. Roper?"

"Katie is living in my cabin. That part's true enough, but I didn't force her to do anything, Judge. She cooks for me and keeps my place clean and she's staying there of her own free will. She was mistreated by—"

"That's a lie," Agnes Schrader shouted and her husband echoed the words in a thundering voice that could have shaved the bark off a tree, John thought with a grin he hid behind his hand.

"Well, that's what we're here to find out, ma'am," the judge said politely. "Now, if you and your mister will just settle down, we'll talk to the girl and get the truth of the matter."

"She won't tell the truth. He's got her scared to death and she's afraid to speak for herself," Jacob Schrader said darkly.

The judge pounded his gavel once and stood. "I will not repeat myself. Settle down or leave the courtroom."

Katie stiffened her shoulders and stepped inches closer to the desk. "May I speak, sir?" she asked, and the judge sent a keen glance the length of her.

"You don't look abused to me, young lady. This fella leave any bruises on you?"

"No, sir. The bruises I had from living with the Schraders faded once John took me home with him."

"These folks left marks on your skin?"

As she nodded her agreement, Jacob Schrader growled a muffled threat and Katie blanched, her eyes widening as she cast one look in the man's direction. Her arms crossed over her breasts as if she would protect herself, and a fine trembling caused her to shiver.

"Empty the court, Deputy, all but this girl here in front of me. I'll talk to her alone."

At that, Bill Stanley took John's arm and led him from the office. Dragging him would have been a better description of their short walk into the street, but John did not speak, only stayed as close as possible to the door behind which Katie stood.

"She's alone in there," he said quietly. "What's that fella going to do to her? She's scared out of her shoes, Bill. That damn Schrader has a lot to answer for."

"The judge isn't going to hurt her, John. He wants to get to the bottom of this, and Katie's not about to be abused by the law."

There was nothing to be done. He knew it as well as he knew his name, but his heart ached as he thought of Katie's fear as she faced the judge on her own.

"ALL RIGHT, YOUNG LADY. Let's hear what you've got to say. Where did you meet the young man…John Roper's his name, right?"

"Yes, sir. John's the man I'm working for. I met him in the Dogleg Saloon one night after I ran from the Schraders' farm into town."

"Why did you go home with him, girl? Did he make you big promises or threaten you any?"

"No, John only promised to look after me and take care of me. He didn't threaten me, not one bit."

The judge looked down at the papers he held, frowning a bit, then peered over his glasses once more as Katie shifted from one foot to another. "Why don't we sit down, girl, and talk like friends, just for a minute."

Katie felt at a loss for words, but did as the man asked and settled on a chair across from the desk. "I don't want John to be in trouble because of me, sir."

"How do you feel about the Schrader family? Did you have a nice room of your own? Enough to eat?" And then he looked at her closely, perhaps noting the pale complexion, the fear that clouded Katie's face.

"I slept in the washroom, on the floor, under a bench where they kept the washtubs. And I had one dress to wear. I ate whatever I could find after the family finished their meals. Usually not much."

"How'd you happen to meet this fella? How long did you know him before you went home with him?"

"I met him in the saloon, like I said, when a drunk pushed me through the door. A couple of other cowhands were making remarks and I was scared and John made me sit down by him and talked to me. He asked me was I hungry, and when I said I was, he took me back to the kitchen where Molly is the cook. She gave me some supper and a bed to sleep in."

The judge's eyes narrowed and his lips thinned as he listened to Katie's tale. "You stayed in the saloon overnight? In a room upstairs?"

"Yes, sir, I did. Molly said no one would bother me while I was in her bed, and she gave me a nightgown to wear. And when John came back in the morning, I'd made up my mind." She paused, realizing she needed to backtrack, and her hands folded in her lap, her teeth sinking into her bottom lip as she thought of what she would say.

"He'd asked me the night before if I'd go home with him and keep house for him, and Molly seemed to think it was a good idea and he looked kind. His eyes are real soft and he speaks nicely, and I wasn't afraid of him. So I went with him."

"Just like that. You just trotted yourself out to the Stanley ranch and moved in with him."

"Yes, I did. And when he took me home to his cabin, his own place out there that Mr. Stanley gave him when he made him the foreman on the ranch, John told me I could fix it up any way I wanted to, and he bought me clothes in town, because all I had were the rags on my back." She looked toward the door and her voice seemed to plead her case for her, the tones trembling as she asked for that which her heart craved.

"Sir. Judge. Can John come back in here? I feel better when he's with me. He takes care of me and I don't want anything to happen to him out there. If folks think he's done something wrong they might not be nice to him. And Mr. Schrader is mean enough to use his knife on John if he gets a chance. I've seen him come close to killing a man for less than what John's done."

"He's used his knife on a man? For what reason?"

Katie was visibly trembling now, but her voice grew stronger as she told a story she'd hidden in the back of her mind for over three years. "Once there was a man who worked on the Schrader place and he took something from the house. I don't know what it was, but Mrs. Schrader was mad at him and when he tried to leave, her husband went after him and cut him up something terrible. The man laid right there in the yard and I thought he was going to bleed to death. I don't know what happened to him, but he was gone the next morning and we never saw him again." She looked again toward the door and shivered visibly.

"Sir, they told me if I said anything about it to anyone, I'd get the same treatment."

CHAPTER EIGHT

"DEPUTY." THE MAN leaning against the wall stood at attention. "Bring John Roper in here."

The deputy nodded and opened the door, calling John's name in a stern voice. In less time than Katie could have imagined, John crossed the threshold and stood behind the chair where she sat.

"Yes, sir." His voice was deep, dark and strong, and Katie was so proud of him, she felt she could burst.

"This young lady wants you in here while I speak with her and I don't have any objection. How do you feel about it?"

"Whatever Katie wants is all right with me." John's voice resounded from the walls and ceiling and the judge only smiled.

"All right now. Let's clear up the rape charge first off." He eyed Katie and then shot a long look at John, as if warning him to be silent.

"Young lady, do you know what rape is?"

She shook her head. "I know it's something bad, 'cause Mrs. Schrader accused Mr. Schrader of thinking about it one time and they had a big fight."

"Who did she say he was thinking of when she accused him?"

Katie swallowed and her voice was very small as she answered. "Me, sir."

"And did the man ever hurt you in any way, Katie?"

"Yes, sir. He used to hit me with his belt when I didn't do my work fast enough or if he thought I looked at him the wrong way."

John jerked upright, the hand resting on Katie's shoulder tightened and a sound passed his lips that sounded like a curse word to Katie. With a quick gesture she turned her head, her lips brushing against the back of his hand and the pressure on her shoulder lessened and became a caress.

The judge appeared to ignore her slight movement, but he smiled as he spoke to her again. "And what about this man you work for, Katie? Has he ever hit you? Or hurt you in any way?"

She frowned and shot him an accusing look as if defying his suggestion, but her words were respectful. "Oh, no, sir. John wouldn't hurt me. He's good to me. Bought me clothes and I have a whole pantry full of food to choose from when I get ready to cook. He even got me new shoes. And I've never had more than one pair at a time in my life, and sometimes not any at all when the weather was warm, and now I've got my boots, and shoes to wear in the houses, too."

"All right, Katie." She thought he hid a smile behind his hand as he looked once more at the paper he held and then he laid it on the desk and leaned forward.

"Where do you sleep at night, Katie?"

The hand on her shoulder moved a bit and she felt the fingers grip her firmly. "John's only got the one bed, sir. So I sleep on the sofa by the fireplace."

"And do you sleep there every night? John doesn't make you sleep in his bed?"

"No, sir. Like I said, John's bed is the only bed, so there isn't anywhere else for me to sleep but the sofa. But he's going to build a room for me before long so I'll have a real bed of my own."

The judge cleared his throat. "That's fine, Katie. Now, I must ask you another question. Has John put his hands on you? Does he touch you?"

She looked puzzled, then smiled. "He touches me sometimes. Puts his hand on my shoulder or touches my arm."

"Does he kiss you?"

She felt a flush climb her cheeks as she wondered just what business it was of this man's if her John kissed her. Surely John wouldn't get in trouble because of that. "Yes, he kisses me sometimes. But not very often." *Not often enough.*

The judge leaned forward, his eyes more alert now, his forehead creasing in a frown. "Where does he kiss you?"

"He kissed me a couple of times in the kitchen and next to the back door a time or two and once in the bedroom." Her smile was brilliant. "No, twice in the bedroom."

She thought the judge was having difficulty swallowing, for he seemed to choke and then he recovered and bent a stern look upon her. "Where on your body does he kiss you, Katie?"

"My body? Like on my cheek, you mean? Or my forehead? Or maybe you mean the last time he kissed me and it was on my lips."

"I think that's enough on that subject, Katie. I want to know if John has forced himself on you, if he's made love to you."

"I'm not sure what you mean, sir. John doesn't love me. He's just the man who hired me on to cook for him and keep his house clean. And sometimes he doesn't even seem to know what a housekeeper is supposed to do. In fact, he got upset when he thought I was working too hard cleaning his floors."

"And you sleep with him in the next room, every night?" As he spoke he looked over her shoulder at John, and his eyes were warm.

"I told you where I sleep, sir. Every night, just as regular as can be, he sends me in to change my clothes and then I come out and wrap up in his quilt on the sofa and he goes to bed in the bedroom. He leaves the door open, should I need anything during the night. But I can't think what I'd need that I don't already have."

"And does he make advances to you, ask you to do things with him?"

She looked puzzled, then turned back to John and her whisper was barely loud enough to be heard, but the judge seemed to have very good hearing. "John, what's he talking about? What kind of things? Like do we talk, or what?"

John exchanged a long look with the man behind the desk and then said words to Katie that told her all she needed to know. "Just tell him the truth, Katie. Have I ever asked you to do anything you didn't want to do or hurt you in any way?"

"You know you haven't, John." Then she turned back to the judge. "All we do is talk when we sit by the fireplace of an evening. You know, John sits in his big chair and sometimes I sit on the couch or on a stool by the fire and we talk. Once in a while I make coffee for us or we have our sweet things there. John's real fond of my pie, and I can bake good cookies.

"Oh, and once in a while, we talk about what I'm doing to the cabin, like what I'm making for the bedroom or such, and John tells me about the horses and cows and the work he's doing on the ranch." She seemed to run out of words for a moment, and then her mind turned to the best parts of their evenings together, and she elaborated on those times to the judge.

"Pretty regular, John pats me on the shoulder after I get undressed and lay down on the couch, and he always pulls the quilts up so I won't be cold. Oh, and he tells me how much he likes my cooking and how nice it is to have a clean house and all, and best of all he always listens to what I have to say." She paused, as if searching her mind for anything more to add, and then her sigh was deep, her smile soft. "And then he just usually tells me to go to sleep, once I'm all tucked in on the sofa. Is that what you mean?"

"Yes, Katie. I think you've told me all I need to know about John Roper. If I understand you properly, he's been kind to you and taken care of you and hasn't threatened you or hurt you in any way. Am I right?"

She shot him a weary look and shook her head as if his logic escaped her. "That's what I told you, sir, and I don't tell lies."

"John Roper, I must advise you to keep this young woman as far as possible from Jacob and Agnes Schrader as you can. They are dangerous to her well-being and it would behoove you to keep a close eye on her at all times. Do you understand?"

John nodded quickly. "Yes sir, I understand what you're saying." His eyes were unwavering as he faced the man behind the desk.

"Furthermore, John Roper, you have my admiration," Judge Henry said quietly, his face sober, his eyes warm. To which John only nodded.

"I think we can call the other folks back in now, Deputy," the judge announced and his look was stern as the deputy smiled at John and then shot Katie a look of admiration.

Bill Stanley filed in with the sheriff behind him, the Schraders bringing up the rear.

The judge stood and banged his gavel one final time. "The court has reached a decision in this hearing. We find no fault with John Roper and give Katie over into his custody and care.

"We also recommend that in order for John to protect the young woman who is living in his house, that he marry her today. In that way, she will have the rights of a wife and will no longer be in fear of being returned to the family she lived with before the past three weeks. We also order a restriction against Jacob and Agnes Schrader, forbidding them to have any contact with this young lady at any time. That'll be all. Court's adjourned."

He sat back down and watched carefully as Katie stepped to John's side and whispered soft words as he bent his head to hear her. "Did he mean it, John? You have to marry me? Because I don't think it's right that you should have to tie yourself down to a wife just because I'm living in your cabin. I just want to go home now. I'm late starting dinner but if we have time I'd like to stop at the general store and maybe we can get some oilcloth, like you said."

John's face was grim as he listened to her words and then he took her hand in his. "Katie, the judge didn't give us any choice when he said that about you and I getting married. He meant it for your protection, so that you'll be a married woman and no one can treat you like a child any longer."

"I'll do whatever you say, John. If you want to marry

me, it's all right. Just so long as we can go and get my oilcloth afterward. You promised me a covering for the kitchen table, remember?"

John laughed aloud, shaking his head as if Katie's words pleased him. And in truth they did, for she was so honest, so simple and open, he could hardly believe it. Had he asked her to jump from a second-story window, she would have done it. Marrying him was but a simple request to her mind, and she was willing to do whatever he asked of her.

"We'll do whatever you want, Katie. If you want oilcloth, we'll go pick it out, and Berta said you needed a teapot, too, and a tin of tea."

"He's buyin' her affection, is what he's doing. Don't our time count for nothin'? We kept her and treated her like our own kin for twelve years and this is what we get for our trouble." Jacob Schrader's voice was loud and clear, and Bill Stanley had a job on his hands as John turned quickly, his eyes hard as he headed toward the older man.

A strong hand grasped his arm and halted his progress. "John, he isn't worth it, and he's not going to cause you any more trouble. Let it go."

"I'll say one thing to you Schrader, and only once. Hear me well," John said, his voice a threat in itself. "You ever come near Katie, I'll hang you out to dry. If you ever threaten her or do anything to harm her, you'll answer to me. I hope you've listened well to what I say because this is the only warning you'll get."

"See what I mean?" Jacob Schrader's shout was raucous, his eyes bulging from his head. "The man's a lunatic. Is this the sort of fella you're giving that girl to? This is against the law."

Judge Henry banged his gavel again and stood erect, pointing a finger at Jacob Schrader. "You've just earned yourself three days in jail, Schrader. That's called contempt of court and you're about as guilty as hell. Take him away, Sheriff."

John tugged Katie to the door and she was spared the sight of Jacob Schrader as he glared in her direction and spewed saliva as he swore.

Judge Henry's voice was loud and clear as he faced the angry man. "That's just earned you a solid week in a cell, Schrader. You want to push it to fourteen days? Just keep it up."

The crowd outside had been treated to the full display within the sheriff's office and they talked busily among themselves, repeating the judge's words and speaking loudly of Katie's plight. When the young couple came through the doorway, a cheer arose from the crowd gathered and loud calls from men and women alike cheered them and congratulated them on the decision that had been made.

Katie clutched John's arm then and he steered her down the sidewalk toward the general store, where he opened the door and ushered her inside. He halted there, almost on the threshold, wrapping his arms around Katie for a long moment, bending his head to inhale her fragrance, thankful that the store was empty but for Shandy Peterson and his daughter. But had it been filled to the rafters with customers, John wouldn't have cared. His only concern was the girl he cherished..

"Let's get your oilcloth and then go find the preacher, sweetheart," he said, fighting for control, aware that he would not rest easy until he'd heard the words spoken over them that would tie her to him legally. Jacob Schrader would no longer have any link to Katie, no reason to ever see her again.

And John Roper would be a married man once more. Perhaps not the happiest man in town, but willing for this moment to do as he'd been bidden. There was no choice, not only from a legal standpoint, but John's own sense of fairness dictated that he should protect Katie by the bonds of matrimony, no matter his own qualms on the subject. He would no doubt spend many an hour in worry over the situation he'd managed to get into, but there was no help for it.

Katie looked up at him uncertainly. "There's just one thing, John." She bit at her lip and her hands twisted together, her fingers seeming bloodless to his discerning eye.

"What else do we need, Katie? What did I forget?"

"You said maybe we could buy enough material to make curtains for the kitchen, and I saw some pretty checkered stuff when we were here before and…"

"Show me," he said, his smile gleaming, and followed her across the store until they reached the countertop where bolts of fabric lay. She slipped her fingers down one pile, and lifted a bolt of yellow and white gingham for his approval.

"This looks like sunshine, don't it, John? And if we were to get a piece of oilcloth with some yellow in it, I think your kitchen would look right nice."

John lifted the bolt of gingham and carried it to where Shandy Peterson stood, awaiting their decision. "We'll take enough of this for curtains. Tell him how much you want, Katie. And then a piece of oilcloth for our table, whatever Katie wants."

Shandy Peterson smiled broadly, apparently pleased at the prospect of a good sale. "Yes, sir, John. I'll have my girl cut a length for you." In moments he'd called Jessica from the back room and she carried the curtain material Katie had chosen to a table where she conferred with Katie for a moment and then measured out six yards of the checkered percale with a long yardstick. Her scissors sliced through the fabric in seconds and she folded it, then sought out thread to match for Katie's use.

"I need needles and pins, too, John. I borrowed Berta's last time when I did the bedroom curtains, but I'd ought to have some of my own, I suspect, if I'm going to do much sewing. And if it isn't too much money, I could use a pair of scissors."

He turned at her voice and nodded. "Just pick out what you want," he said, and smiled as he noted the happiness that wreathed her face.

Katie tugged at Jessica's arm. "I want a piece of oilcloth, too. What do you have with some yellow in it?"

The two young women stepped to the rolls of oilcloth that hung against a wall and Jessica displayed several patterns for Katie's approval. Their heads together, they made a production out of finding the right color and pattern to grace John's kitchen table. Yellow daisies on a white background won, hands down, and Katie watched with eager eyes as Jessica cut a length Katie thought would fit the table with enough to hang on either side.

As if she'd discovered a gold mine, Katie gathered up her purchases and placed them on the counter, waiting for Shandy to figure out how much John owed him. "I'd like to bake a pie, John, and we're almost out of sugar. Can we get a small bag?"

"Ten pounds, Shandy," John said quickly. And then turned back to Katie. "Do you need lard or flour or anything else?"

She shook her head. "No, there's plenty there to last a good long time."

Jessica approached from John's far side and held out her hand, displaying a small wrapped object in her hand, smiling as he nodded quickly and took it from her.

"What's that, John?" Katie's curiosity was piqued and she stood on tiptoe to peer past him at the object he held.

"A couple of things for you. A bar of soap, for one, sweetheart. Jessica thought you might like it."

"You've got soap enough, John. You don't need any more."

He shook his head. "It's not for me, honey. Here, smell it."

She sniffed at the paper-wrapped bar in his hand and her eyes widened as the scent of flowers met her nostrils. "I can't imagine using that on my skin, John. I'll smell like a garden patch of lavender."

"Yeah." His grin teased her as he made his purchase, including the soap in the bundle Shandy wrapped, noting with interest the small package he slid into his trouser's pocket.

Flustered at John's extravagance, she walked by his side as they left the store, then waited as Bill Stanley brought his wagon to the entrance of the general store. "I put your gelding on behind," he told John, and then waved at the wagon bed. "Set your bride on there and climb on, John. We're going to see the minister and then we'll head for home."

Shandy followed them out with their bundles, and in moments they were rolling down the street, Katie blissfully contemplating the making of curtains for her kitchen.

THE MAN WHO PASTORED the church answered John's knock and welcomed them into his parlor, shaking John's hand, then that of Bill Stanley, nodding nicely to Berta as she looked on.

"This man and woman want to get married, Parson," Bill said politely. "What do we need to do to make that happen?"

"The young lady must give me her consent, agreeing that she has in no way been coerced into this union, and then we'll go ahead with the ceremony."

He looked at Katie kindly. "Are you old enough to be married, girl?"

"Yes, sir," she replied firmly. "I'm almost eighteen and John Roper here wants to marry me."

"Do you want to marry him?" the parson asked softly, searching her face.

"Yes, sir, I do."

"And you, John Roper, are you willing to take this woman as your wife?"

John looked down at Katie and his lips formed a smile, one he could barely generate. But his answer was firm. "I want to marry Katie, sir."

And give up my freedom, take on a woman and try to put my faith in her. Trust her to be honest and above-board with me.

"Katie, repeat these words after me," the minister said quietly, and the girl before him trembled as she promised to love, honor and obey the man she'd vowed to wed. Her eyes flew to John's, meshed for a moment with the dark beauty of his, and then her eyelids fluttered and she caught her breath, stunned by the gravity of the vows they took. She'd vowed to give herself into John's keeping, and for a moment she felt a quick stab of fear, knowing that from this moment on she would answer to him, would be dependent upon him for her happiness.

John heard the words of the ceremony as if through a mist, answered at the appropriate times, and at the preacher's bidding he bent to touch Katie's lips with his own. She caught her breath as he did and he touched her shoulder, a gesture that seemed to give her assurance that all was well. They left the small parsonage, John leading the way with his arm across Katie's shoulders, Bill and Berta behind them.

THEY REACHED THE RANCH in the late afternoon and the sun was nearing the horizon before Katie had put together a meal. She stepped out onto the back porch, her eyes peeled for a glimpse of John. She'd kept her new shoes and stockings on, careful not to stain her dress with food as she cooked.

The man fussed overmuch, she thought, her mind traveling back to the days when she'd been told more than once that shoes were a luxury, to be worn out of doors and only when the weather was too cold to go without. It was hard to break old habits, but for John's sake she'd do her best, and if wearing shoes pleased him, then wear them she would.

John had told her he would be doing chores with the men and she'd just caught a glimpse of Shorty with a bucket of milk heading for the milk house. Surely John wouldn't be far behind.

When he walked through the barn door, as she'd expected, his gaze dropped to her feet before seeking out her face. She watched him from the porch. As if he knew she would be there waiting for him, a grin lit his face and his stride lengthened as he made short work of the hundred yards between house and barn.

"Supper ready?" John asked, opening the door for Katie to enter the kitchen. He hung up his coat on the hook, put his hat over it and he sat on the chair and took off his boots. "Smells good," he said, sniffing the air, his nose twitching as the aroma of potato soup reached him. The scent of bacon she'd used in the making of it tempted him and he went to the stove, lifting her spoon and dipping it in the kettle.

She laughed and took it from his hand. "Just get washed up and I'll fix you a bowl," she told him, her mood one of happiness such as he'd never seen.

Her eyes sparkled and her cheeks were flushed; whether it was the warm stove or some stray thought that had brought color to her face, he couldn't guess. He only knew that his Katie was happy, that she exuded joy that spilled over on him and gave him the courage to speak to her about a subject dear to his heart.

After they ate, he decided, would be time enough to talk to her, and maybe he'd be better able to gauge her willingness to accept his thoughts by then. Perhaps she was ignorant of the marriage bed, but surely she had heard some hint of what went on between men and women. And if she feared what might happen in his bed, he'd do well to speak of it beforehand.

They ate, John consuming two bowls of the soup, spreading jam on his bread with a lavish hand and finishing with a generous piece of the apple pie Katie had spoken of in the general store. He pushed his chair back from the table and sighed. "You sure are a good cook, sweetheart. I'm awfully glad I married you."

"Because I can cook?" she asked with a teasing smile as she rose to clear the table.

"That, too," he admitted. "But mostly because I just like having you here in my house. And from now on, in my bed."

"In your bed, John?" she asked carefully, dunking the bowls in warm dishwater. "I've been in your house for pretty near a month now, and you never mentioned me sleeping in your bed before." She turned to him then, and her expression was troubled.

"We've never been married before today," he said carefully. "You're my wife now, Katie." he said, recognizing that she was pondering something and wanted to speak her mind. "What is it you're thinking of right now," he asked, intent on knowing what was bothering her.

"I need the clothes you took out of the bedroom, John. The ones I wore when I came here. What did you do with them?"

"I told you they weren't fit for anything but rags, honey. They're out in the barn, and I'm going to use them to wipe down the tack when I oil the leather."

"Well, I'm needing them right quick, John. Probably by tomorrow."

"I know you have a clean dress to wear, Katie. I saw you doing the wash just yesterday."

"I don't want to wear those old things," she said quickly and a flush rose to color her face, and she bit her lip as though mightily embarrassed. "I need them for rags."

"To clean with?" He was puzzled by her insistence.

"No, just for me." She turned away from him, as if she were unable to meet his gaze and her shoulders hunched a bit. "I just need them, John."

"All right, if you say so." He spoke slowly, unable to determine her meaning.

"John, I know you're a man and you might not know about such things, but I'm about to have a problem and I need my old petticoat to tear up for rags. I thought to use a towel, but I don't want to ruin your things, and…"

A glimmer of knowledge lit his mind and he smiled, suddenly understanding her need. A need that was purely a woman thing, the subject one he'd never discussed before, and actually only knew of from bits and pieces he'd heard through the years, and from the marriage he'd shared with Sadie.

"Katie, you can use my towels if you want to, and the next time we go to town, we'll buy you some white outing flannel to cut up for you to use when you need it. Will that be all right?"

Her face was fiery red when she turned to face him. "Yes, all right, John. I just can't talk about this with you right now. But I don't feel well, and I'm all out of sorts and I'm going to need…well, by tomorrow sometime, I'll have to have that petticoat."

He laughed, his amusement overriding his good sense, and she cast him a long look that told him he'd stepped on her toes. "I'm sorry, honey. I'm not laughing at you, only relieved that there isn't anything wrong. You can talk to me about anything you want to. We're married folks now and there shouldn't be any secrets between us or anything we can't talk about when we're by ourselves. Anything that goes on in this house is private and no one else needs to know what we say or do."

And it was his sincere hope that her "problem" would not come into being tonight, but that it would evidence itself tomorrow or perhaps the next day. A wedding night was a special occasion and he had a vision of his being postponed by an act of nature.

But Katie nodded at his words and he noted the look of relief she wore. "All right, John. I can agree with that."

He went to her then, his hands on her waist, his lips speaking soft words just inches from her own. "I hope you're as agreeable when we talk about something else, sweetheart." She was soft against him, her pliant body forming to his, her smile welcoming him.

It was more than he could resist, and he bent to her, tasting freely of the sweetness that seemed such a part of her. Her lips blended with his and she moved them against his, imitating the kiss he'd begun. Her mouth opened at his silent urging, allowing him to delve into the warmth that lay just beyond her lips, and she stiffened for only a moment as his tongue explored the secrets of her mouth. Perhaps he was moving too rapidly for her, he thought, with the invasion of her mouth, but she seemed to be welcoming his touch and the advances he'd made thus far.

He lifted his head and looked down at her, her wide eyes and soft lips, the soft rise of her breasts beneath the dress she wore. And watched as she trembled at his touch.

Even though a shiver ran the length of her spine and she felt a weakness that was new and almost frightening as his hands left her waist and curled beneath the rounded lines of her bottom, she reveled in his touch, his wide palms holding her close. Then one hand left her backside and moved upward with gentle care, until it reached the curve of her breast. She froze, unmoving for just a moment as he cupped the soft flesh in his palm and a murmur of satisfaction passed through his lips.

"John? What are you doing? Why are you touching me there?"

"Am I hurting you, sweet? I only want to know your body as well as I know my own. I want to touch your curves and find out what feels good to you. I won't hurt you, Katie girl."

She nodded, holding her breath as his long fingers moved against the taut flesh he held, flesh that had, up until moments ago, been soft and familiar to her. Now it ached, the crest of her breast growing tight and needing the attention of his fingertips. And wasn't that a foolish thought, she wondered, then drew in a shuddering breath as he teased and plied the tender morsel he held.

"Will you come to bed with me, Katie?" he asked quietly. "I think you already know that husbands and wives sleep together, don't you?"

At her nod, he took heart and continued on in that vein. "I want you to be in my bed with me tonight, sweetheart. I want you to sleep in my arms. Will you do that?"

CHAPTER NINE

"YOU WANT ME TO SLEEP in your bed with you? Instead of on the sofa?" She seemed perplexed and he would not have it.

"That's the way such things are done, Katie. Men and women share the same bed after they're married."

"I don't have to do anything? You won't…" She hesitated and his heart dropped, the thud taking his breath as he recognized her fear.

"I won't do anything you don't want me to, Katie." It was a promise, a binding vow, as firm as the words he'd spoken just hours ago before the minister in town. If Katie feared his touch, he would not lay a hand on her, but her presence in his bed was the only way to begin this marriage, to his way of thinking.

She seemed to consider his words, her mind working, her face a puzzle as if any number of thoughts were scurrying through her mind. "You're gonna sleep under the sheet with me?" she asked finally.

He nodded, watching for the trace of fear he knew would be apparent, and was not surprised when she inhaled sharply.

"I never slept in a bed with a man, John. When old Jacob tried to crawl in with me, he scared me something fierce. I didn't want him to touch me, no how."

John considered the girl who had only hours ago promised to "love, honor and obey" him. And his words were ones guaranteed to bring about her acquiescence to his bidding.

"You told the preacher you'd obey me, Katie. Remember?"

Her eyes widened and her mouth tightened as if she wanted to speak but feared his wrath should she allow the words to pass her lips.

"What is it, Katie? Tell me what you're thinking." He spoke mildly, measuring his words, softening his tone, knowing she was tensed and ready to bolt, should he allow it.

"Did that mean I have to do whatever you say, John? That 'obey' part of the wedding."

He only nodded, waiting for movement from the small, tensed body before him. But to his amazement, she seemed to relax before his eyes and her gaze lifted to touch his.

"Are you telling me you want me to get in your bed now, John? Shall I get undressed?"

He nodded. "Put on your nightgown, Katie, and then get under the sheet. I'll be in there with you in a couple of minutes. I'll just bank the fireplace and make sure the cookstove is ready for morning."

"All right."

So easily she did as he asked, so immediate was her response, he was stunned. He'd thought to find her stubborn, at least reluctant to sleep in his bed. Instead, she had turned and entered the bedroom and lighting a candle, pushed the door halfway closed before she readied herself for sleep.

He heard the water poured from the pitcher into his china washbowl, heard the sound of a cloth being squeezed out, the dripping of excess water signaling her preparation for washing herself. And he closed his eyes, thinking of the soft curves that would receive the touch of the cloth she used. The urge to open the door was great, but he clenched his fists and stood before the fireplace, waiting for some signal that she had finished her nighttime routine.

He'd seen her, many times, the bedroom door ajar behind her as she made ready for the night. Watched the door she left partway open as she bustled about behind it, doing his best to imagine the flurry of preparation she underwent. And then watching as she came out, garbed in the white gown he'd bought her at the general store, her face flushing as she caught his gaze on her. Her short walk to the sofa where she'd been sleeping was generally fraught with haste, for she did not feel comfortable with his eyes touching her in her nightgown.

That it was totally unrevealing, that he stood not a chance of glimpsing her through its fabric was not the issue. It was a nightgown, and she felt uneasy with only that single layer of material between the two of them. As if her mind were an open book, and he had been given the right to read each page, he knew her thoughts.

And in knowing, recognized that his responsibility tonight was to assure her of her safety in his bed. She would be frightened, of that there was no doubt, for her only exposure to a man had been the hated Jacob Schrader, and John had no wish to be associated with that man in any way.

He rapped lightly on the bedroom door, standing half-ajar, giving him only a view of his bed, and heard Katie's soft whisper. "Come in, John. I'm ready to climb into bed now."

He did as she had given him leave, entering the room, leaving the door open to catch the heat from the kitchen, lest she be cold. And then wondered at his own judgment, as he recognized that cold might be his ally tonight, that perhaps if Katie was chilled, she would curl close to him, seeking his warmth.

But the deed was done, and he would not second-guess himself. She was sitting on the side of the mattress, her eyes wide, the thoughts that filled her mind all too apparent to his view. And then, as if she bowed to his edict, she slid her feet beneath the sheet and quilt and curled up on the farthest spot on his mattress.

"Close your eyes, Katie. I'm gonna get undressed now." His words were a warning she heeded, pulling the sheet and quilt up to cover her head. He undid his shirt, then his trousers, pushing them from his body with a single movement, leaving him clad only in his drawers and stockings. A quick movement allowed him to shed those two small bits of apparel, but his drawers he kept on, fearful of frightening her beyond redemption should she catch sight of his masculine arousal, or perchance feel it prodding against her body.

On the edge of the mattress, he reached to her, his hand warm against her arm, and his words were meant to soothe her fears. "I won't take up much room, Katie, but I'm used to sleeping alone and if I crowd you, you'll have to scold me and make me move over."

She laughed softly, as he had intended she should, and then as he slid beneath the sheets next to her, he heard the indrawn breath she tried to conceal with a cough. He felt her weight scoot even farther from him and with a sigh, he spoke her name again.

"Katie. Listen to me. I'm not going to hurt you, or even touch you if you don't want me to. Just let me hold your hand. All right?" Unmoving, he lay on his back, awaiting her decision.

It was not long in coming, for she slipped the sheet over her shoulder and offered him the slender length of her fingers, her palm touching his forearm. "You can touch me if you need to, John," she offered. "I know there's a lot more to being in the same bed than just sharing the sheets. I heard too many times when Jacob was giving Agnes a hard time of it, and she'd holler at him and make a fuss."

He chuckled softly and took her fingers between his

palms. "I won't give you reason to holler at me, Katie. Or make a fuss, for that matter. I only want to be next to you and maybe help keep you warm."

"Oh, I'm warm enough," she protested. "This nightgown is right warm, good heavy flannel."

He smiled, aware of her tension, willing her to trust him, needing her to seek him out beneath the bedding. And knowing that such a thing was probably not going to happen tonight.

In that he was right, for she turned from him and held herself away from his body's warmth. He felt the shiver she could not conceal, knew that she was chilled by the night air, the cracks in the logs allowing cold to seep into the room.

"If you let me, I'll keep you warm, Katie," he offered, his tone nonchalant, as though it mattered little one way or the other, and knew he had succeeded somewhat in his ploy when she scooted back toward him in small increments, an inch at a time, until their bodies were almost touching.

"That's better, sweetheart," he whispered. "Let me put my hand on your side here, and we'll both be more comfortable." And as he spoke the words he lifted his hand from his grip on hers and curved his palm around her waist, turning her from himself. Then, easily, neatly and with no other movement to reveal his need of her, he placed his big hand on the bend of her waist, feeling her indrawn breath as if she acknowledged his claim on her flesh.

And indeed she had, for Katie stilled at the touch of a male hand on her body and closed her eyes. "I know it's you back there, John, but it feels funny to be having your hands on me."

And yet, she craved the warmth of that broad palm, knew for a moment the comfort of his hand bringing heat to that small portion of her body. And she relaxed, softening herself to sink farther into the feather bed.

"I'll be right here," he whispered. "All night long, Katie. I'm not going away. I'll just keep you warm. All right?"

She nodded, not able to speak, for her throat was dry, the words she tried to form stuck somehow in her craw, as if she were mute. A soft chuckle from the man behind her was a comfort, one she had not thought to hear, for he did not mock her fear, but accepted it as a part of her femininity. And how she knew that was a conundrum, but yet it was true. John would not mock her, only understand her as well as a man could.

And for that she was thankful, easing herself another inch in his direction, until she felt the heat radiating from his long form behind her, knew the comfort of being safe and secure within the boundaries of his bed. For John had promised not to harm her or cause her to fear him.

And if she could believe nothing else in this life, she could count on John Roper keeping his word.

KATIE'S EYES FLEW OPEN, her heart in her throat, sensing that she was in a strange place, and not knowing her whereabouts this morning. Before her was a window, beyond the glass was the barn and a flurry of movement as men came and went through the wide doors.

And if she turned, John would be behind her, for he had slept with her in this bed last night. She held her breath, turning her head, seeking his face, and felt an overwhelming disappointment when she discovered the other side of the bed was empty, John's pillow against her back, the covers tucked over her neatly.

"John?" As if he might be somewhere in the cabin, she called his name, even as she recognized that he would be out with the hired hands, doing his morning chores. And it was time and past for her to be out of bed and making his breakfast.

When he came into the cabin, she was at the stove, turning pancakes with the metal tool she'd found atop the range. A pan of bacon sizzled on the back of the black stove and a small pan emitted the scent of syrup, bubbling next to the griddle.

"I tried to put together some hot syrup for your pancakes, John," she said brightly. "But I don't think I got it right. Berta told me how to make it the other day and she must have left me some of the flavoring, for I found it in your pantry."

"I can show you how to do that," he offered. "My mama used to make it all the time with maple flavoring and sugar and water. Can I help?"

She turned to him and her smile was wide. "I'd be ever so glad to learn how your mama did it. We never had syrup when I was living at the Schrader place." Her laugh was harsh. "We were lucky to have pancakes, let alone anything to put on them."

"Well, you can have all the syrup you like living here, sweetheart," he promised, and then made a production of demonstrating his skill at mixing the ingredients and putting the small saucepan over the heat till it came to a boil. Katie watched him, praising him for his skill and he bantered with her, making her smile, then chuckle at his antics.

She turned from him then and his approach behind her was slow and careful, not willing to startle her with his presence, yet wanting her to become accustomed to him. His hand touched her shoulder and he peered over it to see what she was cooking, watching as she turned the pancake in the pan, pleased to find that she softened beneath his touch, as she turned her head to smile at him.

"You're as sweet as that syrup, I'll warrant," he said softly. "I can smell your soap right here by your ear, Katie."

She turned her head and his lips touched her forehead lightly. "Yup, right here, too," he said, his lips nuzzling that spot.

"I'm not sweet," she replied, as if she must protest his words. "No one ever in my life said such a thing to me."

"Well, you've never in your life had a husband before, Katie Roper. And since I'm the man in charge here, I can say anything I want to, and all you have to do is listen."

She turned the pancake one more time and then slid it onto a plate in the warming oven. "I'll listen to anything you tell me, John, but I don't have to believe it."

"Well, you'd better believe me this time, girl, for you're one sweet specimen of womanhood, and I'm proud as I can be that you're my wife."

Her head tilted back a bit and she lifted the other pancake hastily from the griddle, as if she feared for its safety. "Don't get me all flustered while I'm cooking, John. I'll be burning your breakfast if you're not careful."

He laughed softly, kissing the small ringlet that dwelled against her temple. "I wouldn't want that to happen, Katie girl. I'm a hungry man this morning."

"Well, sit yourself down at the table and I'll feed you then," she said brightly, sliding the plate from the warming oven, then adding four slices of bacon to the offering she'd readied. Four pancakes were piled high and she placed the plate on the table and, using his knife, placed a goodly portion of butter on top of the steaming cakes.

She quickly poured a cup of coffee and John looked down at the meal she'd completed for his comfort. "Are you going to eat, too?" he asked, looking back at the stove for her plate.

"Soon as the next pancakes get done," she said, pouring batter onto the steaming griddle. The remaining bacon in the pan was taken up to drain on a piece of brown paper and she watched as bubbles formed on the sizzling cakes. Within a minute, she had flipped them over, exposing the brown side and allowing them to complete cooking. She poured coffee into a second mug and settled it on the table, then turned to take up her breakfast.

"I'll make you some more if you like," she said readily, eyeing his plate, already half-empty.

"After you've eaten yours," he said firmly. "I want you to sit down while they're still warm."

She did as he said, spreading butter and pouring syrup from the small pan onto her plate. And then with a smile that warmed him, she cut a bite and lifted her fork to her mouth. "I'm glad Berta thought of the flavoring for the syrup," she said. "I'll need to see if she brought vanilla over for me, too. I like to put a good swig of it in my cakes when I bake. Makes them taste right fine."

John swallowed the bite he was relishing and grinned at her. "You're gonna bake me a cake? Are you going to frost it, too?"

"Frost it? With what?" she asked, obviously stymied by his query.

"You make icing out of some sort of fluffy sugar and a chunk of butter and a bit of milk," he said easily. "I used to watch my mama make it when I was a boy. She put some sort of flavoring in it, too. Maybe it was vanilla. And then she'd spread it over the cake, once it was cool. She used to make some other sort of icing, cooked it in a pan on the stove, and then whipped it up before she put it on."

His thoughts went back readily to the childhood he'd all but forgotten, only the movements of the girl before him bringing back memories of his home and the mother who had made life so enjoyable for her family.

"I never made any icing, John, but I'll try. I'll ask Berta how to do it." As though she would go to any lengths to please him, Katie smiled and offered to do as he would have her.

He sensed her willingness and his words were encouraging. "Well, if you just keep on the way you're going, I'll be a happy man. You're a good cook, Katie, and you sure can clean up a storm, and my clothes have never been so well cared for. I'm a lucky man, sweetheart."

Her face softened and her voice was but a whisper. "I'm the lucky one, John. And I know it as sure as I know my own name. I've never had it so good in my life, and I'm thankful to you for making my life such a pleasure."

That she could be happy with so little, that her wants were so few, was a puzzle to John, and yet, he knew that she spoke the truth. Katie was happy with him, and it would be in his own best interests to keep her that way.

He pushed the thoughts of his youthful marriage from him, determined to concentrate on Katie alone, to give her every chance to please him. He'd not planned this situation, but events had brought it about, and he'd be less than a man if he complained and grumbled about his fate.

AGAIN, HE AWAITED THE completion of her nighttime ritual, the time when she washed and prepared to climb into his bed, and rued the fact that the bedroom door kept his vision from her. "You about done in there?" he called out, his impatience showing in the tone of voice he employed. And then winced as she answered with a fearful tone.

"I'll just be a minute more, John. I'm putting on my nightgown right now." And then after a moment's silence, she opened the door, casting him a glance of apology. "I didn't mean to be so long. I had to take care of something."

He walked closer to her and his words were soft and coaxing. "Will you let me make love to you tonight? I want to be your husband."

"I don't know what to do," she whispered, wishing she knew the secret knowledge he held within himself, hoping against hope that he would share with her the meaning of the words he spoke. That making love, as he called it, would be as pleasurable as the feelings his hands drew forth from her body right this minute.

"You don't have to know a thing, love. You only have to let me love you. I want to make you happy, Katie. I want to make you my wife instead of just keeping you a bride."

"I am your wife, John." She was confused by his words and she felt near tears suddenly.

"No, Katie. Right now, you're my bride. I'll ask you tomorrow morning if you know the difference. If being my bride is the same as being my wife."

"I'm sure I don't know what you're talking about," she murmured. "But I'm willing to find out, if it's what you want of me."

John felt his grin widen as he lifted her from her feet and carried her through the doorway into the room where he had spent the past weeks alone, with her just twelve feet away, but totally separate from him. Where he intended to show her the pleasure her tender body was capable of.

"I know how to walk, John. I've been doing it for a lot of years. Put me down."

Impatience shimmered through her words. Although it would have been a simple matter to quiet her protests—a glance through narrowed eyes would do it, he thought, or even the speaking of her name in a tone less than gentle—he could not bring himself to use those cruel devices to control her.

Instead he stood her on her feet just inside the bedroom and pulled her against himself, not making any attempt to hide the aroused state of his masculine parts. Whether or not she would feel them against her belly, he didn't know, nor did he worry overmuch about her reaction to it. For he knew, deep in his heart, that this girl was not aware of the changes in his body being any part of his reaction to her.

She was as sheltered as a newborn babe when it

came to men. Though she'd known the dark, cruel side of Jacob Schrader through his violence and beatings, hopefully she had been spared his sexual attentions being turned on her. Perhaps he got his fun by beating on her, John thought with a flare of hatred toward the man.

There were those men who delighted in physically hurting women. He'd seen the results of that very thing once in a saloon, when he'd visited a young woman who'd still borne bruises and carried a fear of a man's touch with her because of such treatment at a customer's hands.

That memory caused him to use his gentlest touch as he held Katie's body close to his own. His hands were careful against her back as he felt tense muscles beneath his fingertips. His mouth delivered only the lightest of caresses as he ran his lips down the taut line of her jawbone, and his breath spun a web of soft words against the curve of her ear. "Lie down on the bed for me, Katie, just like you did last night. We're going to sleep together from now on."

She looked at him quickly, and then looked down at the mattress beside her. "We're going to sleep together from now on?"

"If you say so, I'll only hold you, Katie, like I did last night. I won't do anything to upset you or cause you to be angry with me." And then bent his head, the better to kiss the line of her throat.

She tilted her head back, dislodging him from his chosen spot, his lips having chosen to press against the place beneath her ear where her pulse beat in an uneven pace. "I'm not angry with you, John. Only caught off guard when you swooped me up in the air. You surprised me, but I kind of liked having your arms around me that way. Not like the way old Jacob felt when he tried to crawl into my bed."

He looked down into blue eyes that wore the shine of innocence, and his heart beat heavily in his chest. "When did he do that, Katie? When did he try to crawl into your bed?"

"A couple of times this winter. He said he'd keep me warm, and I should be quiet and let him lay down with me."

"What did you do?" John asked, his voice deep, the tone bordering on anger.

A tone she responded to with a quick look of fear. "I didn't do anything wrong, John. I told him to leave me alone and when I hollered at him, Agnes came in and made him leave me be." She shrank within herself then, as if a memory overshadowed her.

"He beat me something terrible the next day, kind of like he was mad because I yelled at him."

"He beat you?" John felt anger wash over him, and released her from his touch, fearful that he might clench his hands against her flesh.

"It wasn't any worse than other times, but he was really mad at me. That was a couple of weeks before I left there. I was afraid maybe Agnes wouldn't hear me the next time, and I don't know what he'd have done to me."

"I do," John said tightly, and then cursed himself that he had the same urges in mind when he looked at the girl before him. There was a fine line between lust and desire, and the thought that he might in any way resemble Jacob Schrader made him cringe. And so he determined to rein his desire to a level pleasing to Katie.

Her next words made him grit his teeth as she spoke her innocent query. "Was Jacob wantin' to do to me what he did to Agnes at night? Sometimes I'd hear her scolding him and him yelling at her and then she'd holler that he was hurting her."

John shook his head in despair. "What did those animals do to you, Katie girl? What sort of memories did they leave you with? Marriage shouldn't be that way. Men and women should be happy to be together, not angry or mean to each other."

"Well, I don't have to worry about them anymore, do I?" she said smartly. "I only have to be a good wife to you, John. And I'm willing to do whatever you want of me."

Her flushed cheeks invited him to touch their fine surface with his mouth, and dark hair seemed to beg for his fingers to flow through its length. She'd taken down her braid and the waving mass hung past her waist, holding his fingers captive in the wealth of dark silken texture as he drew her near once more.

It was more than he could resist. He'd waited, tested his patience and cursed his need even as he'd ached for her slender body to lie beneath him. He knew she would be acquiescent, knew that she would do whatever he asked of her, was certain that he could take what he needed and she would not deny him.

And in doing so, he would risk himself once more, accept her words of acquiescence to his will, hope for her honesty and offer her his trust. If she proved to be unfaithful, he would curse himself for offering up unto her his name and his support. But of that, he would not think tonight. For now, he would simply take what she offered and give her whatever pleasure he could in this bed.

But there was a proud bit of him that would not take advantage of her innocence, that needed her to come to him with a desire to seek out his touch. And so he kissed her carefully, not willing to turn loose his passion until she responded in some way. And ached for that moment to arrive.

CHAPTER TEN

BENEATH HIS LIPS HER own were soft and welcoming and John spread a carpet of light, teasing kisses over her face. From her temple to the tiny dimple in her chin, he left damp, warm evidence of the heat that burned within him. She turned her face, lifting one hand to his jaw to hold him in place, and her mouth was firm against his as if she were leading his lips to the very spot that craved his kiss.

And then she imitated him, taking the journey he had taught her in reverse. Her mouth touched lightly against his cheek, his forehead, her lips coasting across his eyelids, her tongue tasting of the vulnerable spot at his temple. He stifled the urge to take control, to seize the tender mouth that teased him now, and instead let her find her own pace.

As though she'd discovered the pleasure in touch, she drew her hands over his cheeks, through his hair and then clutched at the nape of his neck, drawing his face to hers, standing before him, reaching upward to wrap her arms around his neck.

"Unbutton my shirt, Katie." His voice was hoarse, but

soft and coaxing and she responded quickly, her fingers dropping to the front of his shirt, seeking out the small buttons and undoing them without hesitation. And then his undershirt underwent the same treatment as she undid, more slowly, those few buttons that held it across his chest. She brushed with the lightest of touches against the hair that lay beneath his shirts, her fingers moving carefully, her head bent to watch as she explored the width of his shoulders, the breadth of his chest, the small male nipples that stiffened at her inadvertent touch.

His indrawn breath brought her gaze upward, her eyes wide as she met his, and she halted her movement. "John? Did I do something wrong?"

His head moved but slightly, turning from one side to the other in a motion that denied her fear of wrong-doing. "No, you're doing everything just right, Katie. I like feeling your hands on me." He bent his head and lifted her hand in his, holding it to his mouth and brushing his lips across her knuckles. "I'd like to touch you in the same way, but you'll have to let me know when. Are you ready to lie down on the bed now?"

He paused and his eyes sought hers, the glow from the kitchen lamp casting a soft gleam of light on her skin as it shone into the bedroom. A pink tinge touched her cheekbones and her eyes sparkled, as if she were on the brink of discovery, as if she were anticipating crossing a boundary into an unknown place.

"I think so. And…" Her voice was hesitant. "You can touch me any way you want to John," she said softly, her smile shy. Yet her eyes stayed on his, and he marveled at the trust she granted him. *Touch me any way you want.* What doors those few words opened, what joys she gave him to discover. And what responsibility her words offered him.

He placed her fingertips against his chest once more, aware of more than just the slight pressure of her hands, aware that she would venture further if he but coaxed her along the way.

"Let me take off your dress, Katie. Let me undo the buttons and figure out how to take your petticoat off, and find you underneath all those layers you wear." And even as he spoke, he took from her the necessity of responding aloud to his request, instead allowing his fingers to slip beneath her uplifted arms and work at the pearl buttons that fastened her dress, sliding them quickly from their moorings and then reaching beneath to where her chemise lay. His hand barely touching the finer fabric there, he moved to her waist where tapes were tied, holding her petticoat in place.

Her dress gaped open and drooped from her shoulders, holding her arms captive and she lowered them for a moment, allowing the fabric to slide down to the floor. Her petticoat followed in short order and she was naked, but for her chemise, her slender arms once more reaching for him.

The brief garment hung only to her thighs and beneath it were the stockings she'd fastened with pieces of cloth, tying them above her knees. Not even a pretty little garter, he thought, and rued the fact that she lacked any sort of feminine frippery, but had made do as best she could.

"Sit down on the bed for a minute, sweetheart," he murmured, his voice soft lest he startle her. She did as he'd asked and he knelt before her, taking her shoes off and placing them under the edge of the bed. Then running his hands up her legs, he placed warm hands on her knees, his fingers reaching upward just a few inches to untie the fabric she'd used as garters. He tucked his fingers beneath the edges and pulled the stockings from her, exposing rounded calves and slim ankles, sliding the coarse cotton hosiery from her feet.

"We'll buy you some nicer stockings at the general store," he said, eyeing the heavy fabric with disdain as he tossed the shapeless things aside. "And a pair of garters with lace or flowers or something pretty on them."

"I don't need such expensive things," she protested, frowning down at him as he allowed his hands the privilege of coasting the length of her calves and ankles once more, lifting her feet to hold them in the palms of his hands.

"They don't cost much, Katie, and they'll look nice on your pretty legs, and won't leave such deep marks on your skin when you take them off." His hands moved gently against the reddened areas where her stockings had been and he bent to kiss the flesh there, eliciting a soft protest from her lips.

He grinned up at her. "I like kissing you, sweetheart. I'd like to kiss you all over in just that same way."

"All over?" She looked aghast at the prospect and he laughed softly.

"You might like it, Katie. Can we give it a try?" Without waiting for her permission or seeking out a further opinion, he straightened and lifted her chemise, pulling it from beneath her and tugging it over her head.

"John!" It was a single word of protest and he blithely ignored it as he bent closer and placed his lips on her waist, touching the tender flesh with his tongue. Her hands cupped his head and she tugged at him, only to find her palms the recipients of his mouth as he turned from one, then to the other, his lips dropping soft caresses across the width of her hands and then up her arms, until his mouth halted on the inner bend of her elbow.

He nuzzled there and his murmur was almost lost against her skin. "You're so soft, Katie, so sweet and fresh."

"I haven't even washed up yet tonight, John. I'm not fresh at all," she protested.

"You washed this morning. I saw you in here just scrubbing away at yourself, honey. You're the cleanest woman I've ever known."

"I haven't had a good bath since you hauled water in here for me three days ago," she reminded him. "But that surely was a pleasure for me, John. I liked being able to sit in warm water and just soak all over."

"Next time I'm going to watch you and wash your back for you and dry you off when you've finished," he promised.

"You can't watch me take a bath." Her voice was high and uneven, and he wondered if she weren't protesting because she thought he expected her to.

"One of these days when the weather gets warm, we're gonna go down to the creek the other side of the near pasture and take a bath together there," he told her. "I've been swimming out there more than once. It's nice and private and the water gets warm in the spring once the sun hits it at high noon."

"John, where on earth do you get such ideas? I've never heard of such a thing. Just using a tub to bathe in is pure heaven to me. I had to sneak around when the Schraders weren't home to wash myself all over at the same time. They said it was a waste of hot water to be scrubbing your body in it."

"Well, you don't live with them anymore, sweetheart. You're here with me, and you can do most anything you want to. One of these days you'll come to believe me and you won't fuss and worry."

"I'm not fussing, John. I just can't get used to the idea that you're so nice to me."

He'd done his best not to stare at the soft flesh before his face, but now he reached to touch the curve of her breast and smiled as she quickly lifted her hands to cover herself.

"You forgot for a minute that your chemise was

gone, didn't you?" he teased. And then his hands covered hers and pulled them to her lap, where the soft curls at the juncture of her thighs brushed against his knuckles. She jolted, jerking back and he lifted her to stand before him.

"I'm naked, John."

He grinned, unable to hide his amusement at her simple protest. "I know. I was the one who took your clothes off, remember?" And now his hands made short work of his shirt, dropping it to the floor, then working at his trousers and his drawers, scuffing them off his feet, leaving him clad in nothing but his stockings.

Her eyes stayed purposefully on his face, her cheeks turning a more violent shade of crimson and she swallowed with a visible effort. "I want to feel you against me, John. Feel your body and have your arms around me, but I...I can't look at you." Her eyes closed then, and he felt a wash of pure joy as he pulled her into his arms, as his hands ran the length of her back, brushing tender caresses over her bottom, then up her sides to where her breasts lay plumped against his chest.

He eased from her just a bit and allowed his hands to cover those round, soft places that had drawn his gaze so often over the past weeks. The stiffening of the soft crests drew his attention and he yearned to look down at what his fingers cherished, but bent instead to brush his mouth over her shoulders, first one then the other.

"You're so soft, Katie, so smooth and pretty. Will you lie on the bed and let me love you?"

"*Love me?* Is that what you meant when you said you wanted to make love to me?" Her voice was trembling, as if she must not take anything for granted, as though his words left her puzzled.

"Yes, Katie. It's something I've wanted to do for a while now, and especially since yesterday when we got married. We've had some time to get to know each other, and the main thing is, I need you to trust me. The night we met, when you came bursting through the doors of the saloon, I knew you were somebody very special, someone I wanted to have in my life. It didn't take me long, about ten minutes or so, to know that I wanted to take care of you and keep you safe. Now I can only think of possessing you, making you mine and holding you in my arms in the middle of that bed."

"Then do that very thing," she said firmly. "I told you before that I'd do whatever you asked of me." She took his hands in hers and drew him with her, sitting on the bed and then lifting her legs to scoot across the mattress. "Come lie down with me, John. I want you to hold me tight, I think I need you to put your arms around me."

"I'll do more than just that, sweetheart. And if you don't like anything that happens, all you have to do is say so and I'll stop and think of some different way to make you happy."

"No one's ever really cared before if I was happy or not," she whispered. Her hands reached for him as he rolled to lie beside her and her fingertips were lost in the curls that matted his chest, curls she'd found so fascinating just minutes ago. "I wasn't going to look at you before. But I've changed my mind. You're beautiful, John, all strong and brown and with such pretty eyes…"

Her voice trailed off as her hands crept up to his face and rested there, one on either side of his jaw, and though he knew he was but a shadow in the twilight of the room, he sensed her gaze against his skin. She lifted herself a bit so that her mouth was but inches from his and he tucked her closer, his arm against her back. That their bodies meshed in a most satisfying fashion was much to his approval. That she stiffened and then relaxed, laughing softly as she curled closer was more to the point. The point being that the girl was losing a good share of her modesty with him.

Not that she was in any way lacking in that virtue, or comparable to those women who sold themselves for a living, but for the fact that she was willing to give all she had, all she could be, to the man she'd married. To John Roper, the man who had taken the giant leap yesterday to become her husband, who'd made the decision only a short time ago to become her lover. She was eager to please him, generous with her kisses and willing to follow his lead.

His heart swelled, fit to burst with the joy that filled him. He took her lips in a kiss of unrestrained desire. He didn't want to frighten her, but he was unable to touch her with any degree of forbearance, for his body was needy, his manhood primed and ready and the prospect of another night with Katie in his arms was like a glimpse of Heaven to his soul.

Her mouth was soft, her breath sweet, her lips plush beneath his. He suckled for long moments at her bottom lip, its plump flesh between his teeth, until he felt her jolt, knew the presence of her hips pressing against his in a gesture he recognized. His whispered words were soft against her skin, there where her scent dwelled, on her throat and beneath her ear, a blend of a woman's desire and a girl's simple needs.

For if ever a girl had needs, it was Katie. The joy of touch had been denied her, the pleasure to be found in a simple caress had never been offered, and the thrill of knowing that she was wanted simply because she was lovable was foreign to her. If it took him forever, he'd see to it she tasted of all the simple ways in which a man could bring pleasure to his woman. Whether it be the brush of his palm against her belly, the hungry presence of his lips against the soft flesh of her breast or the touch of his manhood at the verge of her thighs; she would know the extent of his ability to please her, to gift her the quivering rapture of making love with the man who cherished her beyond all else.

His mouth opened against the curve of her breast, his fingers curled beneath it, cherishing the soft weight in his hand. A man who had eaten a thousand meals, tasting much of what life offered, a man whose hunger had been tempted in many ways, found satisfaction now in soft flesh that warmed to his touch, offering a delight for his appetite, at a table unlike any other.

The table—a bed with clean sheets, still bearing the scent of cold, winter air; the meal—a banquet for the senses. His mouth opened on flesh that enticed him, his tongue tasting the innocence of a girl on the threshold of womanhood, teasing the tender crest of a breast, growing taut beneath his touch. With a patience he hadn't known he possessed, he found nourishment for his hunger, and in so doing unknowingly lost his heart to the fragile creature beside him.

He held her close, his hands moving carefully over her skin, down the length of her back, to the rounding of her bottom and then even lower, caressing the curves of thigh and calf, the slender legs that trembled in his hands. He made the return trip, up the length of curving legs, long fingers touching the crease of her body where hips and buttocks joined. His fingers ached to sweep to the front of her slender form and he chanced the need, hoping he would not frighten her overmuch.

His fingers trailed over the line of her hip and his wide palm almost spanned the slope of her belly, his fingertip dipping into the tiny crater midway to his goal. She shivered when he touched her there, as if she had not realized it could be a source of pleasure. And then his fingers moved carefully, tenderly into the patch of curls that hid the treasures he determined to uncover. She was slick, damp beneath his caress, obeying his unspoken urging to open for him. He felt quick relief that she was not unwilling to be touched in such a way, for her hips rose a bit as if she would meet his fondling fingertips and she sighed against his throat as though she had discovered a sensation unknown to her. Her arms curved to enclose him, her body yearning closer as if to narrow the gap between them.

He lifted a bit, bending to her, his mouth at her breast once more as he pressed his fingers against her hot flesh, seeking out the sheath that welcomed him. And then hesitated as she stilled beneath his touch. He would not take her to himself until she was ready, would not force her to take his flesh within her until she could hold him without pain. His fingers moved just within her body, stretching her a bit, pressing on sensitive places that were virgin, heretofore untouched.

"Do you like this, sweetheart?" His voice was a low murmur, and he waited, careful to move in slow increments, readying her for what was to come. For should she fail to soften for the strokes of his surging masculinity probing against virgin flesh, he would wait. However long it took, he would woo her, court her to his will, male coaxing female, desire seeking response.

The pattern of his caresses changed, his touch more intense now, increasing contact with her tender flesh, as she joined the rhythm he'd found. To his joy, she cried out, a sound of surprise, of anticipation.

"John, it feels so strange, almost as if I'm floating, and yet…something's happening, and I don't—" Her breath caught in a gasp of delight as he sought her pleasure, and she rose in a spasm that seemed to fill her with exultation, for she groaned and then sobbed, her body twisting beneath his silent leading, her words broken and hushed.

She cried aloud again, clutching him to herself, eager in her movements as she pulled him atop her body. "I need more, John. I need you to be closer to me. I want…I don't know… Please, John."

"I know what you want, sweetheart. Hush now, let me do this…." He covered her, his big body casting its shadow over her slender self, his hands gentle as they moved her thighs apart to make room for his body there where it yearned to be. And then he lowered his hips against hers, his manhood thrusting carefully at the opening he prayed would admit him without giving pain to the body she'd offered so generously into his keeping.

There was no help for it. John was a big man, his arousal was far beyond that of an early-morning reminder that his manhood functioned normally. And in this moment when he yearned for a simple task, he was faced with the knowledge that his wife was small, totally untried and woefully ignorant of what was to come.

But she was intelligent, and willing, two attributes that promised success in his taking of his bride. She twisted beneath him, feeling the pinching discomfort of a man's throbbing arousal, there where she was the most sensitive, and as if she knew what she must do, she calmed herself, breathing deeply and curling against him to meet the invasion he offered.

It was more than he could control. He was suddenly lost, loosing the taut rein he'd held so firmly. His body surged forward and she was penetrated with one swift movement by the evidence of his passion. She was pierced to her depths by his manhood, and he held still as he recognized that his bride lay without moving beneath him.

But, if he'd thought to hear her cry out, if he'd expected tears of anger at the dissolving of his forbearance or rebellion at the feel of strong hands on her body—if he'd had any fear of Katie's response to his loving, his worries were dissolved in but a moment. For beneath him, his bride inhaled deeply, then curled her legs around his hips, drawing him deeply into her feminine warmth, held him close with arms that imprisoned his body even as she came nigh unto capturing his heart.

Her whisper touched his ear, and he lifted from her, his eyes seeking out the tears he feared would be his reward, and finding only the radiance of a woman who has found a joy she had not known existed. The knowledge that Katie meshed her movements with his, that she luxuriated in the feel of his skin against her own, thrust him past the boundary he'd thought to place on himself, cast him into the deep waters of fulfillment, into a place where his good intentions were of no use, where his passion held reign.

For long moments he felt the rush of blood through

his veins that foretold the spilling of his seed, and then he was lost. Lost in the arms of Katie, who held him with the strength of a woman, who clung to him with the tenacity of a bride, luminous, basking in the ecstacy of joining with her chosen mate.

He lifted his weight from her and she rolled toward him, rising over him, triumph alive on her shadowed features. "I'm really your wife now, John." As though she were well pleased with her chosen position, Katie leaned against his chest, her arms crossed, her face close enough to kiss should he lean upward just a bit.

"Did I hurt you badly, sweetheart?"

Her eyes filled now with tears, tears he'd thought to see there long moments past. But their presence seemed not to give evidence of pain or fear, but the heartfelt joy of a woman who has tasted the confidence of pleasing her mate.

"Oh, no, John. It hurt a little when you—you know, when you came inside me. But then it was just…it was good, John. I felt like you were a part of me, like we were all of a piece, the two of us."

"Katie, have you ever heard anything read out of the Bible? Did you ever go to church?"

"A couple of times, not often. The Schraders weren't much for churchgoing. He said it was a waste of time, all that hymn singing and that preacher man telling folks what to do."

"Well, in the Bible there's a line that speaks about married folks. It says something like '…and the two of them shall become one flesh.' I think that's what He meant Katie. The act of coming together in bed and joining our bodies."

"Well, even if it did hurt a little, it was nice, John."

He smiled and his hand brushed the hair back from her temple. "Next time it'll be better than nice, Katie. I promise you."

WHEN THE SUN ROSE it shimmered off new-fallen snow, almost a foot of the white stuff covering the ground.

"There's nothing much worse than a late-winter storm," John said as he ate his breakfast. His gaze traveled to the window, the worry evident upon his face. "We'll need to ride over the meadows and pastures, anywhere the cows may have gone to seek shelter to birth their babies," he said.

"Will they live in this cold weather?" Katie frowned as she thought of tiny calves in the snow.

"They will if we find them and bring them into the barn." He stood and circled the table to where she sat and bent to kiss her, long and lingeringly. "Are you all right, Katie? I didn't hurt you?"

She smiled, her spirits leaping as she recalled the bliss he'd offered her, the joy he'd given with a generous heart. "You didn't hurt me, John. Well, just a bit, but I didn't mind. It was a good hurt."

"You take my breath away, girl," he told her, his eyes darkening with a look she cherished, as though he saw and approved all she was. "With just a little encouragement, I could be persuaded to stay here with you today. But I can't neglect my work, honey.

"I'll be gone till well past noon. It'll take that long to make half a circuit of the pastures. We'll go in pairs and cover as much ground as we can."

"I'll fix something to eat that I can keep warm for you. Take a biscuit along with you, John, in case you get hungry before dinner. I'll wrap it up for you."

She found a thin dish towel and folded two biscuits into it, then tucked it into his pocket as he slid his arms into the sleeves of his warm jacket.

The cabin seemed chilled without his presence, for his body moving across the porch, then down across the small yard and toward the barn held a warmth she craved. That she would ever yearn for a man's hands on her, his mouth against hers and his arms circling her in a warm embrace was far from any expectation she had ever dreamed of. The touch of another's hand against her skin had heretofore heralded pain to some extent, either that of a man's blow or a woman's sharp, pinching fingers if she did not respond as quickly or as efficiently as their evil minds required of her.

A warm bed, a mattress beneath her body at night and clothing to keep the chill of winter from her skin— those were the things dreams had been made of. A relief from fear, of physical abuse at the hands of another.

Until now. Until John's care and concern had made her aware of so much more.

And now she became aware of an aching deep within

her belly, one she'd known was imminent; the cramping announcing the time of her woman's curse, as Mrs. Schrader had called it.

And she was without the old petticoat she needed that would keep her clothing protected from staining, for John had forgotten it. A towel would have to do, she decided, and she set about the task of tending to her physical needs.

By the time she'd put a batch of bread to rise atop the warming oven, she was aching in a familiar way. When the soup she prepared for their noon meal was simmering on the back of the stove, she recognized that the cramping she knew as normal had increased to more than mild discomfort.

And when John appeared at the back door, stomping his feet and brushing snow from his jacket, she was ready to find a corner in which to lay her weary body.

His concern was quick and to the point. "What's wrong, Katie? You look kinda peaked, like a good, stiff wind could blow you away. I've never seen you look so pale, honey." His arms reached for her and she sought the haven of his embrace, her head resting against his heart, her arms circling his waist as she leaned on the strength he offered.

"I don't usually feel so puny when I have this problem, John, but today's just a bad time for me." She shot him a wry look, one he seemed to be able to easily interpret.

"You need that doggone petticoat, don't you, sweetheart, and I forgot about digging it out for you. Let me fetch it from the tack room. It's not dirty or greasy or anything. I just stuck it in the bin and haven't used it yet."

"After you eat, John. Your soup is hot and I made corn bread to go with it. It's not a very good dinner, but there'll be fresh bread for supper tonight.

"John?" The speaking of his name was a query and he responded in but an instant.

"What is it, Katie? What do you want?"

She wriggled against him, lifting her face to meet his gaze. "I need to tell you something, John. I want you to know that I've never felt this way about anyone in my life. You know just how to make me happy. When I look at you I feel good, like all my wishes have come true. I just want to spend my life with you and live all my days and nights in this cabin." She looked away, over his shoulder and a blush covered her cheeks.

"That sounds foolish, I know, but it's how I feel, John."

"You couldn't sound foolish no matter what, Katie. You make me proud to know that you care about me."

She lifted her hands to her eyes, wiping away the traces of tears and backed from him. "You need to sit down at the table and let me get you a bowl of soup. You must be hungry. Did you find a lot of calves out there?"

"Only one that worries me," he said, stepping to the sink and washing his hands quickly. "One of the cows didn't make it and the calf is in need of a mama. I thought maybe you'd come out to the barn this afternoon and take a turn at feeding him."

"Could I? Do you think I'd be able to do it right? I've never done such a thing, but I'll try." Her excitement was vivid, her eyes lighting with pleasure as she spoke. "As soon as we eat and I clear up, I'll put on warm clothes and come out to help you."

"I don't want you to be chilled. Make sure you bundle up good."

His head bent and his kiss was warm against her lips, a comfort she hadn't known she needed so badly. That John should so readily comprehend, that this man understood her and sought to solve her problems without question was a small miracle, she decided. Her heart fluttered within her as she buried her nose in the warmth of his throat, her mouth opening to press a damp kiss against his skin, inhaling to catch the scent of all that made up the aroma that was uniquely his. Hay and horses, leather and the cold bite of snow; a blend that meshed man with the elements, and gave to the woman who held him a memory to hold to herself for the whole livelong day.

CHAPTER ELEVEN

KATIE FOUND THAT THERE was not a lot of talent involved in feeding a newborn calf, only the small creature's will to live and ability to suckle from a bottle. And that she could handle, she discovered, with a great deal of satisfaction and delight. Bill Stanley, who had been passing by the stall while she was figuring her way through the procedure, informed her she was doing a "damn good job" of it, and he assigned her the task of twice-daily feedings over the next little while.

Reporting to John on her success, she caught a frown on his face and backtracked hurriedly. "Don't you think I can be trusted to do it well?" she asked dubiously.

To which he only grinned and then grabbed her around the waist for a quick hug. "You'll do fine, sweetheart. I just don't want you to wear yourself out on a newborn calf. If you want to play mama cow for a while, it's all right with me."

And so it was that Katie spent an hour or so a day in the barn, gaining confidence in her own abilities, and delighting John with her happiness at being able to help. It was after one of these sessions, when she had returned to the cabin and washed up, readying herself for the baking of bread, when she found a box in the bedroom that had not caught her notice until now, having been buried beneath a blanket in the corner.

She opened it without thinking, only mildly curious as to its contents and was stunned to find books stacked neatly and closely, probably twenty or so volumes of literature, none of them familiar to her. But then, she'd not had access to any books in her short life, not having been schooled properly, but she was delighted that such a treasure trove was now available, should John set his seal of approval on her perusing them.

"I've dragged that box with me all over the countryside," John told her, entering the room behind her. When he turned to face her, his look was almost shamefaced, as if apologizing for setting such store on them. "My mama was a great one for reading and we always got a new book for Christmas, along with new socks and trousers and such. She read to us in the evenings and when I learned how to make sense of all those letters, it was a big day in my life."

He lifted the cover of the box and drew forth a thick volume. "This is one of my favorites. Tells about a man marooned on an island, how he survived and about a friend he found there. We can read it together one day. Or perhaps I can read it to you during the evening."

Time had slipped away and Katie made haste to prepare their evening meal.

After supper, they sat before the fireplace, a respite

during which she planned her approach to him regarding his collection, and he asked her a question that had been in the back of his mind for the duration of their marriage.

"Katie, didn't you ever go to school? I mean, regular, everyday schooling in town? You told me you had a sister, I remember, and that she went to school. But weren't you sent along with her? And where is she now?"

Katie looked abashed, perhaps ashamed, he thought, and then carefully cleared her throat. "She's still out at the farm, so far as I know. I think about her every day and wonder if she's all right. I'd give a lot to see her, but I'm afraid to go out there, lest old Jacob should get his hands on me again." She shivered and her sigh was deep as she looked up at him.

"So far as school goes, Agnes and Jacob said I was not fit to be out in public, what with my being such a dolt and with nothing fit to wear, so they kept me at home. They sent Jane though, and she…"

"Whoa! Back up there, honey. Let's explain a little about Jane. Why did she get schooling when you didn't?"

"She's my sister, kinda," Katie said carefully. "Well, not really my sister, but one of Agnes's shirttail relations, a girl who didn't have a family when her folks died and the Schrader pair took her in to raise. She helped some with the work, but being family, so to speak, she didn't have as many chores as I did. And

Jacob didn't very often beat on her, just once in a while. They sent her to school because she was blood-kin to Agnes and worth schooling. She brought her books home with her to read and study.

"She used to sit at the table at night and work on her sums and letters and I used to wish I could be as smart as she was." Her eyes brightened then as another memory entered her mind and she spoke it aloud.

"When the Schraders didn't know it, she let me see her books, too, and taught me some of the words she could read, and pretty soon I was doing pretty well myself at it. Until Jacob caught me one day in the hayloft with a book and he beat the livin' tar out of me for wasting my time with such foolishness."

John gritted his teeth and managed to speak calmly, even though his heart raced and his hands itched to be alone for five minutes with the beast who had so abused this child bride of his. "So did you quit looking at the schoolbooks?"

She cast him a look of total disbelief. "My word, no. I just was more careful where I was when I was reading them. I can do pretty good, John. My writing isn't much to brag about, but then I've never had any reason to write down many letters or numbers, only just to practice on Jane's slate once in a while. But I know all the letters and I can read a bunch of words. I remember real well, though. Like with what groceries we need and such, so I don't have to do any writing."

She looked at him pensively, her heart in her eyes.

"So do you think I can look at your books? Can I see if there's any words I can read, maybe? I'd be real careful of them, John, and make sure my hands are clean when I open the covers and everything."

He felt his throat tighten, knew that the tears he had failed to shed for any number of years were too close to the surface to bear, and reached for her, pulling her into his lap. She settled there, as if she had been born for such a place, curling against him, her breath warm against his chest through the fabric of his shirt. It was almost more than he could bear, that this blessed child should have been so neglected and unfairly treated. And his voice threatened to tremble as he spoke.

"Sweetheart, anything I have is yours. If you want to look at those old books, and read them you're more than welcome to them. Maybe we can read them together if you want to. There's some good stories in there, real exciting stuff, and I think you'd enjoy it."

She hugged him, her arm sliding around his chest to grip the flannel of his shirt, anchoring herself as close to his sturdy form as she could get. "John, you're so good to me. I just don't know how to tell you how much I appreciate all you do for me. And if you'll read with me once in a while of an evening, I'd sure take pride in it."

"Whenever you like, Katie," he said quickly. "And now I want you to tell me more about Jane? Did you get along well together? Is she still living out there at that place?"

"Far as I know, she is. I just hope that old Jacob

don't take it out on her 'cause I'm not there anymore to do all his scut work. She didn't have to do as much as I did, but then she was blood-kin, and I was just a throwaway."

"A *throwaway!* Whoever called you that?"

She laughed, a sound that held not a smattering of cheer. "That wasn't the worst thing I got called, John. But that's all right. I like *sweetheart* and *honey* a whole lot better and those seem to be what I'm gettin' called these days."

Her arm tightened against him, her face turned fiercely into his chest and she sighed. "John, I just like you so much. I don't know what I'd do without you. You make me happy."

"You provide your own happiness, sweetheart," he said quickly. "I just give you a place to be yourself, and you've done the rest. We all have to do the best we can with what we have, and that's what you do. Give you a nest and you settle right in, I've noticed. And that's what I wanted for you; a place of your own to fix up any way you wanted it. All you do here is what makes you happy, and I don't have an awful lot to do with it, just sit back and enjoy you."

"You enjoy me?" She peered up at him, surprise lighting her face.

"You bet I do. I like to watch you sashay around the stove and table and I like to see you with that churn, making butter for us, and I especially like to watch you when you're getting ready for bed at night and you're washin' up and scrubbin' yourself to a fare-thee-well, just like you've been covered with dirt all the livelong day. And you're already the cleanest little bit of woman I've ever laid eyes on."

He hugged her closely, his heart beating at a furious pace as she softened and curled into his warmth. "I like everything about you, Katie girl. You're the best thing that's ever happened to me."

"John…I don't know what to say. Nobody's ever talked to me like you do. Like I'm somebody worth something. I used to think about what the preacher at the church said, one time when we went there on a Sunday morning—even though that only happened a couple of times that I can remember—anyway…" She paused, thinking and then she bit at her lip.

"John, do you think there's really somebody up there in the sky who cares about us folks living here in the world? That this God fellow the preacher talked about really is there? Or is he just a story like Jacob Schrader said he was? Could he really care about people like you and me?"

John held his breath for a moment and then made an offer that surprised him with its simplicity and wondered for a moment why he hadn't thought of it sooner. "Would you like to go to the church in town where the minister preaches on Sundays? The same fella that married us? I've never heard him, but Berta goes every week and she seems to hold him in good regard."

"I could maybe go with Berta someday?"

He shook his head. "No, I won't let you go to town alone, sweetheart. I'll take the both of you if you'd like to go. I don't trust things enough to turn you loose, even with Berta to look after you. I'd feel better if you went with me in the wagon or maybe Bill will let us use his buggy." And no one would be giving her long looks of appreciation with Berta along. Katie was blossoming and he wasn't about to turn her loose where other men could look their fill and perhaps approach her with foolishness in mind.

As if she had been considering the idea of a Sunday morning in town, Katie sat up suddenly, her face glowing. "I've even got a dress that'll look just fine for Sunday to go to meeting, John. When I went there the one time or two, the ladies were all dressed in pretty things. I think my new shoes will be just like the other women are wearing. Can we go, do you think?"

"I said we'll go, Katie. If you like, we can ask Berta to ride with us and go on Sunday morning."

She sighed and settled back in his lap, his arms holding her close and he felt the shiver of anticipation she could not withold. "You cold, honey?" he asked, knowing that it was not a chill that had caused her to tremble.

"No, not cold, John. Just excited, I think."

"Could you get excited about going to bed with me, you think?"

She looked up into his face, her eyes wide, her cheeks pink. "John, I can't do that love stuff tonight, not with my woman's curse on me. Don't ask me to do that, please."

He hugged her tightly and laughed. "Going to bed is for more than making love, Katie. Besides, I can make love to you by holding you close and rubbing your back a little and kissing you. It doesn't take any more than that to keep me happy." And then he thought quickly. "Well, for a few days, anyway. After that, when your woman's time is over, then we'll talk about the making love thing again. Will that work?"

She giggled and he was touched by the simple laughter that marked her a girl, for he suspected that there hadn't been much in her short life to bring that sort of sound from her lips.

"Anything you say is all right with me, John. I like sleeping in your bed. You know that. And when I'm done with this messy stuff, I'd be honored if you'd want to do the loving thing again with me. I sure didn't know what it was all about, but I think I could get to liking it real quick."

Satisfaction soared through him as he rose and carried her in his arms, across the wide floor to the bedroom door and into the small area that had seemed to be a place of infinite pleasure last night. Just having Katie in his bed was like a miracle. Just the presence of her soft, curvy little body next to him had been a temptation he could not resist. And now that he had tasted the essence of her beauty, known the joy of coupling with her, his time here in this place loomed ahead as a part of marriage he planned to enjoy.

As they lay together beneath the quilts, their bodies

tangled in a most comfortable fashion, he said as much to her. "Katie, did you ever hear about a story of two people called Adam and Eve and a place they lived called Eden?"

"You mean like the town? Like the Eden where we met, where we got married?"

He chose his words carefully. "Not exactly. This place was a garden, and it was made special for a man and woman to live in. It was way back, so many years ago we don't even know for sure just when it was, but this fella named Adam and a woman called Eve lived in the place, and called the whole shebang The Garden of Eden, and it was a beautiful spot, just made for two people to be happy in."

"Did they live there forever?" she wanted to know, peering up at his face in the faint light that glowed through the open doorway from the fireplace.

"No, not forever, but while they were there, they were happy. Anyway, I was thinking about something else."

He was silent and he felt her prodding him, poking a finger in his chest. "What were you thinking, John?"

"Well, I was thinking that we're living here in this little cabin, just you and me, and it's gotta be kinda like the Garden of Eden. A place for a man and a woman to live and be happy and have some joy of their own that belongs to them and nobody else. I like to think that maybe we've got our own Eden, right here, Katie."

She was silent and he bent to her, touching her cheek

with his fingertips, only to feel a damp spot. "Katie? Are you crying?"

"Oh, no," she said with a half laugh. "I was just thinking how lucky I turned out to be, what with having you to take care of me. And—"

"I'm the lucky one, Katie girl, and don't you forget it. You've brought me so much joy. And I didn't even know what that word meant before I found you in the saloon that night. I just lived from one day to the next and did my best to be a man and do a good job at whatever I set my hand to. And then, there you were. And I knew that you were the woman I wanted in my life for all the years to come. And it was the smartest idea I ever had."

Errant thoughts of another time and place, of betrayal and lies besieged his mind for a moment and he pushed them aside, holding them in abeyance, as if they had never been. And hoped that he was not being foolish in giving his trust so readily.

Katie's voice was soft, the words like music to his ears. "I think it was the best thing in the world that could ever happen to a girl, John. I'm so glad it was me that fell in the door of the saloon that night. I thought sure I was at the end of my rope, and then you were there and I just knew you'd take care of me."

He held her close, his big hand in the middle of her back, holding her in a sudden frenzy of emotion that startled him. Whatever there was about this woman, this particular woman, of all he'd ever seen in his lifetime, he didn't know. But she struck a chord within him that resounded with a melody he felt to the depths of his soul. That he should have been the recipient of such a blessing was almost not to be believed, but since fate had sent her to him, John Roper was not dolt enough to refuse such a gift.

"Close your eyes, Katie. Morning comes early and that calf is gonna be waiting for you to get yourself out there right early."

She mumbled a word against his chest and he recognized that she had already gone close to slumber without his admonition. He buried his face in her hair, catching the scent of soap and woman that surrounded her and his joy was complete.

BERTA ANNOUNCED IN EARLY April that it was time and past to get the kitchen garden put in, with a resultant flurry of activity that astounded Katie. She was enlisted to help, and felt a sense of real joy that her knowledge of gardening and working out of doors would be a bonus to the hardworking housekeeper and cook from the big house.

So it was that Shorty, one of the cowhands, was drafted to plow up the space that had long years ago been designated as right and proper for the kitchen garden, a plot of nearly half an acre, not far from the back porch. He turned up on a fine, sunny morning, complete with horse and plow and Berta went out to show him the place she wanted to have ready for planting.

Although he could have done without her guidance, being a man who had plowed many a patch in his lifetime, he bore with her gracefully, and between them the space was roughly plowed by early afternoon. Along with the able help of Katie, who lugged bottles of water to and fro, and helped with the dinner arrangements while Berta supervised outdoors, it was a productive event.

After dinner was cleared away, Katie and John having joined the men in the big kitchen for the meal, the dishes were washed and put up and then Berta found two rakes and she and Katie began to work. With the promise of his return in the morning, once chores were out of the way, Shorty left them to it, and they raked industriously at the big clumps of dirt, smoothing the area for gardening. The huge piles of weeds gathered and before long Bill Stanley appeared, pushing a huge wheelbarrow, then filled it with the residue of their raking and lugged it away behind the barn.

It would take longer than the two of them could manage easily, Berta said as she and Katie quit for the day in time to put together a supper of sorts, but do it they would, with some help from reluctant cowhands. In two days of hard work the area was smooth and weed-free and Berta announced that it was time to haul out the seeds she'd collected from last year's crop and then decide what they might need to add to the mix from the general store in town. It was an exciting project to Katie's mind, for she had always been the laborer who did the dirty work in the past, and now she was given a voice in what might be planted and how much of each crop she would want for her own use in John's kitchen.

That she was truly married, a real part of such a project gave her confidence a boost such as she'd not expected, and between Berta and John, she made a list of the foods she'd like to store up for the following winter, given Berta's help with the canning process. A good space was designated for corn, for all agreed that it must be a staple. Not the field corn that the men strewed across a five-acre lot in the north pasture, one fit for crop feed, but a small, carefully tended patch for the house.

The first seeds to go into the ground were peas and carrots, and then Berta planted a long row of morning glories along the fencerow, where they could twine as they chose through the scrub there. Another spot was designated by the outhouse and string was placed in upright rows to contain the plants as they grew, providing a screen for the necessary building.

Green beans were next and Berta announced they would plant a new crop every two weeks for a couple of months, ensuring a steady supply for the entire summer, lasting until fall, when the remainder would be canned up quickly. Tomato plants had been ordered from the general store, since growing them from seed took forever, so Berta said, and one morning found John with the reins in his hands, atop the wagon, with Berta and Katie by his side on the wide seat.

Clay Thomas, a new ranch hand had volunteered for escort duty, but something about the man's manner put John's teeth on edge, and he'd put a stop to that plan. Clay had sent long looks in Katie's direction more than once when she worked outdoors, and John had vowed to keep an eye on him, sensing that the man might have ulterior motives where the young woman was concerned.

Now, with Bill Stanley's approval, John organized the shopping trip, their destination Eden, the general store being the first stop.

They arrived midmorning and Katie and Berta went inside while John settled the team at the hitching rail. Berta's list of supplies needed was long, for they'd been so busy with the gardening they hadn't been to town for over two weeks, and the flour bin was almost empty. Sacks of sugar and coffee, tins of lard and canned peaches were soon piled on the counter of the bustling store, and as Katie held the list and tried to decipher Berta's writing, the order was filled.

She'd watched as Berta wrote down the necessary items they would purchase, looking over her mentor's shoulder as they thought of what was needed and so recalled easily just what each item was. Delighted at her own prowess with the words written on the paper before her, she checked each item off as Shandy Peterson brought it to the counter. Stacking them high, he stood back and she beheld a satisfied grin on his face, for the items were many and his store stood to make a tidy profit on this order.

Katie's words were soft, spoken beneath her breath, pleased by the excitement of the shopping trip. "This is more fun than a…" Her voice trailed off as she thought industriously just what such an occasion could be compared to. It was certainly more enjoyable than many a day she'd spent in her short life, not as wonderful perhaps as her evenings with John or the meals they shared over the oilcloth-covered table in his cabin, but nevertheless, a day to remember fondly.

"You sure don't require much in the way of entertainment, young'un," Berta said with a laugh. "Buying supplies is hard work, and once we get back and we have to lug all that stuff into the pantry and sort it out to store it, you'll change your tune, I warrant."

Katie only smiled, well aware that the happiness she'd found in Berta's kitchen was worth any hard work that might fall to her. Shandy loaded up the supplies in cardboard boxes and when John approached the counter, the storekeeper was ready to begin carrying out the merchandise. Together the two men loaded the back of the wagon and then Shandy brought flat boxes of tomato plants from the back of the store and placed three of them carefully at the far end of the wagon, positioning the boxes of supplies so that nothing would fall on the fragile stems.

Katie could hardly contain herself on the long ride back to the ranch, so keen was she to begin the planting on the following day, for Berta had said that the tomatoes must go into the ground right away. It would be a daily task to water them for the first little while, at least until they got a good spring shower to dampen the whole garden.

Their arrival at the ranch was accomplished in time for preparations for supper, as Berta said when they turned into the long lane that ran toward the ranch buildings. She began telling Katie what they would fix, letting her know that she and John were more than welcome to join with the ranch family for the evening repast. But Katie's mind was seized by another matter as the wagon turned the corner of the house and the porch appeared in her line of vision.

Upon the back step of Bill Stanley's big house sat a young girl, brown-haired and thin, seeming to shrink within the dowdy, homespun bit of apparel she wore. Her head was bent, her hands folded in her lap. A single word passed by Katie's lips and it brought John's attention to her with a swift motion of his head.

"Jane." She swallowed hard and then repeated the name, more loudly this time. "Jane." The speaking of the word caught the attention of the child, for surely she was not more than fifteen years of age, John thought, and she looked up at the approaching wagon. Her eyes lit with pleasure as she caught sight of Katie and she stood, unmoving for a moment, as if she were unsure of her welcome, and then as Katie uttered a cry of happiness, Jane ran to the wagon and Katie almost fell off the seat, so eager was she to be on the ground.

They hugged and whispered excitely together as

John watched, Berta alert to a major occasion here, and then Katie turned Jane to face the couple who sat on the seat and observed their reunion. "John, Berta, this is Jane, my sister."

"Didn't know you had one," Berta said shortly, but her brusque words were tempered by a smile as she nodded greetings at the newcomer. John grinned and dropped to the ground.

"Hello there, Jane. Good to meet you. Katie's told me about you, but I'll have to admit I'm a little surprised to see you here."

The girl shivered and her eyes filled with quick tears. "Can I stay? At least long enough to see Katie for a bit? I've missed her a lot, mister, and I just couldn't stand it no more without seeing her."

John was puzzled. Whether or not Jane was here as a runaway or had come for a visit, he wasn't sure, but he suspected that the Schraders were not aware of her presence here. And said as much.

"Your folks know where you are, Jane?"

She paled and shot a quick look at Katie. "I ran off. I was afraid of what—"

Her sudden pause alerted John and he touched her shoulder, a touch she flinched from, causing his eyebrows to lift a bit. And yet, it was a familiar reaction, he realized, for Katie had been in much the same condition when he'd first found her.

"What were you afraid of, Jane?" he asked quietly, lowering his voice so they would not be overheard.

Berta sauntered to the back of the wagon and called out to Ben, one of the hands who had walked up from the barn to get the wagon and team, and asked his help in taking the supplies into the house. Leaving Katie, Jane and John to their discussion, she directed proceedings and in short order the wagon was emptied, the tomato plants on the porch and the foodstuffs in the kitchen.

Jane trembled as she looked up into John's face, and even as he watched, her skin pebbled as chills ran over her body. "I was afraid to stay there any longer, sir. Things were getting mighty bad and I was afeared of what old man Schrader was gonna do to me next."

"Was he beating on you?" Katie asked quickly, touching Jane's arms and bending close to check the young flesh that was discolored and stained with dirt. She brushed at a dark spot and looked up with fire in her eyes. "He hit you with a board or something, didn't he?"

Jane only nodded and tears began to flow, as if she had held them in as long as was possible, and the simple query had been enough to prime the pump and turn the deluge free. She bent her head, making no attempt to halt the waterworks, and Katie reached for her, holding her close and whispering gently in her ear.

And then she looked up at John, and her eyes pleaded silently for that which was the cry of her heart. "John, don't make her go back. Please, John."

"Katie, don't you know me better than that? I wouldn't do such a thing. She's your sister. Of course she can stay," he said.

Katie released Jane from her embrace and stepped closer to her husband, reaching to touch his face—her fingers against his lips.

"Don't say any more, John. I should have known better than to doubt you for a minute. You're so much a part of my life, sometimes I forget how much I depend on you to always do the right thing. I know you'll take care of both of us—both me and my sister."

John bent a bit, dropping a quick kiss on her forehead. "You've got it right, Katie. I'll always be here for you."

CHAPTER TWELVE

IT WAS LATE EVENING before the tub of water was drained off onto the ground by the back porch of the little cabin. John had filled it with hot water from the reservoir on the cookstove and Katie pumped cold water from the kitchen sink's pitcher pump to cool it for Jane's bath, and then John had disappeared. The two girls spent an industrious half hour, with Jane in the tub, Katie washing her hair and using her new bar of soap to ensure that her sister would look clean and smell good by bedtime.

The thought of such luxury was obviously an unknown to Jane and she made much of the soap, sniffing the suds on her hands and then washing her face until her eyes watered from the soap that would not stay out of her eyes. With tender, gentle touches, Katie helped her to dry off, frowning as she caught sight of several large bruises on Jane's backside and upper legs.

"He had a good time whacking at you, didn't he?" she muttered, not needing an answer to her accusation to know the truth of the matter.

"Wasn't too bad," Jane said sullenly. "I've seen a lot worse on you in the old days."

"No more of it, though," Katie said sharply. "I decided the night I walked away from there that I'd die before I went back, and if by some chance he ever got ahold of me again, I'd shoot him, right where he stood."

"That's murder," Jane said, stricken, as she lifted her head from the towel that had been drying her hair.

"Just a good payback, to my mind," Katie said. "The man ought to be gut-shot and left to die, to my way of thinking."

Jane considered that idea for a moment and then nodded firmly. "Guess I'll have to agree with you. He sure is one nasty man."

"He's not a man. He's no more than a worm," Katie said with fire in her voice. "John is a man, and let me tell you it's like night and day to compare the two of them."

"I didn't want to be nosy, Katie, but I gotta know how you met him, and how come he brought you home with him like he did." Her laughter rang out, clear and spontaneous. "You shoulda heard the hubbub when the Schraders found out what had happened. They thought you'd run off, sure enough, when you weren't there in the morning, but it took 'em a couple of days to find out that you'd got tied up with John Roper and were living out here on the Stanley place. And then when she came back from town after you had to go see the judge, she was having a regular fit, saying that John was gonna force you into marriage and you was nothing but a slave for him."

Nudging a chair into place, Katie put a towel-wrapped Jane onto it and then worked at drying her hair. Within ten minutes, she had divulged the whole of her story, leaving private portions where they belonged, in the secret places of her heart.

"So after they found out that they couldn't get me back from John, old Jacob got himself tossed in jail for a week and we came home," she finished with a flourish, pulling her brush through Jane's tangled locks.

"And was Agnes ever mad," Jane repeated with a muffled laugh. "She had a pea-pickin' fit over the whole thing. Told me she'd get you paid back, one way or another." And then her laughter quit, and she looked up at Katie with fear on her face. "You don't think she'll hurt you, do you? Can she get to you?"

Katie shook her head. "Not so long as John's alive, and he's not about to lay down and die anytime soon, barring an accident." That thought sobered her as she spoke and she slid another chair nearby and sat by her sister. "I worry about him some days, but he says not to, that he's got something to live for, what with me here with him and our house all getting fixed up and having everything so nice."

"You're sure enough lucky, ain't ya? But I'm not jealous, Katie. I promise you I'm not. I just think it's grand that you got out when you did. I'm afraid that old Jacob had plans for you that weren't nice at all. He was so mad when you left, said he'd just got you raised to a good age and now you were gone when you coulda been some use to him."

Katie was puzzled. "What do you suppose he meant by that?" And then her face cleared. "I'll ask John what he thinks. Maybe he can figure it out."

"Well, whatever it was, I'll doggone guarantee you it wasn't something good," Jane said bitterly. "He was already startin' in on maulin' on me. Tried to climb in my bed the other night. That's when I knew I had to get out of there. One of the boys at school was talking about stuff one day and the boys were laughing about pokin' at girls and what they'd do to some girl who was willing to let them."

"Pokin' at girls? What on earth are they talking about?"

Jane gave her a long look. "I swear, Katie. For such a smart girl, you sure don't have much of any idea how men's minds work, do you?"

"Only John's," Katie said with a warm smile. "And I like the way he— Oh, my." The memory of what might be involved in the *poking* process occurred to her suddenly, and she felt her face redden and then shivered with distaste at the thought of such a thing in connection with Jacob Schrader.

"You don't think Jacob would have…" She shuddered again and buried her face in her hands.

"I think he would have done a lot of things, given a chance. If old Agnes didn't keep such an eagle eye on him, he'd probably have been even worse than he was."

Katie's eyes lit with a militant light. "You're not going back there, no matter what. You'll stay here or something, but you'll not be back in that house again."

"We can't always do what we want, Katie. I don't relish the idea, but unless I have somewhere to go, I might get dragged back."

"Not if we have to go live in a cave in the hills," Katie said stoutly. "I'll talk to John. Maybe he'll have an idea. Besides, won't they be wondering where you are at school when you don't show up pretty soon?"

"My teacher said I'm doing real good," Jane said with a trace of pride. "I told her I wanted to learn how to be a teacher someday and she said I could go to Normal school and get a certificate to do the job. Said it wouldn't take long, not more than two years at the most. But I know the Schraders won't hear of it. And it costs a lot of money, I'll warrant."

"Well, you need to be back in school. Land sakes, you're almost ready to finish, and heaven knows you're a smart one, Jane. I'd be so proud if you could be a real teacher."

"I sure wish I'd thought to bring my schoolbooks with me when I left there yesterday," Jane said. "I just skedaddled with the clothes on my back and a sackful of stuff I could carry." She looked stricken for a minute. "I left it under the back porch when I got here. Maybe I can sneak out after a while and collect it. I'll scrub stuff out in your bucket if I can. My things need washin' real bad."

"We'll get the washtub out in the morning and fill it with good hot water," Katie said. "I've got John's things to do up anyway and we'll put up a line between the trees out back if it's nice out. If not, they'll dry on the porch."

"You sure got it nice here," Jane said, looking around the neat kitchen, running an admiring hand over the cheery oilcloth Katie had put on the table, the first thing she had added after moving into the cabin. And then she ran her hand over the six yards of fabric Katie had brought home for new curtains.

"I'll cut these to length tomorrow and sit down and sew them up first thing, once we get your clothes into some hot water," she told Jane.

"You done a good job, Katie fixing this place up. Looks real homey, like."

Katie preened silently and then couldn't resist a bit of bragging. "My John says he never had it so good. He's proud as can be."

"Your John is a lucky man," came a low, deep voice from outside the back screened door.

Katie jumped up and spun around. "John. You scared me to death."

"Serves you right for talking about me when I can't even defend myself," he said with a grin, opening the door and stepping into the kitchen.

"I was just telling Katie how nice you've made it for her," Jane said quietly, her eyes unable to meet the gentle blue of John's gaze. As though she had been well trained to keep her eyes downcast and her thoughts to herself, she spoke hesitantly, yet her words were sincere.

"Katie's done her own nesting, Jane. I just gave her a place to do it in. What you see around you is the result of her skill."

"I'm not all that good at stuff, John," Katie said, chastising him abruptly. "You're just trying to make me look good to my sister."

"I don't have to do a thing to make you seem what you are, Katie," he told her with a smile that belied his scolding words. "You are talented and smart. I'm not telling tales when I say that, and I'm sure that Jane would agree with me. She knows you probably far better than I. She knows what strength and courage it took for you to leave the place where you lived and strike out on your own. And I'll guarantee she's more than aware that you've made your own way here, with me. That you've been the best wife you could be to me and taken care of me."

Jane laughed aloud and her eyes crinkled with the sound of her happiness for her sister. "You surely do know a lot of pretty words to say, John. No wonder Katie's so taken with you. She's thinking the sun shines right out of those blue eyes of yours, and I can't say as I blame her. You've made her into a new person, what with her smiling all the time and being so happy. I'm thankful, and more than pleased for her."

For the second time in his life, John Roper was smitten. Smitten to the core, by the lissome charms of a young woman who had not even achieved eighteen years of age, whose stature was small, whose frame was slender, but whose heart was as big as the back forty, and maybe even measured larger than that. And if he wasn't careful, he'd be letting this little girl gain a place of too much importance to him. It wouldn't pay to accept her at face value, any more than he would any other person in his life. But allowing her the presence of her sister in her life would surely be a small thing to do for Katie.

Perhaps he could see if Bill Stanley would allow him to keep Jane here. Katie would be able to offer her sister the shelter the girl so desperately needed. And it was possible that Jacob and Agnes Schrader would keep their hands off the pair of girls and allow them the freedom they had fought so hard to gain.

And maybe pigs would fly.

He smiled at his own foolishness. It was gonna be a tough row to hoe no matter what he did about the situation. First off he'd better check with Bill, then know what he could offer to Jane before he made any promises to Katie concerning her sister.

Bedtime found Jane on a pallet in front of the cookstove, a pillow offered by Berta beneath her head and a warm quilt pulled up over her shoulders. Katie eyed her with concern. "Sure wish we had another bed to offer you, but this is the best we can do for tonight. It's either this or the sofa." And Jane had turned down that offer, seeking the warmth of the big stove instead.

Berta had offered a bedroom in the big house, a plan to which Bill Stanley had nodded his approval after a long, searching look in John's direction. But Jane had turned hands down on that idea, stating that she'd rather be near Katie, where she could keep a good eye on things. And made John wonder privately just how long Jane had been doing such a thing, for the girl seemed to have an almost maternal instinct where Katie was concerned. Their relationship was a mutual thing, it seemed, for Katie's concerns were real and valid, and the assumption that they would tend to each other seemed deeply ingrained in each.

The bedroom door was closed, a condition they had not set into place before, instead allowing the heat from the main room to raise the cold temperature in the room they slept in. But John wanted his privacy, and he wanted to be able to speak with Katie if needed, without the benefit of an audience.

And so, in the dark they found each other beneath the covers, the big man with gentle hands and the girl with a desperate need for those hands to touch her and assure her of her position in his life. He might say the words, and say them well, but it was the warmth of John's caresses and the strength of his tender touch that assured her of his need and made her yearn toward him nightly.

He held her close in the middle of the bed, his mouth touching her hairline, there where her temple smelled sweet and fragile, where her life's blood throbbed in a steady rhythm. His lips touched the skin, brushed through her thick eyebrows and then made a fanciful trail down to the tip of her nose.

She giggled softly and scolded him. "John, don't be doing foolish stuff tonight. You don't want Jane to hear you making monkeyshines in here, monkey-doodling around like you do."

His whisper was a vibrant temptation in her ear. "And why not, young lady. You're my wife and I like to monkey-doodle around with you. And what does *that* mean anyway? Monkey-doodle, indeed. What a word to attach to what we do in this bed."

His words made her laugh all the more, her hand against her mouth to muffle the sound. Then she touched his cheek with her palm, spreading her fingers wide over his jaw, lifting herself the mere inches it took to reach his mouth with her own. Her kiss was still youthful, innocent, but held a trace of knowledge yet untapped, of a siren's lures and a woman's yearnings. He let her plunder a bit as she wanted, then lifted over her, laying her back on the pillow and spending a deluge of kisses over her face and throat.

She sighed and responded as he'd known she would. "John, you surely do know how to make me feel good," she whispered, careful to keep the quilt almost over her head, lest the sound travel to the other room where Jane slept.

"Well, you'll have to be real quiet for the next little while now, Katie," he said with a solemn purpose. "For I'm going to make love to you and we don't want any noise to disturb your sister, do we?"

She pushed at him quickly. "John, we can't be doing that stuff with Jane on the other side of that door."

His lips touched her ear and his murmur was soft and pleading. "She's so tired, she's no doubt out like a light already, sweetheart. And even if she's awake, she'll not know what's going on if you just cooperate with me and let me do this nice and quiet."

"John, you know I have a hard time being nice and quiet," she remonstrated softly. "You get me all excited sometimes and I make noises and say things to you, even when I promise myself I'm not going to act so foolish."

He chuckled and held her close. "That's not foolish, honey, just acting the way you should when your husband makes love to you." He moved to lie atop her and held his weight from her slender form, holding himself up on his forearms and bending to spread another layer of kisses over her face.

She slid her arms around his waist, apparently deciding that she'd argued enough and was willing to accept his choice, for her legs moved to make a place for him, settling him there where he fit so well. She lifted her knees and her nightgown pulled up, aided by his hand as he tugged it from beneath her. It was no effort at all to touch her warm parts while his hand lay beneath the covers and he used the moments to good advantage, caressing her and plying the soft, plush surfaces with careful touches.

Her whisper was soft, almost unheard, but it made

his heart joyous to sense her pleasure. "John, that always feels so good. You know just how to make me wiggle and make me want you right there, inside me where it feels so good."

"That's the whole idea, sweetheart," he managed to mumble, his thoughts speeding rapidly ahead to the details of making love to his woman. It would of necessity be a hasty coupling, but not without pleasure to Katie, for he knew her body well.

And yet, there was with Katie, a joy beyond any he'd ever known before. A sweetness he'd sought and never found, a satisfaction he hadn't known was missing in the areas of his private life. From the first time they had come together in this bed, he'd sensed a newness of his vision as it pertained to the art of making love. There was more to it than the simple slaking of passion, the need for completion, the scratch of a nagging itch.

With Katie it seemed that his whole self was tied up in the act he instigated here, the marriage ritual that was so much more meaningful to him than the simple sharing of his body with another. For Katie was *his*. A soft, completely responsive woman who completed his life, who gave unstintingly whenever he needed her, who offered herself as the answer to his physical urges and his emotional cries. Cries he could not speak aloud, but kept buried in the depths of his soul. Her giving spirit, her generous outpouring upon him of physical and emotional bounty had made the difference for him between existing and living.

And now, he took again what he needed from her, not failing to give the joy that was available at his fingertips for her pleasure. She rose to his touch, moving more rapidly as he shifted over her, his mouth at her breast now, his body against hers, not capturing her where she lay, but loving her as he held her beneath himself. Until he felt the waves of passion come together in a final outpouring of gasping ecstacy, until he knew she was sated with the trembling rhythms that still fluttered against his hands and mouth.

It was then he entered her, carefully, gently and with a degree of patience he found incomprehensible. For he was on the cusp of release, his body aching to plunge and take, madly and desperately, having held back as long as he could in order to ensure her own culmination of pleasure.

He slid within the narrow channel, his breath rasping in his chest, held close by the warm arms that circled him, his chest the recipient of a rash of kisses and murmurs he could not decipher, but accepted with the full knowledge that she was more than willing to travel this road with him.

It took very little to push him over the edge, a simple matter of moving slowly, holding back the rush, breathing carefully and then finally turning loose the beast within himself that always seemed ready to burst free, the animal within that he kept on a tight leash. The part of himself that he would not turn loose to ravage her tender flesh, or frighten the joy from her heart.

For John knew that deep within a man lived a part of him that could cause pain and irreparable harm should he not rein it in and control it. His kindness was not a facade, but a real part of him, one bit of himself he had honed and refined until it became his finest quality. And it was that single trait that had drawn Katie to him in the beginning. He would not abandon it now to become another version of man before her.

CHAPTER THIRTEEN

THE GARDEN TOOK UP much of their time over the next weeks. The plants were separated and placed in small holes, watered daily and tended with all the care two young women could spare. Katie looked down at them with pride, holding the watering can high, so that the spray would cover a wider area, and thought greedily of the crop to come. She knew how to can tomatoes, and Berta had said she could use a supply of Mason jars from the fruit cellar for the task.

They would do up green beans, too, in fact there would be beans to pick in a matter of weeks. The carrots were ruthlessly culled, the smaller shoots pulled from their places to leave room for the sturdier plants to grow and develop. Katie felt guilty as she pulled the skimpier bits and pieces from the rows, but knew that the space she was making would enable the crop to grow to its fullest effect.

The peas were going to be ready to pick soon, a fast-growing crop, one that Katie was not overly fond of, but which provided a fresh vegetable early in the spring. The morning glory vines were flourishing, growing rapidly along the strings they'd been provided, and before long the shabby outhouse would be shielded by a mass of early-morning blossoms when the sun came up over the trees and touched the greenery. Even the hired hands commented on the flowers that added color to the backyard, one man venturing into the garden's boundaries several times to speak to Katie and Jane. A man she did not trust for some reason, for his eyes seemed to seek her out, and she felt a chill run the length of her spine when she saw him looking at her.

She knelt now in the middle of the garden, her eyes ever vigilant, and she kept Jane in view. It was Saturday and Jane was home, not at the school in town, where John had decided she should still attend as much as possible. He made it his business to speak with her teacher. He let her know that Jane was staying at the Stanley ranch and he would take her into town two mornings a week to attend classes, and then pick her up to bring her back to the ranch and allow her to study at the small cabin with Katie as companion.

Whether or not it was the proper way to do things, he didn't care. If it was beyond the boundaries of legality to keep Jane from the Schraders' reach, he was not concerned. Only the fact that the girl be kept safe, that Katie slept well at night, and that Jane might be assured of a future of sorts concerned him.

The teacher was willing to go along with the unusual procedure, coming out to the ranch on Saturday or Sunday for an hour or so to work with Jane, and to his surprise to listen to Katie's efforts to read and be an encouragement to her.

Jane looked forward to seeing her teacher, and Mrs. Rice would be here later on today if all went as scheduled. She had promised to show up in time for supper and Katie thought now of the meal she had planned for the teacher's visit. Fried chicken was always a favorite with everyone, she had decided. And she could cook a chicken to a fare-thee-well. She'd have a bowl of fresh peas if there were enough of them ripe and then open a jar of applesauce that Berta had canned up late last fall.

A sack of potatoes, a bit withered but still eminently edible, sat in her pantry, and her plan included having Jane peel and slice enough for supper once they got in the cabin and washed up after their gardening chores.

And that time was upon them, Berta coming out onto the porch to wave and suggest that they might stop laboring in the spring sunshine. "Getting pretty hot out there," the housekeeper said, looking up at the azure sky overhead that promised fair weather.

"We're about done for now," Katie said. "It's most time to get ready for Mrs. Rice. She'll be here in a couple of hours and I got work to do, fixing supper."

"You can bring her in the house if you want to, Katie," Berta told her, and Katie only smiled and shook her head.

"Naw, she can't stay too long, and me and Jane want to take advantage of her while she's here with us. Got to learn all we can while we got her handy."

Berta nodded, as if she understood the need for learning that drove the two young women. And then, at a cry from Jane's lips, Katie looked up to see the buggy Mrs. Rice used to convey herself back and forth, coming down the long lane from the main road.

"She's early today," Jane said. "I'm glad we're about done here."

"Go on ahead and I'll finish up taking care of the litter," Katie said, gathering up the strewn, feathery carrots they'd culled and the weeds that had been stripped from around the tomatoes and corn.

Slender and bright, the green stalks were above the ground, leafing out in proud display as the cornfield gave a small intimation of the stature it would achieve over the next weeks. They'd hoed carefully around each hill, mounding the dirt and cleaning up the eager weeds that would threaten the corn crop should they let them have their way.

Now she piled two buckets full of the residue and watched as Jane went to the cabin and took off her heavy shoes outside the door before she went in, barefoot on the clean, wooden floor. She'd scrubbed it early on in the morning after the dishes were washed and the sun had been allowed to shine in the doors and open windows to aid in the drying of the wide boards.

Having help in the house was a boon, Katie decided. And Jane took on the chores assigned to her with a cheerful mien that spoke well for her innate sense of goodness. So thankful for a safe place to lay her head at night, she gladly pitched in and did more than her share in keeping the small house neat and clean.

Now, Mrs. Rice climbed down from the buggy, tying the lead line to the hitching rail and lifting a hand to wave at Katie. "You coming in the house, honey?" she called. "I brought you a book to use this week."

Katie's heart lifted with anticipation as she heard the words. The teacher was quiet, unassuming and didn't offer any criticism for Katie's lack of schooling, but offered her help as if it were the girl's due to be assisted in her studies. And now, she'd brought a new book. Katie's steps were rapid as she carried the buckets to the dump pile behind the barn where all such refuse was spilled out to dry, and eventually be burned. Her quick nod at Mrs. Rice seemed to assure that lady that Katie's presence would very soon be felt in the cabin, and the teacher rapped on the screened door and entered the cabin with a muted word to Jane.

The refuse was dumped quickly and from the back of the barn Katie saw the shadowed form of the ranch hand, Clay Thomas. Bill Stanley busied the man with general chores and he seemed to fit in well with the rest of the crew. But today he'd appeared to pay special mind to Katie's presence behind the barn, and as she emptied her pails of weeds onto the refuse pile, he approached her.

"You need any help there, missy?" His eyes seemed bold, she thought, scanning her form with heat, and she clutched the pails tighter in her hands and made to move past him. Being rude was not called for, but she simply didn't like the man.

"I'm fine, Clay," she said shortly, unwilling to tarry longer.

"I'd be glad to lend a hand with your work," he said softly, his dark eyes intent as he stepped before her, blocking her path.

"My work's done for now. I'm heading back to the cabin to get ready for supper."

His gaze stayed on her, his jaw taut, as if he were riding a fine line. "Maybe I can give you a hand."

A shiver of apprehension shot through Katie and she shook her head. "I don't need any help, Clay. Jane's in the house, waiting for me."

He stood before her in the doorway leading to the darkened barn, the shadows behind him seeming threatening to Katie, her skin pebbling with a sudden cold that frightened her. As if she were once more cast into the past, with a vision of Jacob Schrader before her, she looked over her shoulder, seeking a path of escape.

"Come on in here a minute, girl," Clay said with an urgency in his voice that brought Katie's senses to a sharp edge. And then the man reached for her, his big hand seizing her forearm. "I want to talk to you for a minute."

Katie pulled back from him, but to no avail, for he was strong, a good foot taller than she, and had the husky build of a man who had worked hard making his way in the world. He tugged her closer to him and she jerked away, the pail in her left hand hitting the side of the barn with a clatter.

His head bent to her and his mouth touched her forehead, even as she pulled away from his touch, and shoved the other pail between their bodies.

With a low growl that expressed his anger and frustration with her reticence, he pulled the bucket from her grasp and tossed it aside, then clamped his hands on her waist and lifted her from her feet.

She flailed against him, crying out and pushing against his shoulders with all her strength. From behind her she heard a sharp sound of anger, a word that she'd only heard before from the lips of Jacob Schrader and she twisted in the grip of the man who held her, turning her head to see who was behind her.

John stood in the corral, his hands fisted against his sides, and as the ranch hand deposited her quickly on the ground, Katie's husband caught her against himself.

"I see Mrs. Rice has arrived. Are you going in now?" he asked, his voice harsh, his eyes narrowed as he glared at the man before him.

Katie shivered in his grasp, her heart racing, her body trembling. "Yes, I'll go to the cabin, John. I was just—"

"Never mind, Katie. I saw what you were doing."

With a quick movement, he put her to one side, pushing her out of the barn, toward the cabin on the other side. "Go on now."

She hastened to do as he bid, not hesitating as she heard the low sound of his voice behind her, heard the answering words of Clay as he spoke a challenge. And then came the sound of a body hitting the wall and with a quick glance over her shoulder, Katie saw the ranch hand on the ground, John standing over him with the glare of anger, the fury of a man who seeks revenge on his face.

She scurried out of the front of the barn, across the yard to John's cabin, and her heart pounded with fear, knowing that John was involved in a fight with a man who was taller and larger than he.

The cabin was before her and she hastened to enter, listening to the muted sound of Jane's voice humming a song as she climbed the single step to the porch and went inside. Jane was sitting at the table, peeling potatoes, a piece of brown paper salvaged from the purchase of supplies holding her work before her. A kettle of water held the two potatoes she'd already pared and cubed, and now she looked up at Katie.

"I don't think we'll need many more, Katie. Do you? These are good-sized spuds."

With a look of greeting to Mrs. Rice, Katie nodded. "Should be plenty," she replied. "I'm going to use the stale bread to make up a little batch of dressing to put in the oven so we should have plenty with one more."

Jane and Mrs. Rice watched her closely as she washed her hands and found the half loaf of bread from the last baking that sat on the kitchen dresser, as if they sensed that she had more than supper preparations on her mind. Cutting the bread quickly into cubes, Katie tossed them into a pan to lose their last bit of freshness while she washed and floured the chicken she planned to cook for supper.

Her hands trembled as she worked, thinking of John and his anger, hoping against hope that it was not directed at her. Even the joy of cooking escaped her today, it seemed. She only thought of the men in the barn, of John's fists and the fury she'd seen on his face.

Her hands moved with automatic precision. A small pan of peas was quickly cleaned, the pods discarded, the small, green specimens put in a small saucepan to cook quickly and then be set aside till suppertime. She watched from the corner of her eyes as Mrs. Rice reached down to the voluminous bag she was in the habit of carrying with her, and from its depths drew a book, an obviously unused textbook of sorts, placing it on the table and then looking up at Katie. Her smile was bright, but her eyes held a trace of worry, as if she sensed that Katie was troubled.

"I brought you a reader, Katie. I know you've learned a lot of words, but this has many of the easiest words for you to practice with. You can read through it quickly, I'll warrant, for the stories are simple, but I think you'll like it, and it's not so challenging that you'll get weary in well doing."

Mrs. Rice was fond of such wording as she spoke and Katie usually enjoyed hearing her opinions. She admired intelligence and Mrs. Rice was a smart lady, one who was more than willing to share her knowledge, and seemingly had much to share. That her mind was filled with John and the scene behind the barn was keeping her from her usual interest in the teacher and her kindness.

"I surely do appreciate your thinking of me," Katie said, aware that her voice trembled as she spoke. The time before supper would be long, she knew, for she felt the need to see John, to know that his anger was not directed at her. But for now, she must put it aside and think about the task at hand.

Deeming that she had a good half hour until she needed to begin frying chicken, Katie sat down at the table and took up the book she'd been entrusted with.

She inhaled the scent of the text she held, her thoughts calming as she felt the binding, the fresh pages of text. Books. They had an odor of their own, an aroma like no other. That of new paper perhaps, of dried printer's ink, of the binding and the glue that held it together. She inhaled the rich smell, taking it in as she might a nourishing meal, and escaped for a moment into the world offered by the kindness of Mrs. Rice.

For it was just that to her. Nourishment for the soul, and Katie's soul was starved for such a thing. Her hands were clean, her fingers careful as she opened the first page and cast her eyes on the letters that formed the words on the page.

Her fingers trembled as she held the page in place, and she saw the look of pleasure cast in her direction by Mrs. Rice. "I know some of these words already," she ventured, pointing at several familiar arrangements of letters. Jane told me a lot of stuff and I got so I could figure it out by myself, too."

"I'm sure you have, Katie. You have a sharp, open mind, and learning comes easily to you. I'd be pleasured to teach you right along with Jane if you like. I'll be out here on a regular basis, anyway."

Hope filled Katie's heart with a surge of joy. "I want to learn so bad, Mrs. Rice. I really do. There's so many of John's books in there in a box that I'd like to open up and find out all the things he already knows. All those things he's already read. I could kinda get to know him better if I know what's already in his head, I think."

"I think you already know John Roper quite well, Katie. At least all the important things about him. He's a fine man."

"He's a *good* man," Katie said emphatically, thinking again of his quick movements as he'd taken her from harm's way.

"Do you think I'll ever have a husband like Katie does, Mrs. Rice?" Jane asked in a small voice. "I'd like to do something with my life, like teaching or having a family of my own."

Mrs. Rice smiled widely, nodding her head. "I can see you at the State college, gaining your certificate in just a few years, Jane. I've already written to the powers that decide such things, asking for a scholarship for you. Your mind is sharp and keen and by the time this year is over, you'll be ready to consider such a step. We'll speed up your studies a little, throw in some more math and science and before you know it, you'll be ready to pack your things and go off to school."

"Where will I live?" she asked, wonderingly, as if her mind could not contain such thoughts.

"They have dormitories for the young women there, and the dean will help find work for you to do to help earn your way. And the state will hopefully pay for enough of your schooling to make it easier for you to earn your certificate. Two years will do it if you work hard."

"Oh, I'll work like a piker, Mrs. Rice. You know I will. I can't wait till the day I get to stand in front of a class of young'uns and start to teach them all the things they need to know about reading and writing and doing sums and learning the right way to speak and say their words. I want to teach them how to sing songs and say poems, like the ones you read to us in school."

"You'll do all of that one day, Jane. Your goals are in place and opportunities will be opening up. Just you wait and see."

JOHN STOOD ON the porch, listening, thinking that he really should let his presence be known to the three females inside his kitchen, but too filled with pleasure at their words to move. He settled down with his back against the upright post, folding his hands on his knee and thinking of the one small creature inside that house that was his to call "wife." The girl he'd thought was devoting herself so fully to him and his comfort.

The girl whose actions were at the center of his thoughts, his mind scanning her behavior behind the barn. That Clay had touched her was a given, for he'd seen the man's hands on her waist, lifting her against himself. Just how much Katie had cooperated with the man was the question, for if she had encouraged Clay in any way, shape or form, John would consider it as treachery, as a mar against their marriage.

He tried to recall each moment of time as he'd watched Clay speaking to her, her responses to the man and the way in which she'd pushed at him and tried to escape his touch.

Perhaps Katie had lured the man on, perhaps she'd smiled at him and tempted him against his better judgment. It was possible, he decided. For Katie was friendly, had made quick friends with the men who had helped with the garden plot. She'd been trying her wings, making her own place here, and maybe she'd thought to see if she could entice Clay into paying her some particular attention.

He felt a chill of anger touch him as he considered what might have brought about the scuffle he'd come upon behind the barn. And he looked down at his fists, knotted against his knees, the scuffed surfaces showing bruises already forming, blood at the surface, and knuckles aching from the pounding they'd given to the man who still lay on the floor of the barn.

Bill Stanley would be fit to be tied when he found

that two of his men had had a fistfight, although John knew he'd gotten the best of the deal, with only one small mark on his jaw from Clay's left fist. Anger had fueled his strength and Clay had suffered at his hand, with both eyes blackened and his nose bleeding and probably broken.

Now he faced entering his own cabin, seeing his wife and the other two women who worked in his kitchen. He must put on a good front, not bring his fury to bear on the women who were inside, for he could not bring himself to embarrass them by his anger. He would save that for a private time with Katie, when he could bring out into the open all of his thoughts and fears.

How he'd come to this place in his life, he didn't know, didn't understand and was usually thankful for. He'd felt that the presence of Katie was a blessing and he knew a moment of thanksgiving that it was so. Still a small part of his mind wondered if she was all she had purported to be, if she was indeed honest and faithful to him.

From inside he heard the shuffle of feet, the movement of a chair and then Katie's words of warning. "Land sakes, it's getting right on to suppertime and I'm sitting here, lollygaggin' like I got nothing to do. John will be in right shortly, hungry as a bear, and I won't have his supper ready."

But, as it turned out, she did. John went into the cabin and washed quickly, sitting at the table with a cup of coffee, watching Mrs. Rice and listening to the women speak of the meal they prepared. Mixing the dressing and then browning the chicken took a mere half hour, and the peas cooked quickly and then rested atop the warming oven to stay hot while Katie finished the chicken in the big oven. Fresh bread was sliced, a jar of applesauce opened and a pat of butter appeared from the pantry.

Jane mashed the potatoes deftly, adding cream to the mix, a dab of butter and sprinkling a dash of pepper over the top of the offering. "Looks pretty that way, don't it?" she asked with a grin, settling the bowl on the table. "I like to make the food seem kinda special sometimes. Agnes always says I'm foolish, but I don't care."

"You don't have to care one whit about what Agnes says or thinks anymore anyway," Katie told her. "You can do whatever you want here, and John won't give a good gol dern. He just likes folks to be happy." Her eyes touched John's as she spoke, and he caught a glimpse of the fear she held within. And wondered if she hid some bit of treachery within that slender frame, if there was a need within Katie for approval from other men. Wondered if she had been somehow intrigued by the attentions of the ranch hand. He'd sure hung around the garden enough over the past week or so, and even though John hadn't seen any sign of her encouraging the man, the possibility was there.

And then he heard Jane's words as she spoke to her sister. "You're so lucky, Katie. And so is John. I think this is about the nicest place I've ever been in my life. Everyone is nice to each other and you don't even have that sad look in your eyes anymore."

Perhaps Jane was right, John thought. Maybe he was looking for trouble where there was none to be found. And for a moment, he vowed to withhold his doubts lest he cause discord where there was no reason.

Mrs. Rice finished bundling up her paperwork in her bulging bag and turned to the girls. "It's a peaceful place, Jane. A place where you can grow and be yourself and know that you are loved and accepted. And that's what all of us need. I'm so pleased that you're here. I was so worried about you. About Katie, too. Even though I didn't know her as well."

She settled her bag near the door, looking up at John "I just spoke of you a few minutes ago, John. I'd like to think that Jane could come to school on a more regular basis if it can be arranged. She's doing well, but I'd be able to use her in the classroom, helping with the younger children sometimes, and I think it would be good for her training."

John knew his expression was dubious. "I fear to let her ride to school alone, ma'am. She's not able to take care of herself should someone lie in wait for her or meet her along the way. I feel better if I just ride in with her a couple of days a week and then come back to bring her home later."

Mrs. Rice pursed her lips. "I understand that. I truly do. I just know that she needs everyday learning. But

I'll bow to your better judgment on this matter. I'm sure you're more aware than I of the circumstances."

"We'll see how things go," John said easily, pulling out his chair to sit at the table. His eyes ran over the food already there and then at Katie, who was dishing up the chicken from the big pan she'd taken from the oven. She drained it for a few moments on a large piece of brown paper salvaged from store wrappings, allowing the grease to soak from the tender surfaces of the meat, then brought it to the table. A little more of the grease was poured from the pan into the skillet where she'd stirred gravy to a creamy, aromatic finish, and now she poured it into a large bowl and carried it, steaming, to the table.

"You sure can cook, Katie," John said, giving in to the urge to touch her hand as it lay on the table while she looked over the presentation and considered her meal. No matter his thoughts, he could not seem to keep from establishing his claim on her, and he silently cursed himself for his weakness where she was concerned. "That chicken looks good enough to eat," he said with a last look in her direction.

Her response was a smile that teased. "That's exactly what I expect you to do with it, John. I know how much you like fried chicken."

His thoughts went to the owner of the ranch, recalling a conversation they'd shared only this morning. "Bill said he's gonna have the fellas help Berta slaughter a bunch of the young roosters in a couple of weeks, while they're still nice and young, and he wondered if you'd like to can up a few of them for soup later on in the year."

Her eyes lit and she grinned. "I never canned chicken before, but I'll bet Berta can help me with it. She's so smart. She does things better than Agnes ever did, makes the food taste so much better and look nicer. Half the fixing of food is the way it looks anyway, once you're ready to put it on the table."

John spoke in tones that bore traces of the anger he struggled to keep under control, and he stifled it as best he could. "Well, yours is getting cold, Katie. Come sit down now. You've got it all finished, haven't you?"

She nodded, pulling her chair out and settling next to him. Across the table, Mrs. Rice was waiting, her hands folded neatly in her lap, Jane next to her, grinning to beat the band, and Katie thought that life was grand, indeed. At least she sincerely hoped it was, for John was a puzzlement to her right now, what with his jaw so tight and his eyes so cold.

He bowed his head and offered brief words of thanksgiving for the meal and Mrs. Rice smiled at him as he finished. No words were needed, Katie thought, for the teacher's look of approval said more than a hundred nice phrases could have.

They ate, John answering Mrs. Rice's queries, speaking of his books, with Mrs. Rice's encouragement, telling of the classics he'd carried about with him over the years, comparing notes with her on the authors he enjoyed best. If her looks of surprise as he spoke pleased him, it was not obvious, for John was accepting of his own worth, and Katie knew that he was confident in his knowledge. He didn't brag or boast, but John was intelligent, and he knew it.

She felt pride fill her as she watched and listened to him talk of his travels, of the places he'd visited in his young life. Of the parents he'd left behind and his mother especially, who had influenced his life.

"Did you never want to do anything other than work on a ranch?" Mrs. Rice asked, her query not degrading his choice of work, but a measure of curiosity, as if she knew he was capable of most anything he chose to lay his hand to.

"I was raised on a farm, a ranch really, for my father ran a herd of beef and raised horses. I'd thought to be a ranch hand and worked my way north from home. Took me a couple of years to get this far, and my job here was a stopgap for me for a while," he admitted. "But I enjoyed working for Bill Stanley. The men here are good company and hard workers. When the foreman went on to his own place and Bill offered me the job and this cabin to live in, it was like a new door opening and I knew that all my years of working with livestock and men was just leading up to this. It's been a good opportunity for me. If things go well, maybe sometime in the future I'll find a place of my own.

"Anyway, I went to town that night, stopped by the saloon to celebrate with a quick drink…something I don't do frequently, by the way," he added with a quick look up at Mrs. Rice.

She nodded, encouraging his words, as if she were eager to hear his tale.

"Anyway, I saw Katie right soon after I got in there, kinda like she fell almost into my lap, and it was the biggest surprise of my life, finding her there. I knew she marked a changing point in my life."

"You did?" Katie's words of astonishment burst out without thought. "I didn't think you knew that right off, John. You were just feeling sorry for me, I figured."

He glanced at her, and his smile was taut, as if he held back his thoughts. "I wasn't about to walk away from finding a woman to work in my house. You were what I needed right then, Katie. I had a cabin to take care of and no one to lend a hand at it."

Mrs. Rice cut in, as if she could not resist adding her own bit of thought. "I'd say that you did the right thing, John. Katie was meant to be there that night, as were you. Some things we really don't have any control over, you know."

Katie spoke softly, awe coating her words. "I'm just thankful things worked out the way they did."

"Does John take you to church?" Mrs. Rice asked, although Katie was positive that the woman knew very well that such a thing was not in the cards yet.

"Not yet, but we'll go one day soon, I think," Katie answered. "He promised me he would and he always keeps his word."

John flushed, overcome by her words of praise on his behalf, words that made him ashamed of the anger that still filled his heart. "I don't know about all of that, ma'am, but I know that my mama taught me to be good to folks, and always treat others the way I'd want them to treat me.

"By the way, Mrs. Rice. I'll be escorting you back to town after supper. I don't like the idea of you being out alone after dark."

With a quick smile, the teacher agreed to John's plan, and between the four of them, they made short work of the chicken dinner.

JOHN WAS LATE COMING back to the cabin that night, having ridden his gelding beside the teacher's buggy, all the way back to town, to ensure that she safely reached her destination. The breeze was soft, with the chill of early spring in the air, but the promise of warm days to come, and Katie looked up as a waft of fresh air washed in the kitchen door.

"I'm glad you're home," she said. "I was just about to get ready for bed."

"You tired?" he asked, his eyes regarding her with interest. "You've been working hard lately, what with the gardening and fixing things up around here."

"I'm sleepy, not tired," she said. "And that sounds foolish, but it's like my body needs to stop working for a while and just spread out on that bed and soak up the night."

Jane sat before the fireplace, a book open on her lap, her eyes on the pair who spoke quietly by the doorway. "Why don't you go on to bed, Katie. I'll get my pallet ready and lie down soon anyway. I can read by the fire so long as it stays bright. By then it'll be time to sleep, anyway, and maybe I'll move to the sofa."

The bedroom was dark, but the light of a candle lit beside the bed was sufficient to see what she was washing, and Katie stood before the dry sink and poured warm water from John's pitcher into the bowl provided there. She stripped to the waist, standing in the dim light, washing industriously at her upper body and arms, rinsing and drying with pleasure on the soft cloths John had purchased at the general store for her use.

He watched her from the bed, indulging his senses in the joy of watching her lithe figure, her firm young arms and the soft flexing of the muscles on her back as she moved. She was so feminine, so very different from himself. Her body was formed as was his, true, with arms and legs and a torso that held all the inward parts that functioned to make her a living being. But she was more elegantly put together, her skin more finely pored, softer, her body pale against the darker flesh of her arms, and he admired the difference, knowing the soft feel of that tender skin against his own.

Her hair hung long against her back now, with the braids and pins removed, the length waving in silken luxury against the slender waist, the fullness of her hips, yet covered by the dress and petticoat that were caught on the cusp of her womanly form. There where her hips widened and curved into the lush lines of her bottom, covered now with layers of fabric, soon to be naked beneath the white gown she would don over her clean flesh.

She bent, her hair falling to either side of her shoulders as she lifted her gown from the chair beside her and her arms held the white muslin before her, slipping it over her head and her arms into the sleeves that would contain them. In a practiced move, she slid her dress and petticoat to the floor, her drawers with them, and then stepped from the circle of clothing, tossing the whole of it into the basket she kept there for such a purpose.

It was a ritual he never wearied in watching, a series of movements that touched him with the graceful gestures she employed, the smiles that touched her lips as she considered whatever private thoughts raced through her mind. In the small mirror before her, he could see her face; unknown to her, he watched her, admiring the shadow of her lashes as she looked down before her, his gaze resting on the soft oval of her features, her nose so small, with just a tilt at the end, her lips, full and soft and ever ready for his touch.

And then his heart nudged him with remembrance of the scene behind the barn and he looked at Katie with eyes that took special note of her grace and the confidence she had gained over the past weeks. Perhaps she sensed more than ever her own beauty, he thought. Maybe she thought she could have done better than to be married to a ranch foreman and be stuck in a small cabin.

He sensed his thoughts turning once more to the man who had held her against himself earlier in the day, of the look of avarice in Clay's eyes as he beheld the beauty of the woman before him. And John's anger was ignited once more at the thought that Katie might have encouraged the man's attentions.

He watched as she looked a final time in the mirror, leaning forward to wipe at a spot that caught her attention on her cheek.

"Come to bed," he whispered, catching her ear with his soft words, her eyes lifting to touch his through the magic of the mirror before her. Gleaming in the candle glow, they offered warmth and beauty he could barely resist, and he held out his hand to her, watching as she turned and made her way the few feet to where he sat on the edge of the mattress.

And rued the spell she cast over him so easily, the softening he felt as she stood before him.

CHAPTER FOURTEEN

SHE STOOD BETWEEN his knees, her thighs captured there, her hands making their way to touch his shoulders, then his nape and the rough layers of hair that covered his head.

"You need to have your hair trimmed," she said softly. "I'll sit you down in the kitchen or maybe on the porch, if it's warm enough in the morning and clean you up a little."

"Do I need cleaning up?" he asked, softening the rough edge of his voice. "I'd thought I'd washed up pretty well already."

"You know what I mean. You just need to get the rough edges smoothed out. I've got my new scissors I can use on you." As she spoke, her fingers ran the length of his dark hair and measured it against her palms, and he felt a chill travel the length of his spine at her touch.

Her eyes softened and she looked down at him. "I can't tell you how I feel about you, John. I don't have the right words. I just know I want to make you a good wife and keep things just the way you want them."

Not prone to deny himself the warmth and comfort

of her body, no matter how his doubts raged within him, he only forced a grin to his lips as he wrapped his hands around her waist. "I'm more interested in you keeping me warm right now, Katie. Not my back or my chilly feet, but way inside me, where I get chilled sometimes, where I need to feel your warmth. I need to hold you in my arms and know that you think more of me than any other person in this world, that you…"

And wasn't that foolish? He could take what she offered without needing assurance of her tender feelings. In fact, he'd be better off if he didn't worry overmuch about her wants and needs.

"I like you, John," she said, surprise alive in her voice. "I've always liked you, from the very first day I ever saw you."

He shook his head, knowing that they spoke of two different things. "I know you hold me in high regard, Katie. But I'm talking about the love that a woman feels for a man, that one thing that binds them together as husband and wife, man and woman, male and female. The thing that joins them in a way that no one else in the world knows about, that shuts out everything but those two people. The sort of feeling that keeps them loyal and faithful to each other, no matter what.

"My mama and daddy had that. He could look at her and I knew that she was the most important thing in the world to him. And she would touch his shoulder or his arm or lean against him for a minute and I knew that she drew strength from the love that flowed between them. That she would never look at another man the way she looked at my daddy. Sounds kinda silly, maybe, but that's what I've wanted for us."

She turned, settling on his lap and her arms tangled around his neck. "John, that's not silly. It's beautiful. And you know that your strength is what makes me work so well, that keeps me breathing every day and next to you every night. I just…just crave being beside you, like my insides ache when you're not with me. I think maybe that's kinda what you're talking about, John. Don't you?"

"Maybe so, Katie. Maybe one day it will be true for us."

Katie only nodded, but her words showed the thoughts that had been in her mind. "I'll bet your folks were proud of you, John. Do you ever hear from your daddy?"

"Oh, yeah. A couple of times a year, he writes to me, sends the letters to General Delivery in Eden. I try to keep him up-to-date, but I haven't seen him in, oh, maybe eight years or so."

"Where is he?"

"South, in Oklahoma. I was born and raised there. My daddy was a farmer, raised crops and cows and horses and mama had a garden and a passel of kids. We had a good life."

"Don't you ever think about going back there?" she asked wistfully, thinking perhaps that such a place would be warm and welcoming.

"To visit, maybe, someday. But I've got a life here that suits me," he said. "I enjoy what I do and the cold weather in the winter and the long spring and summer."

"It must be so nice to have memories of home, of family and people who care about you." She felt the sting of tears as she fought off the touch of envy that nudged her.

"You'll have your own set of memories to pass on one day," he told her. "When we have a family, we'll teach them all the things we know and show them how to live their lives as they should. I want my boys to ride and explore and camp out with the ranch hands and help with the roundups and the branding and all the sorts of things that men do together on the range.

"I want our girls to learn how to keep house and cook and sew and be a woman like their mama is." He could not escape the warmth that flooded him as he held her close, even with the doubts in his mind.

"Come on, lie down with me now and sleep. I know you're tired." He rolled over with her, catching her giggle in his mouth as she expressed her delight at his foolishness, placing her under the quilt and sheet, tucking her in beside himself. He rose high enough to reach the candle, blowing it out and then, in the darkness, he gathered her unto himself and curled her against his big body, craving in this moment the soft warmth she offered.

His hands roamed her back, pulling at her gown as she softened against him, lifting the fabric to expose the curve of her bottom, the lithe line of her thigh, his touch gentled her. She turned as he bid her silently, allowing his hand to touch as it would, exposing herself to the wandering fingertips, whispering her approval in wordless murmurs as he found places that soothed even as they aroused her to a degree of passion, submitting to his touch

And then Katie spoke words that had been dwelling in her mind for the past hours. "John? Were you angry with me today, out behind the barn? I felt like you were about as mad at me as you were at Clay. And I don't want you to be mad."

"We'll talk about it another time, Katie." He seemed to grow quiet suddenly, his body stiffening against her as the memory of his wife and Clay entered his mind. His whisper was soft against her ear and his voice grew stern, as if some dark thought had entered his mind. And so it had. His words were grim, his voice touched with the threat of anger. "I don't want to speak of it now with Jane right beyond that door. If you led him on, I don't know if I could forgive you," he said, his voice a low growl.

She nodded, aware that he was tense, his thoughts still tangled in the web of his anger earlier. And then was stunned at the fierce movements he instigated as he rolled her to her back and formed his body over hers. His hands were rougher than usual, his touch not as soft and caring, and he did not spend his kisses upon her face as was his wont.

She felt the intrusion of his masculine parts between her legs and stiffened against him. "John? Is something wrong?"

His laugh was rough and did not give evidence of humor, for he pushed against her and even though she was dry and did not receive him readily, he entered her body and quickly found release for himself. And then lay upon her, his weight seeming for the first time since their coming together in this bed to be a burden.

Katie levered her hands against his shoulders and attempted to lift him from her, all to no avail for he was heavy and unwilling to allow her the space she wanted. "John? What's wrong? Why are you treating me this way?" She heard the trembling of her voice and tried to overcome it, not wanting him to think she was on the verge of tears. For indeed, she was, unaware of why his touch was so uncaring, his movements so harsh.

"I'm just treating you as my wife," he said, his words holding not a smidgen of softness, his body releasing her then as he turned to his back and left her uncovered and trembling. "Can't I take what I want from you without you getting all in a snit?"

Katie looked into the darkness, and felt it encompass her like a shroud. This was not the man who had, until today, treated her with tender care and concern. This man was an angry mass of masculinity who frightened her beyond words. She turned her back to him, unable to look upon him, and felt a chill of foreboding travel the length of her body.

"You have the right to take whatever you want or need from me, John. I'm your wife and I won't deny you your rights." She trembled then, feeling cold and unwanted, knowing the violence of anger from the man she'd married. "I don't know what I've done to make you feel this way, but whatever it was, I'm sorry."

He was silent behind her and she gripped the edge of the mattress, unwilling to seek the warmth of his body, shivering with but a thin sheet to cover her.

With an angry sound of frustration, John reached for her, pulling her against his warmth, his arm firm about her waist, his hand flat against her belly. "So long as I'm in this bed with you, there's no need to be cold," he said firmly, his voice as chilly as the fingers of ice that crept up her spine.

He held her close to himself, silent and morose, as though he performed a duty that might be distasteful, but necessary. Katie twisted in his grasp, but to no avail, for he was larger, stronger and able to physically restrain her without any obvious effort on his part.

"Please, let me go, John," she begged, wriggling her body in a vain effort to release herself from his hold. His hand only pressed more firmly against her soft belly, his arms tightening their grip, and his voice was without expression as he spoke.

"Lie still, Katie. I'm through with you for tonight. You need not fear that I'll pounce on you again."

His words struck with brutal force and she shriveled within herself, fighting the tears that begged to be shed.

Not for anything would she let him know how deeply his scornful decree had hurt her. Not for the world would she beg again, not for anything from this man, she vowed silently. He had turned against her without just cause, his hands had bruised her without reason, for she knew she would bear the marks of his fingers on her body when morning came.

Her own fault, she admitted to herself, for she had twisted and turned in her attempts to escape him, and only her own movement had caused his hands to tighten on her flesh. That she had brought about that small amount of pain to herself was not important, only the fact that he had delivered it so casually, so readily had he clutched at her arms and formed her to his purpose.

His invasion of her body had been harsh, yet she would not speak of it to him, for he seemed to have found little satisfaction in their quick joining. Only the sound of his rapid breathing had announced his release from the tension he'd spent upon her body, and she knew he had not received any great amount of pleasure from it.

As for herself, she felt somehow stained, besmirched and soiled by his behavior, as if she had become only a vessel for his use. No longer a cherished wife, but a woman he only tolerated.

When she arose it was to find the bed empty, with John apparently already gone to do chores and direct the hired hands in their work for the day. She dressed quickly, washing the tender places on her body, feeling twinges she was not accustomed to, and noting the bruises that stained her skin. She covered them with a long-sleeved dress and was thankful that only the marks on her throat were visible, there where he'd suckled at her skin, biting the tender surface and leaving a trace of his anger behind to remind her of his rough hands and mouth. Katie hid those marks beneath a high collar, buttoned to the top, so that there would be no marring of her skin to signal Jane of her distress.

She made biscuits quickly, speaking softly to Jane as they worked together to put breakfast together, only to shiver when she heard John's step at the back door.

"John. I'd thought you were lost out there," Jane said with a laugh, mocking him for his late arrival, for he normally was gone but a half hour or so after arising.

"I had work to do," he said shortly, going to the sink to wash up, rolling his sleeves to his elbows and bending to cup handfuls of water to spill over his head. He reached for a towel and as he dried off his gaze touched upon Katie. She felt the heat of his perusal and stood with her back to him, unwilling, unable to turn to him. She felt a flush cover her cheeks as she stirred the eggs she'd scrambled in the big skillet, poured the sausage gravy into a large bowl and then slid the biscuits from the yawning heat of the oven.

"Coffee, John?" Jane asked, bearing a cup as she went to the table, and he nodded abruptly, his eyes still anchored on Katie. He accepted the heavy china cup from Jane and lifted it to his lips, sipping at the strong brew, and then as Katie turned, he willed her to meet his gaze.

She bent her head, paying particular attention to the bowls she held and walked around the table to place them carefully on hot pads. The eggs steamed, the gravy sent forth a scent that tempted her and yet made her stomach roll with distress. She returned to the stove and gathered up the biscuits and the coffeepot, intent on pouring a cup for herself.

As she sat on her chair, she winced, her flesh still sore from the misuse she'd received at John's hands the night before, and she covered her lips with one hand, clearing her throat to hide the small sound she'd made.

John looked at her, his gaze intent, as if he attempted to solve some great puzzle, and she merely passed the bowls to his hands, waiting until he helped himself to the food before she took some on her plate.

John watched her closely, aware that she ignored his eyes, that she seemed intent on looking anywhere but at him this morning. And he felt a rush of shame as he recalled his treatment of her last night. She had winced as she sat down, her step had seemed to have a hitch in it, and he thought he caught sight of a bruise at the base of her throat. The kitchen was warm, the stove generating heat with a vengeance, and he wondered at the long sleeves she wore, the dress that bundled her up so thoroughly.

"Why don't you roll up your sleeves, Katie? You look warm over there with your back to the stove." Perspiration dotted her forehead, he thought, and her face was pale, as though she felt unwell. Yet she only ignored his suggestion, speaking quietly to Jane, as if she had not heard his words.

He ate quickly, more aware of her than was usual, noting the strain that seemed to affect her features, her forehead furrowed, her cheeks pale, her mouth trembling as she ate. If he had hurt her last night, if he had caused the bruise on her throat, if her soft parts were sore from his use—he could not bear the thought, and he ate the rest of his meal with haste, then spoke to his wife abruptly.

"I'd like to see you alone for a moment, Katie. In the bedroom, please."

She looked up, her eyes widening, her face turning even more wan, as if some great calamity had come about. "I'll clean up the kitchen, first," she said quietly, and he shook his head.

"I think Jane can tend to things here. I'd like to see you in the bedroom, please."

He knew that his voice had chilled, that his words were firmer than was his wont, and saw the shiver that passed over Katie as she rose from the table. She walked to the bedroom, leaving the door ajar behind her and with a quick smile in Jane's direction, he followed Katie, closing the door firmly behind himself.

She stood on the far side of the room, the bed between them, the covers already pulled into place, the pillows propped against the headboard. Her hands were clasped tightly before her. She refused to meet his gaze; her eyes seeming to seek a spot over his right shoulder.

He went to her and his hands reached for her. She shrank from him, an involuntary movement that made him growl an indistinct word beneath his breath. His fingers curled over her shoulders and he felt the shudder that swept her body as she stood silently before him.

"Katie, I'm not going to hurt you," he said, aware that he had no doubt frightened her the night before, that she was fearful of his actions today.

"Aren't you?" She looked into his eyes then and her own were dull, without the usual warmth he found there.

"I know I caused you pain last night, and I'm sorry," he said shortly. "I took out my anger on you and treated you badly."

"I've been hurt worse other times, by a man angrier than you, John," she said quietly. She tried to escape his touch, twisting from his grip, but he refused to allow it, and only held her the tighter.

"Did I leave bruises on you? Is that why you're wearing your sleeves all buttoned around your wrists?" Even as he spoke, he grasped her hand and worked at the small buttons that held her sleeve secured. She pulled back from him with a small sound of despair, as he undid the final pearl button and pushed her sleeve up. Above her elbow, there where he had held her firmly as he'd taken her body with haste and so little care, he saw the marks from his fingers, four on the back of her arm, a larger one from his thumb on the soft, inner surface.

With care, he undid her other sleeve and pushed it up, searching out and discovering identical marks on her other arm. His breath caught in his throat as he viewed the results of his anger, the marks he'd left on her fragile skin, and he felt a wash of shame that threatened to unman him.

"I can't tell you how sorry I am, Katie. I never thought to do such a thing to you. You're my wife and I had no right to hurt you that way."

"You're right there. I *am* your wife and you have the right to do anything you like to me, John. I'm smart enough to know that. If you want the use of my body, you have it. If you treat me roughly and leave marks on my skin, I'll keep them covered until they fade. No one will know what happens here in this room between us."

Her voice was dull, without a trace of the lilting quality he had come to expect from her. He pulled her sleeves down and his hands held her again, there where she wore bruises from his touch. And then he released her abruptly. "I won't mar you again, Katie. I may use you badly sometime in the future, for I can't promise never to be angry again, but I won't leave bruises on you."

She shrugged, as if it were of little matter to her and busied herself with the buttons at her wrists. Her mouth was taut, the full lips pressed together as though she would not speak to him again, and he bent to her, lifting her chin with one long forefinger. He lowered his head, his mouth touching hers and his kiss was soft and careful, but she refused it, turning her head away, her murmur one of dissent.

"Don't turn from me, Katie," he said curtly. "I'm still your husband, no matter that you're angry with me now. I've told you I'm sorry, and there isn't anything else I can do to make it right with you."

She looked down at the floor, obviously unwilling to meet his gaze, unable to speak, for she trembled before him, and her eyes were overflowing now with hot tears. He tugged her against himself, held her close and his big hands rubbed up and down the length of her spine, lending her warmth and offering the comfort of his touch.

She was rigid in his grasp, unwilling to bend to him and he set her aside, his pride damaged by her unwillingness to allow him to make amends.

With a last look at her bowed head, he turned to the door and left the bedroom, stalking through the kitchen to the back door and then out across the yard to the barn.

Shorty met him just inside the big doorway. "Hey there, boss. We're about ready to head out to gather up all the strays and get things ready for branding. Do you want me to do anything here before I get things under way?"

John shook his head. "I'll go with you," he said, not prone to staying behind, with Katie all in a snit and him in such a bad mood. Somehow it seemed to be a good idea to leave the ranch and head for the open range to the north.

"What about the chores? You gonna leave one of the men here to tend to things?"

"Are you volunteering?" John asked. "If not, just tell one of the men to stick close to the barn and take care of feeding the horses. We only need one man here to keep an eye on things."

"Clay can do that, I reckon," Shorty said carefully, his frown expressing doubt, even as he spoke the man's name. "I'm not sure he's a good one to leave in charge here, though. He's kinda shaky on taking hold the way he should. And there's something about him that doesn't…"

John's gaze narrowed on him. "Has he done anything to cause you to doubt his value to the ranch?" So far as John was concerned, the man had about signed his walking papers by putting his hands on Katie. It wouldn't take much to have him booting him from the ranch and sending him on his way.

"Just a feeling, I suspect," Shorty said slowly. "He's kinda shifty, if you know what I mean. I'm not sure I trust him."

"Well, I can't afford to leave any of the other men behind, Shorty. Clay is the last man hired on and I need all the experienced hands we've got during the next couple of days. That's why I'm going along. I expect Clay can tend to business here and if he can't, he'll be looking for another job when we get back." And if he doesn't behave himself, he'll be dodging a bullet from my gun.

Leaving Katie to the tender care of Jane and Berta

might not be his best plan, but John was torn between doing his job for Bill Stanley's benefit or staying close to keep an eye on Katie. Her abrupt behavior with him was the deciding factor, and he wondered if his absence might not make her have second thoughts about her behavior with him. When she had pulled away from his touch, she had marred his pride, and he felt a hint of resentment gathering beneath the surface of his emotions.

His entry into the kitchen at noontime was abrupt and his words a surprise to the women there. "I'll be gone for a couple of days with the men, rounding up the calves for branding and cutting. Can you handle things here by yourself?" His gaze pinned Katie where she stood before the stove and she merely nodded briefly, almost as if she were uncaring about his plans and his absence here.

"Will we be helping with chores while you're gone, John?" Jane seemed ready to volunteer should her help be needed, but John shook his head.

"You can gather eggs if you like, but Clay will stay here to tend to feeding the stock and keeping the barn clean. Looking after the chickens might be a good thing for you to tackle, but he's pretty capable and I'm sure he'll keep things up. If you've got a problem just go to Berta. She'll be right handy should there be a problem."

He ate quickly, then went to the bedroom and sorted through the dresser drawers, the sound of his rummaging for his clothing audible from the kitchen. Katie thought of offering to help him ready himself for the next two days, and then thought better of it, staying in the kitchen, aware that he was an old hand at this sort of thing. He probably wouldn't welcome her help at any rate. His eyes had been harsh when he'd looked at her earlier, his smile distant, as if Jane were the only recipient of the gesture.

He came from the bedroom carrying his saddlebags over his shoulder, his heavy coat over his arm. "I've got all I need. I'll be back day after tomorrow I suspect. Unless things go wrong out there. Usually doesn't take more than two days to get the calves together, and since we're doing the branding here instead of out on the range, we'll be riding in early on in the day to pen them up. You might want to get ready for some extra men to feed in a couple of days. We'll be taking on several from the neighboring ranches to lend a hand and they'll need to be fed. Talk to Berta and she'll let you know what your share is."

Katie listened in a daze. He spoke of things she had no knowledge of, as if she were to be expected to cook a mountain of food for a crew of men who would need sustenance. But acknowledging her ignorance was not to be considered and she nodded and tried her best to act knowledgeable as he spoke. She'd talk to Berta later on today and get a list of the duties expected of her.

For now, John was leaving and it looked as though he was going without any semblance of a tender goodbye, or a leave-taking that would include soft words or even an embrace. He stood by the doorway and shot her a look of impatience.

"Was there something else you wanted, Katie?" His eyes were cold, his jaw firm, and he watched her with eyes that did not soften even as she stepped closer to him.

He was about to find himself on the outside, looking in, she decided as she stood before him. "We'll be fine here, John. I'll do some extra baking and check with Berta about the food situation. I'm sure we can handle it between Jane and me."

She offered no smile, no melting gaze, no softening of her form, only a tip-tilted chin and a mouth that did not look for his kiss. To her surprise, she received it anyway, for he bent to her and his lips were rough against hers, taking the softness he found there and leaving only the chill touch of a mouth that did not hesitate, only brushed coldly against hers and then tightened again as he stood erect and looked down at her.

"I'd appreciate it if you'd behave while I'm gone."

As a goodbye, his words left much to be desired, Katie thought, and she stifled the words that filled her mind. The man was about as stupid as a man could be.

And then her mind retraced the events of the day before, of Clay's hands on her and her own short and futile battle with him. Perhaps that was the answer to John's angry behavior. Maybe he really thought she'd been too friendly with the ranch hand and no longer trusted her to be a lady.

She turned from the door, refusing to watch as he left the porch and strode across to the barn, already in the bedroom as he called out to Shorty for his horse. Through the bedroom window, she heard his voice, heard the laughter of the men as they mounted and gathered up their reins. The chuck wagon rolled from the barn, and several men followed, forming a line that traveled to the north pastures, where the young calves and bullocks awaited them.

Katie gathered up the soiled clothing from the basket she kept handy for that purpose and headed for the kitchen, intent on using the scrub board and taking out her anger on the items John had left for her to tend.

"What's wrong with John?" Jane asked softly as she watched Katie cross the kitchen. "He acts different for some reason."

"He's about half-mad at me," Katie admitted. And then refused to elaborate on her statement, only settling the big boiler on top of the cookstove to heat water for the wash. She knew that only hard work and the physical labor of scrubbing clothing and then hanging them to dry would keep her from giving way to the frustration of the anger she had stored within her.

She scrubbed on the porch, kneeling before the boiler, her knuckles scraped from the ridges on the board and her hands reddened from the heat of the water she used. Spots were vanquished readily with the lye soap she used and within an hour she had readied the line for John's clothes to hang across the yard. The sun promised to be hot today, the breeze blowing from the west, and the clothes blew in a satisfying fashion, shirts billowing like a ship's sails, trousers drying rapidly in the heat of the direct sunlight.

By midafternoon, she had hauled the basket full of clothes into the house and sprinkled down the shirts for ironing later on. The trousers she shook out, pressing them with her hands and folding them neatly for John's drawer. His small clothes were softer, the wind having blown the wrinkles from them and she thought she smelled a faint aroma of John's unique scent on them, and was tempted to hold his stack of shirts and drawers against her nose to catch the aroma they carried.

Jane watched her throughout the day, silent and wondering as Katie did her chores in a solitary fashion, as if she needed the time to consider some great problem. She knew that Jane deserved some sort of explanation for her withdrawal, but could not bring herself to make one.

The ironing took much of the next morning and Katie found herself in the big kitchen where Berta reigned supreme by early afternoon. She queried the woman as to the cooking chores she would be expected to fulfill and Berta shot her a quick look of surprise.

"There's not all that much for you to do, girl. I'm used to feeding the pile of men who'll show up here tomorrow. If you want to help out, you can fry up three or four chickens for me. I'll go out and butcher them later on tonight and bring you a potful of parts to tend to."

"I can help with the butchering, Berta. I did some of it when I was young and even though it isn't my favorite thing to do, I know how and I'm more than willing to help with it."

Berta nodded. "I'll call you when I'm ready to start in on them. I've got eight young roosters we can kill and clean. It's a big job and if Jane wants to lend a hand it'll be that much easier on you and me."

"She'll be happy to help," Katie said, knowing that Jane would do whatever was required of her. "I'll plan on picking corn in the morning and heating water in my boiler to cook it. How many ears do you think we'll need? I'd figured about forty or so should do it."

"Sounds about right to me," Berta said. "John will have seven or eight men with him when he comes in, and there's four or five of the neighbors will be coming to help with the branding. With fried chicken and a kettle of mashed potatoes and then the corn, we should have a pretty good spread. I'll do a kettle of gravy and put green beans on to cook early in the morning."

Katie nodded agreeably and headed for the cabin to prepare Jane for the work to come. When Berta sang out late in the afternoon, the two girls were ready and headed for the spot behind the chicken coop where Berta did the butchering. Between them, they caught up the young roosters and held them firmly while Berta used her small hatchet.

It was a job that turned Katie's stomach, the stench of feathers in boiling water rising from the big pails Berta had readied for the job. They plucked feathers, the air thick with the sticky things, their clothing covered with the mess. But there was no chance of them not lending their able help to the job, for Berta did more than her share on the ranch, and when help was needed Katie was eager to step in.

From the barn, Clay watched the three women at their chore and at Berta's uplifted hand, he approached, his nose wrinkled as he neared. "Sure is a messy job you ladies got tangled up with out here," he said, awaiting Berta's orders, for she had made it apparent that he was to help.

"You can carry the roasting pans into the kitchen for us," Berta told him. "We've got four chickens in each and they're kinda heavy for the girls to lift."

"I can do that," Clay was quick to agree. "John told me to help out if you needed me."

He lifted the first roasting pan and headed for the house, then returned for the second one, shooting a quick glance at Katie as he picked it up. "You feeling all right? You're looking kinda peaked, ma'am."

Katie swallowed the bile that would not be controlled, rising in her throat as she inhaled the scent of the wet feathers she'd handled over the past half hour. "I'm fine." Her words were short and sharp, and her intent was to discourage the man's attentions, for she knew John was still bearing a grudge over the last encounter she'd had with Clay.

His face was still bruised from John's fists and one eye remained swollen, but his manner was as cocky as before and she was determined to discourage his veiled hints. He'd allowed his gaze to rest on her body in a way that made her embarrassed, his eyes seeming to laugh at her. If he was interested in her, if he thought she was an available woman, he had another think coming, she decided, her own anger on a fine edge.

John would have a fit if he knew that Clay was being so apparent in his attentions, and Katie was undecided what she could do about it. Speaking to Berta about it might be one option, simply ignoring the man was another, and she even considered talking to Bill Stanley upon his return, if it seemed necessary. Yet the thought of causing problems at the ranch, no matter her own inclination, was something she dreaded.

"You girls go on to the cabin and get cleaned up. You'll want to change your clothes before we start in on making dressing and getting those birds ready for the frying pans tomorrow." Berta sent Katie and Jane on their way with a wave of her hand, following Clay into the ranch house kitchen.

Jane washed at the sink and reached for a towel, turning to face Katie, who waited her turn at the basin and soap. Her face was troubled as she dried her hands and arms. "Is it my imagination or is Clay sweet on you, Katie?"

"He's making a pest of himself, is what he's doing," Katie said shortly. "I'm not showing him any mind, but he keeps on watching me. John's gonna have a fit when he comes back and finds out."

"Well, you haven't done anything wrong, or tried to

encourage the man," Jane said stoutly. "Seems to me he's taking a lot on himself, paying special attention to you."

"I'm a married woman and you'd think he'd get that through his head. I'd appreciate it if you'd stay close by tomorrow, Jane. I don't want to take a chance on being alone with him."

Jane nodded. "I can do that. He puts me in mind of old Jacob when he looks at you, Katie. Like he'd like to take liberties with you."

CHAPTER FIFTEEN

THE MEN ARRIVED FROM the far pastures before noon the following day, and Katie heard the sound of their voices as she cleaned the bedroom.

She listened, dust cloth in hand as John's voice penetrated her hearing, his words distinct.

"I'll check in the cabin and see if the girls are all right," he said to some unknown man outdoors. And with that, she heard his footsteps on the porch, then the slam of the door as he came inside. His voice was a low murmur as he spoke with Jane in the kitchen, for she'd been cleaning up the stove, blacking the surface and readying the workspace for the cooking they would do.

He opened the bedroom door and stood in the entryway. "We've brought back over fifty young steers, Katie, and the men will be hungry before long. Have you and Berta got things together for our dinner?"

She looked up from her work and blinked in bewilderment. "Not yet, John. Berta didn't expect to feed the lot of you until suppertime. She'll be working at it now, but you'll have to wait a bit until I can find something for your dinner. I'll go out and pick some beans right away and start them cooking. Berta said she was going to cook up a big kettle of them for supper, too. I'll go to the house and see what she wants me to do."

His brow lowered as he looked at her and his mouth was taut. "You knew we were heading back in this morning. I'd have thought y'all would have food cooked and ready for us."

"Give me an hour, John." She turned her back on him and straightened the screen that shielded the dry sink from the rest of the room. John had bought it one day in the general store, having ordered it from the catalog as a surprise.

"I'll help the men get the bullocks penned up and start the fires for branding. That ought to give you time enough."

He was gone then, back out the door and onto the porch. She heard his deep voice as Shorty called out to him. Her heart thumped unmercifully in her chest as she remembered his dark looks in her direction, his big fists clenched at his sides as he dictated his needs to her.

"He's all in a snit about something," Jane said from the sink, where she was cleaning the last of the dishes. Her towel flapped as she swung it from her shoulder and turned to Katie. "I didn't think they'd be back this early, and I'll bet Berta isn't ready for them, either."

"Probably not," Katie said with a shrug. If John wanted to be ornery, he could just go right ahead and act like a fool. The last weeks had proved to her that she was a woman to be respected. She wasn't about to give in to his orders, not today at least. He'd just have to wait till they could put together a meal of sorts.

In just a few minutes, she was in the big house, listening as Berta stewed aloud over the men showing up so early in the day. "I'll make them some sandwiches, Katie, and you can slice some of that round of cheese for me. They can settle for that and some fresh lemonade to drink. We'll pick the beans and make supper earlier than I'd thought."

Katie did as Berta told her, lifting the heavy round of cheese from the pantry shelf and using the biggest butcher knife to slice it off into slabs. Whether or not John had any dinner at all, she didn't care. Her heart was heavy as she considered the disintegration of her marriage from the way it had seemed to exist in the past. John's anger was all too apparent, and she felt somehow damaged by it. He had hurt her beyond her ability to understand.

Berta carried a tray full of sandwiches out to the back, where the men had hastily set up a table for the food. A kettle of lemonade was added to the accumulating food there, for Katie had filled a platter with cheese and then found leftover potato salad in the icebox beneath the pantry floor for their meal.

Plates from the kitchen dresser were carried out, and Katie's arms ached from the weight of them as she stepped carefully from the porch. "Let me take those, ma'am." Clay was before her, his arms outstretched for the burden she carried and she merely shook her head and stepped around him to deposit them on the big table under the trees.

From the barn, she felt the heat of John's gaze upon her, and she returned it with a somber look, then headed for the cabin. He could eat with the men, and between Berta and Jane, they could tend to the hungry cowhands. She let herself into the kitchen and leaned over the sink, feeling bile rise in her throat. The tension of this morning was more than she could understand, for she'd hoped that John would be back to normal when he returned. Instead he was more wary, his eyes dark with some unknown emotion, and his body taut, his face harsh with anger.

Gathering up the biggest kettle from her pantry, she went the back way to the kitchen garden and knelt between the rows of green beans, gathering them from the lush plants and placing handfuls of them into her kettle. Moving from one row to the next she was surprised to see Berta stepping between the plants and standing over her.

"You all right, girl?" the woman asked, squatting before her and lifting Katie's chin with her blunt index finger. Her brow was furrowed and her voice concerned, and Katie realized she was about three seconds from tears. It would not do, for Berta didn't need to be involved in the problems Katie and John were struggling with.

"I'm fine, Berta. I just thought I'd get the beans picked and get them ready for supper while you fed the men. I'll take them back to the cabin and wash them and snap them before we put them on the stove. Thought I'd put a piece of ham in with them."

"That's good," Berta said mildly, her sharp gaze on Katie's face, her concern apparent. "You go on ahead and I'll take care of things here. Looks like that kettle's about full enough for supper."

Katie stood and lifted the utensil between her hands, then nodded briefly at Berta and headed for the small cabin. Inside, she found a bread pan and carried it to the porch, then settled in the rocking chair there. With the big kettle next to her, she picked up a handful of beans at a time and snapped the ends off, then broke them in half and dropped them in the bread pan.

It was a job requiring little concentration and her thoughts were able to wander as she worked. Only the flash of color at the end of the porch made her aware of the man who watched her from his vantage point. She turned her head and Clay smiled at her.

"You've got yourself quite a job there, ma'am," he said cheerfully, settling on the end of the porch.

Katie refused to acknowledge his presence and lowered her head to the pan of beans in her lap. Her fingers were busy with the task she'd taken on, and she looked only at the food she tended, her mouth taut, her lips sealed.

"You mad at me, ma'am?" Clay's words were soft, his mood seeming to be one of teasing as he leaned against the upright post and lifted his leg to the porch.

He bent his knee and rested his folded hands there in-dolently, as if he had the whole of the afternoon to watch her at her work.

"Please go away, Mr. Thomas," she said bluntly. Her hands moved quickly as she readied the last of the beans for cooking, and then she stood and held the bread pan in one arm as she picked up the kettle with the other hand. Quickly, Clay stood to his feet and hastened to the back door, opening it for her to step inside.

Her look at him was cold, her eyes filled with anger as he waited for her to draw nearer to his tall figure. He had bent to speak in her ear when she heard John's voice behind her.

"Don't touch my wife, Thomas." With a swift move, John was on the porch, his hand buried in the front of Clay's shirt and he swept him from the porch and down to the ground. "I told you before what would happen if you put your hands on her." His voice was soft, deadly and his face held murderous intent as he lifted the man from the ground and held him before him.

Clay was silent, his gaze wide, his mouth working as if he would defend himself, but John gave him no leeway, only dragged him toward the barn. Shorty approached and after one look at John's face, he turned back to the house where the men sat beneath the tree with their food.

The barn door slid shut and from within the sound of men's voices were loud, but Katie did not wait to hear the commotion. She went into the house and deposited her pan of beans in the sink, then pumped the water to cover them so that they would be ready for cooking. She lifted them into the kettle and placed it on the stove, then filled it halfway with water before she went to the pantry for the ham bones she had waiting there.

From the yard, the sound of the hired hands talking back and forth penetrated her solitude and she shuddered at the hubbub of raised voices and sounds from the barn. Behind her, Jane burst into the cabin, her eyes wide, her hands gesturing wildly.

"John's gone off the deep end, Katie. He took Clay Thomas into the barn, dragged him inside is what he did, and then he proceeded to beat the livin' tar out of him. Bill Stanley went out there and put a stop to it, and he told Clay to get his things together and get off the ranch. Then him and John went into the big house and Clay disappeared into the bunkhouse. He was sure a sorry mess, all bloody and tore up."

Katie opened the salt box and scooped out a scant handful of salt to put into the kettle of beans. As if she had not heard Jane's tale, she continued on with her food preparations, then after dumping the bean leavings into the garbage bucket, she washed out the bread pan in the sink.

"Katie, did you hear me?" Jane stood behind her, one hand on her shoulder, the other on the drainboard, as if she could not hold herself erect.

"I heard you." Katie's voice was dull, empty, as if she were bereft of all feeling, as if her heart had been shattered by the happenings today. John was obviously angry with her, whether he thought she was encouraging Clay's attentions or not, she didn't know, but he obviously had taken out his anger on the man.

She would be his next target and she could only wait here for him to appear. "Go help Berta in the house, Jane," she said carefully, unwilling to let the other girl know the extent of her fear. "Tell Berta that I've got the beans on to cook and I'll peel a bucket of potatoes next."

Jane left, seemingly unwillingly, but inured to doing as she was told, she gave no argument. The door closed behind her and Katie drew in a deep breath. She went to the pantry and brought out the pail of potatoes she had brought from the garden only yesterday, thinking they would last her for two weeks, but now intending them for supper today.

She sought out her paring knife from the cupboard and settled at the kitchen table, the bread pan half-full of water to hold the peeled potatoes and a piece of brown paper over the oilcloth to contain the peelings.

She'd finished the biggest part of the pailful when the back door was opened and John stepped into the house. He stood just inside the entryway and his hands were fisted against his hips. "Are you determined to make me out for a fool?" His words were harsh and loud in the small room, and Katie winced at the darkness that filled her heart.

"I'm sure I don't know what you're talking about," she said, her head bending again over the potato in her hands. Her fingers trembled as she cut a swath of the peeling and then he spoke again, his voice loud directly behind her and to her aggravation her hand jerked and the knife cut deeply into her palm.

Gritting her teeth against the pain she dropped both knife and potato on the paper in front of her, rising to step to the sink, holding her hand over the empty basin.

"What have you done?" John's voice boomed against her ears and she leaned over the sink even farther, lifting the pump handle with her right hand, awkward in her movements as her hand dripped blood into the basin. The cut was long, across the whole width of her palm and gaped widely before her vision, blood running in a steady stream. She felt weakness almost overcome her, knew her knees would give way in a moment, and leaned heavily against the drain board lest she fall to the floor.

Over her shoulder John peered past her to where her hand was outstretched beneath the water that streamed from the pitcher pump. "Damn. Damn, damn." His words were harsh and grim against her ear, and she heard them as through a mist, for her head had begun to spin, her legs faltering beneath her weight, and only the clasp of his big hand on her waist kept her upright.

He reached for a towel and wrapped it tightly around her hand, then led her to the table where he sat her down with little ceremony in her chair. "Put your head down,

Katie. Down between your knees." Pushing at the back of her nape, he forced her to the position he had decreed she take, and then held her hand in his, opening the towel just far enough to see the damage done to her palm.

"This will need to be sewn up," he said roughly. "I'll see if Berta has any silk thread." He knelt before her, his other hand atop her head. "Are you all right?" His voice sounded far off, as she attempted to lift her head, but he held it against her knees, his hand careful to keep her in the position that would best keep her from losing consciousness.

Standing, he seemed to change his mind, for he lifted her abruptly, his arms filled with the limp form that seemed to have no strength of its own. He carried her into the bedroom, placed her on the bed and carefully wrapped her hand tighter with the towel, then brought another piece of toweling from the dry sink to wrap around the first one.

"You won't want to bleed on the bedding," he said with a final twist of the towel, adjusting his rough bandage as he settled her beneath the quilt. "I'll be right back, as soon as I get a needle and thread from Berta."

Katie felt her eyes drift shut and she turned her head away from him, toward the window, then heard the faint sound of his footsteps as he left the cabin and saw his shadow pass the window as he ran toward the big house.

He returned in moments, it seemed, for she had only closed her eyes when she heard the door open again and knew that he was inside the cabin. Accompanied by Berta, he came into the bedroom, and Katie was overwhelmed by the sympathy in the other woman's voice as she settled on the edge of the bed and took the injured hand onto her lap.

Berta unwrapped the toweling that bound Katie's fisted fingers, then her own hands were careful as she straightened each digit and viewed the damage done. "Land sakes, girl, you've about cut your hand in two," she said quietly. "You'll have to have some stitches in that mess. I'll lend a hand here and John can sew it up for you. I've seen him doing as much for some of the men who've been hurt, so he knows what he's doing."

Katie lifted her lashes and looked at the woman who touched her with such gentleness and found it was almost her undoing. That Berta should be so tender, so caring of her pain was an eye-opener, and Katie felt tears gathering as she looked up at the woman who seemed intent on pampering her.

Berta regarded John, her gaze sober, her eyes seeming to take in the needle and thread he held in one hand. "You got some whiskey to put on it and maybe a little dish to soak the needle and thread in? You'll want to be sure they're as clean as a whistle so's this little girl don't get any red lines running up her arm."

Jane stuck her head in the door. "I'll bring a little dish for you to use, John," and at his nod of agreement, she turned to the kitchen cabinet and found a dish that would do the job. Berta pressed on the wound with a clean section of the towel, keeping the blood flow to a minimum and Katie turned her head away, the sight of her riven flesh making her feel ill suddenly.

"Don't be looking at this mess, girl," Berta said, holding the piece of towel over the wound. "You look like you're about halfway to a dead faint."

"It'd be easier if she passed out cold," John said gruffly. "I could stitch this thing up without her feeling it."

Katie met his gaze from where he stood beside the bed, noting the color in his cheeks, aware that his eyes were dark, seeking hers with a message she could not decipher.

"I won't make a fuss, John," she said softly, determined not to cry out no matter how great the pain of his stitching. She'd borne pain from whippings that surely were harsher than what pain John might deliver to her rent flesh, for his hands would be careful, his touch gentle. No matter how great his anger with her over the attentions Clay Thomas had shed on her person, he would not cause her more distress than was absolutely necessary, and that she would stake her life on.

Jane held the small dish, looking down at the needle and black silk thread it held. Berta had cut off a length for John's use, probably a foot long and it coiled in the bowl, soaking in a half cup or so of whiskey. The needle was a fine one, for Berta had apparently searched out her smallest from the assortment she kept in her sewing box. And now John neared the side of the bed where Katie lay, his face drawn as if he dreaded the chore to come.

He sat beside her, a pillow on his lap and a clean towel over it to soak up any blood that might be shed during his task. With a clean cloth, he soaked up some of the whiskey and then looked into Katie's eyes. "This is gonna burn like hellfire, Katie. I can't do much about it, but if I don't clean this out good you might get an infection and we don't want that."

"Go ahead, John." She'd thought her voice was strong, but the sound that came from her was strained and sounded puny even to her own ears. She turned her head aside, knowing that she could not watch as he sewed up her hand and waited for the first touch of the needle. But she had forgotten the whiskey-soaked cloth he would use on her hand first and at the first touch of the fabric against her open wound, she cringed and cried out, smothering the sound with her uninjured palm.

"I'm sorry. I didn't mean to do that. I just wasn't ready for it, John."

He looked up at Berta and Jane then, and his voice was ragged as he spoke his request. "Could you both leave us alone for just a minute. I want to talk to Katie before we do this."

Berta nodded, as if she were not surprised at the words he spoke, and Jane backed into the kitchen without a murmur. They closed the door behind them and Katie looked up at John questioningly.

"What's wrong?" she asked, still fighting the tears that begged to be shed. The whiskey had burned more than she'd been expecting and she was ashamed of her cries, unwilling for John to think her a coward. "I'm sorry I made a fuss over the washing out of my cut, John. I just didn't think it would burn so bad."

"That's not what I want to talk to you about, Katie. We need to get something straight between us before I do this. I don't want you to think that I'm gaining any revenge on you by causing you pain. The fuss we've had over Clay is to be forgotten for now. We'll talk of it later, but right this minute, he's the furthest thing from my mind. And I want you to know that I'll do everything I can to make this easy for you, even though it's gonna hurt like hell. There's not much I can do about that, but I'll be as quick as I can with it, and if you'd like a couple of swallows of whiskey for the pain first, we'll wait a few minutes for it to work."

"I don't want any of that stuff in my mouth, John. It stinks and reminds me of Jacob and I don't think I could swallow it anyway. I know you aren't going to cause me any more pain than necessary, and it never even entered my mind that you would take out your mad on me this way."

He clenched his jaw and his eyes were warm as he looked at her. "Will you let me kiss you, Katie? Can we make this up between us for now. We'll have to talk about it later on, but not today. I just want to get this over with and get your hand wrapped up."

"You can kiss me whenever you want to, John. You know that. If you'd like to bend over here, I'll put my good arm around your neck and hang on and kiss you back."

He grinned suddenly at her words, and she responded with a chuckle of her own, knowing that he would feel her pain as much as did she in the next minutes. He bent to her, his lips soft against hers and then his mouth touched her cheek and swept to her throat, pressing the warmth of his lips to every inch of skin he could reach.

"I'll try not to hurt you, Katie. But I can't make any promises. This doggone cut is deep and I'll have to take a number of stitches to close it up good."

She closed her eyes then and clamped her teeth together, holding her hand still in his, awaiting the first piercing of her skin. John called out for Berta and asked her to return to the bedroom, and when she neared the bed, he nodded at Katie, a silent request for Berta to hold her against the bed, lest she jerk her hand away without thinking.

But there was no need for Berta's grasp on her other arm, for her hand lay upon Katie's head, lending sympathy and the strength of a woman who had known her share of pain. Katie lay unmoving, only a quiet whisper of sound leaving her lips when the needle pulled the thread tautly against the flesh. John tied the first stitch off, cutting the thread and moving on to the next area he would close with the silk.

He winced as he drew the needle through her palm, and Katie watched his face as his fingers held the needle, unable to look at what he did to her, but unwilling to look from his profile as he worked. His jaw was taut, his mouth a drawn line and his teeth seemed to be grinding together. He inhaled through his mouth, then exhaled through his nostrils, keeping his breathing even as if he would somehow control his whole body by the discipline he used in this way.

"Katie, take some deep breaths," he said quietly. "Don't try to hold your breath, honey. Just keep your eyes on something other than your hand."

"I'm watching you, John," she said softly, and he halted what he did for a moment of time, his gaze turning to mesh with hers, his eyes filled with the pain he felt for her as he completed the necessary mending her hand required. Eleven stitches crossed her palm, the black thread against her flesh pulling the skin taut, the blood flow almost ceasing as he worked.

"He's about done, honey," Berta said, her hands gentle on Katie's arm and forehead. "It's almost over."

Silent tears escaped Katie's eyes and she smothered the sob that begged to be spent, for the sharp pain of the needle had not been totally contained by the whiskey John had poured on her cut. She looked down at what he was doing as he tied off the last bit of thread, and his sigh was long and harsh.

"That's it, Katie. We're done." He bent low to inspect the work on her hand and then met her gaze, his eyes filled with a sorrow she had not expected. John hurt as much as she did. She knew it without a doubt, knew the pain she had borne had been shared by him, that his long minutes of tending her had caused him an amount of pain she had not expected.

"Thank you, John." Her whispered words were puny, she thought, as if she hadn't the breath to speak them aloud, but he heard her and nodded, placing the needle back into the dish that still held an amount of whiskey.

"Here's some clean cloth to bind it with," Jane said from the foot of the bed. "I tore it off an old petticoat that Katie had in the pantry for some reason or other." She held out the strips of cloth to John and he folded several layers together to form a pad for her palm, then bound it in place with long strips that held it firmly.

"That ought to do it," Berta said, with a sigh of relief. "Jane, let's you and me head for the kitchen and get things going. Did you put those spuds on to boil?"

Jane nodded, for she'd apparently filled the kettle when Katie's accident happened and finished the peeling herself, then settled the pan on the stove.

"We'll get busy with the chicken then, John. If you'll stay here with Katie for a little while, she'll be feeling better and you can bring her to the house so she can sit and watch us work."

John nodded his agreement and Berta gathered up her things and left the bedroom. She and Jane spoke briefly in the kitchen and Katie did not pay any mind to them, her thoughts wrapped up in the pain that seemed to have taken hold with greedy strength in her hand.

John sat beside her, his hands holding her arm, and she whispered the thought that would not be denied. "Thank you for helping me, John. I'm sorry you had to do such a thing for me, but I'm glad it was you and not anyone else."

His smile was lopsided and he caught a deep breath as she spoke. "I wouldn't have let anyone else touch it, Katie. I knew I could handle it, for I've sewn more than one cut on a man. Barbed wire can be nasty and there's been more than a handful of men who've gotten themselves torn up on it. We've been real fortunate that no one has ever gotten an infection, and so long as we're careful and keep things clean we shouldn't have any trouble with your hand."

"Can I get up now?" she asked, thinking of Jane and Berta working in the big kitchen. "I need to see if those potatoes are getting done yet."

"I'll check on them," John said quickly, rising and making his way into the kitchen. He took out a fork and pierced one of the topmost pieces, then used a big spoon to stir them in the pot. "Just about finished, Katie," he said, raising his voice the better for her to hear him.

"Use my biggest lid to hold them in the pot when you drain them, John," she said, sitting up on the edge of the bed, holding her hand carefully in her lap. The throbbing had not let up and she feared that she would be of no use to Berta in the kitchen. And on top of that, she didn't think John would allow her to do much to help anyway. He seemed bent on watching her closely, and she didn't mind one little bit, for his mood seemed to have softened over the past hour or so.

Whether or not she would ever have to see Clay Thomas again was a moot question, for she knew that if he were to stay on the ranch, she would, as before, go out of her way to steer clear of him. And yet, even that had not kept him from her presence. Yet, it might not even be an issue, for she thought she'd heard Jane tell her that John had kicked Clay off the ranch, telling the man to pack his things and get out.

She heard the kettle dragged across the stove, then the sound of John draining the potatoes. "I'll take these to the house so Berta can get them ready for supper," John said, sticking his head in the bedroom door. "You stay right there till I come back, you hear?"

Katie only nodded, unable to speak, for the throbbing in her hand seemed to increase with her movement, and she would not test her strength by rising while she was alone in the house.

Within five minutes, John was back and Katie called out to him, asking him to check on the beans. He stirred them, then came to where she sat and spoke of Berta's doings in the house.

"She told me she'd send one of the men out to get the kettle of beans, and you should just take it easy for a while. I'll wait here with you till you're able to make it into the house, Katie. Then you can eat something in the kitchen. Jane and Berta have everything under control, the chicken is about done frying and the men are washing up for supper."

"I'm going to sit in the kitchen, John," she said, standing up and waiting until her head stopped swimming before she attempted to walk to the kitchen.

He hastened to her side and put his arm around her waist, lending his strength to hers as she walked slowly to the kitchen chair and sat down. "Would you pour me a little coffee?" she asked, knowing that the pot contained leftovers from earlier in the day.

He did as she asked and brought the cup to her. A spoonful of sugar was stirred in quickly and she lifted it to her mouth, knowing that the hot beverage would lend her strength. Coffee always gave her a quick rush of energy it seemed, and she needed such a thing right now.

Shorty came onto the porch and rapped at the door. "I heard that there was a kettle of beans in here waiting for me to carry them to the house," he said, entering the door and heading toward the stove. John found a pair of thick pot holders and handed them to Shorty, then opened the door for him to leave the kitchen, kettle in hand.

"Okay, let's get you over to the house now, Katie," John said quietly. "Can you walk by yourself, or shall I carry you?"

Katie shook her head with a quick movement. "No, I'm fine. Just hold on to me a little and I'll walk by myself."

"First I'm going to put your arm in a sling," John said quietly, seeking out a piece of sheeting from the ragbag in the kitchen pantry. He folded it double, making a triangle out of the square and slid it under her arm, then tied it behind her neck, holding her hand against her breast.

He did as she'd asked and together they made their way across the yard, passing the ranch hands who had filled their plates and were seeking out places to sit with their supper. The big kettle of beans was on the table and Berta used a large slotted spoon to dish up the vegetable to the men who still stood in line. Pieces of chicken were snatched from the platters and mounds of mashed potatoes appeared on every plate, topped by creamy gravy.

Jane brought a platter of sliced bread from the house and passed it to the men who had already served themselves from the laden table. They took the slices from her, thanking her nicely and using them to sop up the gravy.

John helped Katie into the house, settled her at the table and then left her to go outdoors and fill a plate for her. In moments he'd returned and sat down beside her.

"I don't think I can eat all of that," she said, eyeing the huge amount of food he'd brought to her.

"I'll share it with you," he told her, lifting the fork and spearing a piece of chicken. It was a part of the thigh, broken off from a piece that had been too tender to hold together. "Try this," John said, offering it to her and then grinning as she accepted it into her mouth.

"My right hand still works," she told him, reaching for a piece of breast meat that sat atop the beans Berta had scooped up onto his plate. Biting into it, she savored the flavor of the crisp coating, and then replaced it on the plate.

John ate heartily from the plate, offering bites of potatoes and then beans to Katie as he scooped one forkful after another into his mouth. "Sure tastes good," he said. "You want some more chicken, Katie?" he asked, holding aloft the piece of white meat she had tasted just minutes ago.

"I don't think I can eat any more," she told him, leaning back in her chair and holding her left hand carefully against her breast.

John looked to where the bandaged hand rested and his eyes held a wealth of tenderness as he directed his look at Katie. "Why don't we just take you on back to the cabin now, and get your nightgown on so you can crawl into bed. I think you've had enough excitement for one day, Katie."

She could not fault his plan, and she only nodded, willing to do as he directed her. His plate was empty now and he put it in the sink, pumping water over it, then returning to the table to help her to her feet. At the door, he lifted her into his arms and carried her from the house, unmindful of the watching eyes of the men who silently followed his progress to the cabin.

CHAPTER SIXTEEN

BY THE TIME THE SUN was settling below the horizon in the western sky, Katie was dressed in her white nightgown and placed beneath the sheet and quilt in the big bed. John sat beside her, silent, his thoughts his own as he watched his wife. She didn't seem prone to sleep, so far as he could tell, for she lay on her right side and looked out the window, her hand resting on a pillow before her.

He'd helped her undress, even though she protested that it was a task she could handle with one good hand, and after pulling her nightgown over her head, covering the slender curves he'd knowingly exposed to his view, he settled down to watch her.

"Aren't you going to come to bed?" she asked him, not turning to look at him as she spoke, but intent on the window where the twilight seemed to be infiltrating the bedroom.

"After a bit," he said, leaning back in the chair. "I want you to close your eyes, Katie. You've had a shock to your system and you need to rest."

She spoke beneath her breath and he leaned closer,

intent on hearing her words, but she seemed to regret whatever phrases she'd spoken, for she did not repeat them, even though he asked politely. Something about resting better when he was in the bed with her, he thought she'd said, but could not be certain, for she had mumbled the words as if she didn't want him to hear them.

He bent over her, lifting her hand to move the pillow to a better angle, enabling her to cradle her hand on it. She lay in the middle of the bed and he knew that there was barely room for him to sleep behind her, but not for the world would he find a resting place somewhere else. Wrapping his arms around Katie's form was prominent in his plan for this night, and keeping her comfortable was first and foremost in his mind.

He carried in a quart jar of water and a clean glass from the kitchen before he readied himself for bed, and then he closed the door and blew out the candle before he undressed. It was still early, but his day had begun at sunrise and riding with the men, then coming home to the hassle with Clay had worn him to a frazzle. Now he craved the comfort of his bed, and only the knowledge that Katie needed him to be aware of her needs during the night kept him from seeking his slumber too rapidly.

He pulled back the sheet and quilt and crawled in behind her, then wrapped her in his warmth, one big arm around her waist, pulling her carefully against himself. She murmured softly, and he heard his name spoken aloud, then a muffled sound that might have been a yawn.

She didn't quibble over his hands on her, though he feared that she might refuse his touch, knowing that things were still not settled between them. An enormous amount of frustration filled him as he considered Clay's behavior earlier today. It had been obvious to him that Katie was not inviting the man's attention, that Clay had made his presence known to her while she was working on the porch, and then had made haste to open the door for her to enter the house.

Had John not appeared when he did, the man might have gone into the cabin with her, and John felt a surge of anger as he thought of Clay's hands on Katie's flesh. The memory of the man's head bent close to her, his lips next to her ear filled John with a cloud of indignation, that the man had dared to whisper his thoughts to Katie.

She had not seemed to encourage him, but had stood back, waiting for him to move lest she brush against his body. As John recalled the incident, he recognized that Katie had not offered any invitation of any sort to the man, only tried to escape his presence.

That Clay had borrowed a horse from Bill Stanley and made his way to town did not dismiss him from John's fury, for he regretted that he had not left the man with any teeth in his head, that he had not left him unconscious on the barn floor. Had Bill not called a halt to the fight, Clay might not have survived with his vision intact, for John had closed both of his eyes with well-placed blows.

Now he curled behind Katie and held her against himself, yearning for the warmth she offered, knowing that he could not approach her as his manhood demanded, for indeed he was swollen and hard against her back. She moved a bit, leaving a small amount of space between their bodies as if she felt his arousal and would not encourage him in seeking her warmth.

"I'm not going to bother you tonight, Katie," he said softly, aware that she was not able to withstand a session of loving. "I don't mean to be pushing at you, but that thing of mine just doesn't seem to realize that you're in no shape for loving tonight."

She turned her head toward him and her voice was soft, her words spoken in an undertone. "If you want me tonight, John, I'll roll over and keep my sore hand out of the way. I won't refuse you. You know that."

"I wouldn't ask that of you, Katie. There are a lot of nights in our future, and you're not in any shape to be handling a man in this bed tonight." He cuddled her close, his hand moving up to cup her breast, and she sighed, curling against him, her legs against his, her bottom cradled by his thighs.

"Sleep, sweetheart," he said softly. And held her as she closed her eyes, her body relaxing against his, the sounds of her breathing deepening as she slept.

JOHN FELT HIS WAY carefully over the next days, not mentioning the rift in their relationship, his mood ever watchful of Katie, lest she hurt herself by working too hard. She let Jane do the washing up after meals, and then had to sit by as Jane took care of scrubbing their clothing on the board and hanging them on the line. After a week, John unwrapped Katie's hand one evening and with Berta's small scissors, clipped the stitches on her palm, then pulled them from her flesh, watchful as she winced with each move of his hands.

"I'm sorry, Katie. I know it's touchy, but they have to come out. It'll be harder to free them if we wait any longer."

She nodded her agreement and held her hand against her breast, rocking back and forth a bit as if it would bring surcease to her aching palm. John put a fresh bandage on her palm then, wrapping it carefully, telling her that she would need to change it daily, a task he would be glad to take care of in the evenings.

Berta had offered a tin of salve that she said would bring quick healing to the cut and John used it generously on the pad he formed over the long scar. Then, he helped Katie get ready for bed, taking off her shoes and stockings, unbuttoning her dress and blowing out the candle before he helped her get into her nightgown.

She seemed to feel less embarrassment each evening, as John handled her with ease, his hands not straying to her soft parts, but being careful to treat her with care. That he yearned to touch her intimately, that his hands burned to take hold of her breasts and the curves of her bottom was not to be spoken of yet, he decided, for Katie seemed to hold herself from him.

He needed her with an urgent yearning that would not be eased by her body next to his at night, for he ached to possess her, his body hard and aflame with desire. Katie seemed to be unaware of his problem, and he felt a surge of impatience as he drew the covers over her one night, over a week after her accident with the knife.

He circled the bed and crawled in behind her, then turned her to face him, his hands urgent on her as he lifted over her slender form. "I need you tonight, Katie. I don't think I can spend another night in this bed with you and not make love to you."

She did not speak, only widened her legs to make room for him, pulling her nightgown up to allow him access to her body. He felt almost like a marauder as he lay atop her, seeking out the softness of her woman's flesh. He touched her carefully, intent on bringing her to a climax before he took his pleasure within her warmth, but she pulled from him and only murmured that he should take his ease in her body.

With a sigh of frustration, for he had wanted desperately to give her the pleasure that was her due, he took her quickly, then felt a pang of regret, for he had used her as a man might a woman whose body was his by way of money having exchanged hands.

He could not enjoy the relief that was his, for it was not the true essence of loving that he had come to find in Katie's warmth, but a temporary easing of his need. He almost resented her for her disinterest in his lovemaking.

She rose from the bed and washed behind the screen, cleansing herself and then coming back to the bed in silence. He waited there, his mood edgy, his conscience bothering him that he had used her so.

"I don't know how much longer I can stand the distance you've placed between us," he said after long moments had passed, and awaited her reply, hoping against hope that she would give him some notion of her thoughts.

"You've treated me without trust, John, and I find I cannot feel the same as I did a month or so ago. You accused me, perhaps not aloud, but in your heart, for the problems with Clay Thomas, and I find no fault within myself in all of that. Your hands have not been gentle against my body, your words have cut me deeply and I am but a woman, not a machine that will operate to your bidding."

He moved restlessly beside her and his thoughts reflected his ambivalence. "He kept watching you and you didn't seem to discourage him, Katie. Clay seemed to think he was quite a ladies' man and maybe you didn't know how to give him the cold shoulder. It just seemed to me that you were enjoying his attentions, and it made me angry with you. I suspect I'm a jealous sort of man from way back."

"Your first wife wasn't faithful to you, John. But I'm not Sadie. I think you forget that sometimes. Maybe you just don't trust women, not just me."

"I've tried, Katie. For the most part, I've trusted you. But when Clay kept on chasing after you the way he did, it made me think that maybe you were encouraging him."

Her voice trembled as she denied his words. "I never wanted his hands on me. I never asked for his attention, John."

She turned from him then and he found himself viewing only the back of her head, the form of her body beneath the quilt a temptation he could not resist. He moved closer to her, fitting himself against her as he had been wont to do in the past, but tonight there was no softening of her curves against him, no melting of her slender form, no giving of herself to his comfort. She was stiff beside him, her body apart from him as though she were miles away instead of inches.

He could not bear it, this distance she offered and he pulled at her, tugging her close to his body, shaping her to his will. She did not dispute his right to touch her, only remained silent and unresponsive.

He would not have it, for his manhood was crushed by her lack of warmth, her total disinterest in him. He turned her to face him and his hands touched her gently, with care, brushing against her breasts, his lips finding ease on the peaks that formed to his caresses. He was determined to find a response of sorts in her and his touch ventured lower, across her belly to the soft curls that hid her womanhood.

He found the crease there, opened it with gentle care and touched the responsive nub that had hidden beneath a hood of flesh. Bending over her, he kissed her tenderly, his tongue venturing into her mouth, seeking out the hot depths of her throat and moving with a rapid thrusting that only imitated the movement he would soon initiate upon her soft parts.

She caught her breath with a sob and he determined to ignore the small sign of distress and only found new areas to conquer, his hand moving to pierce her body, his palm caressing her mound with gentle movements. She bucked once against him and he smiled carefully, lest she sense his triumph. He had trained her well over the past months, her body attuned to his, her woman-hood responsive, perhaps unwillingly, but nonetheless finding pleasure in his touch.

With long strokes and careful probing touches, he brought her to her pleasure and she moaned against his chest, her sounds swallowed up in the firm muscular lines of his body.

"Katie…don't hold back from me, love. Let me have your warmth tonight." His words were almost harsh, so great was the renewed need he felt for her. For even though he had taken her body less than an hour before, he was more than ready to possess her again.

She lifted her arms to encircle his neck, her breasts firm against his chest, her legs twining about his as she raised her hips to receive him. She was well prepared for his taking, soft and wet, and he slid within her depths easily, sinking to his full length in the heated channel she offered.

Again, she lifted her hips and caught his rhythm as

he blended their bodies in a union such as they had not enjoyed for a matter of weeks. For since his spat of jealousy over Clay Thomas, she had not responded to him in such a fashion. As though her body ached for his possession, as if she hungered for the union they shared in these moments, she clung to him, holding him against herself, her voice a soft murmur he strained to hear.

"I need you, John. You're strong and warm and… Hold me close, please," she whispered. His response was immediate, his arms tightening around her slender form, his body fitting itself to hers, their linking that of a man and wife seeking out the joy only to be found in the marriage bed.

He held her close, unwilling to disturb their union, turning to his side, the better to keep her in his arms, her head pressed against his shoulder, her face buried in his chest, her soft breath warming him in the night hours.

He awoke in the middle of the night, when the sky was darkest, the moon a sliver on the horizon, the stars standing out sharply against the midnight covering them. She stirred against him and he pulled her snugly against himself, aware that she was awake, that she moved in a sleepy fashion to gain comfort for herself, her legs shifting, her arm circling his waist.

He spoke then, words that had been in his mind for the past days, words he had not found it possible to speak when he knew she was not happy in his bed.

When he recognized her pain in the tension that had existed between them.

And so he whispered his query, his voice soft against her ear, and felt for a moment that he strayed into territory that was almost forbidden to him. "Katie, isn't it past time for your woman's stuff to be happening? Seems like it's been a while."

She lay quietly, thinking, and yet he knew she had almost expected this line of questioning from him. "You're right, John. I thought about that the other day, but I kinda forgot it. It has been longer since the last time than usual." As if caught up now in the passing of time, recognizing that the passing of days and weeks had come and gone, she pondered the thought. "I haven't really considered the length of time since my last time being a woman. It's been quite a while, hasn't it?

"In fact, I haven't done that kind of stuff for ever so long, John. Maybe seven weeks or even longer than that. It's mid summer already and I came here early in February. I haven't had my time of the month since April or maybe May. I can't remember for sure. In fact, I cut and folded up all that flannel you bought me to use for my monthly time and I've only used them a couple of times. They're still piled up nice and neat in the drawer waiting."

She stirred against him, worry racing through the corners of her mind. "I haven't even thought about it. Maybe I better ask Berta if she thinks I'm all right. I don't want to be sickening or anything. I suspect I could be having some kind of woman trouble. I know I heard Agnes talking one day to her sister, a long time ago, about their mama, and how she had woman trouble and sickened up and died."

He smothered a chuckle. "You're not gonna die, Katie. You're not even sick or anywhere close to it. Let's just wait and see what happens. I suspect things will work out just fine all on their own."

He held her close, his thoughts awash with the prospect of Katie having his child, and the pleasure that idea brought to his mind was so great he felt almost foolish, for he was but one in a long line of men who had fathered a child. Surely this occasion would be not very different from any other child born to a husband and wife.

And yet he sensed a difference, for Katie was the woman who would bear the child, the one who would suffer the pains of birthing, whose body would provide the shelter for his son or daughter. That prospect gave him pause, for he knew the tales of women who had died during childbirth. Those who had not survived the delivery of their child, and should Katie ever be one of that number, he would not be able to forgive himself for subjecting her to such a fate.

He held her closely, his thoughts a jumble, his heart more involved in this process than he'd thought possible. For the future loomed as an unknown entity, one in which he would either find the joys of fatherhood or perhaps the pain of losing the woman he held in his arms. He knew, in the depths of his mind, that such a happening was not likely, that Katie was strong and healthy, that she would no doubt survive the future that faced her, but his humanity was such that he faced days and nights of worry over her.

And perhaps that was all a part of the marriage vows, the promises he had made to love, honor and cherish this woman above all else. He had failed miserably in that of late, but made a silent vow now to make amends for his bouts of jealousy, his unkind treatment of Katie and the weeks of tension shared between them in this house.

IT WAS A WEEK OR SO later when John again joined her in the bed late one night and spent long moments in caressing her body, fitting her soft parts against himself, and touching her where he would, hearing her soft sounds of pleasure. It was more than his hungry body could bear, being apart from her and he considered whether she would be acquiescent to his needs.

He rolled atop her, his big body pressing hers into the mattress, and his mouth was warm against hers, his arousal pressing firmly against her belly. "Is it all right, sweetheart? Do you mind if I do this?"

She shook her head, her words slurred as she moved languidly against him. "You've already got me halfway there, John, what with all your messing around a few minutes ago, pokin' at me and touchin' me the way you were."

"Well, this won't take long then, will it?" he asked, shifting his body to where it yearned to be, spreading her legs to make room at the shrine he had attended frequently over the past days. He slid within, warm and slick and then lay still, soaking up the rapture of this communion with his woman. But it soon became imperative that he move, and so he did, carefully, gently and slowly, willing to withhold his final pleasure till she should achieve her own. And it was not long in coming, for he caressed her, murmuring soft words of encouragement, dropping kisses where he would, his hands ever careful to urge her toward the ultimate completion of this act that so completely surrounded them, that filled them with the joys incipient in the marriage relationship they were fast repairing.

"John, I asked Berta about things…you know what I mean, don't you?"

He smiled, aware that she was embarrassed. "Did she answer all your questions, sweetheart?"

"She said I was probably in the family way. I told her about missing my monthly and all and she said she'd wondered, that I'd been looking a bit peaked lately. In fact, she didn't act a bit surprised."

"Well, if making love with your husband results in a baby, I'd say that's something to be happy about, Katie. Don't you think so?"

"I reckon I do, John." Her sigh was replete with happiness, with the savoring of the warmth and beauty he showed her with his body, with the expressions of his heart. She clung, for there was no other word for her actions, her arms, her lips, and indeed, the essence of her being. Wrapped tightly against him, his weight easy on her, she bent and flowed, each curve nestling where it would, each rounding of her form blending with an essence that rose about them, the aroma of the loving they had experienced once more in this simple bed of pleasure.

JOHN HELD THE KNOWLEDGE of Katie's pregnancy within himself, aware that even though she'd talked with Berta, she was not totally knowledgeable about such things, that her education in such matters lacked much. And so he waited, not speaking again of the matter, but watching her for signs that her body harbored a child of his making. Two weeks passed, their relationship seeming to be strengthened each day, Jane taking on much of the work that had been Katie's for several months. And then events moved quickly, one morning finding them about their business, John working on the chores in the big barn, Jane gathering eggs and Katie in the kitchen, ready to prepare breakfast.

The smell of bacon and coffee, always the aroma of early morning, ever the call to breakfast, rose above the cookstove, dissipating into the room. And as John entered the cabin, he felt the emptiness of the kitchen. For the back door was still closed against the early-morning air, Jane still in the chicken coop, and Katie nowhere to be seen.

As for Katie, she'd run to the bedroom, leaving the

bacon frying in the skillet, the biscuits browning in the oven. She crouched in the corner of the bedroom, behind the screen, where the slop jar sat before her. With her face lowered, her eyes closed, her stomach revolting against the very scents that normally assured her that her day was off to a good start, she bent low over the slop jar, her very saliva tasting of green bile, her head swimming with the nausea that poked revoltingly from her belly into the depths of her stomach and thence out into the bucket before her.

"Katie?" John's strong voice called her from the back door and she stood upright, holding a damp cloth to her lips, her eyes wide.

"I'm in here, John. I'll be right out."

But he did not wait, whether alerted to some tone in her voice that drew him or perhaps the unusual circumstance of Katie not being where she belonged while breakfast cooked, he didn't know. Only that his bride was not where he was accustomed to finding her at this time of day, where she should have been when he arrived for his morning meal. His heart quickened as he strode rapidly across the small room to the bedroom door.

She was bent over the bucket, her mouth streaming, her hair falling about her face in disarray and her body bent forward. He went to her, sliding his arm around her waist, holding her against himself, his hand gentle against her belly.

"Sweetheart, are you sick? What is it?" His other

hand went to her forehead, fulling expecting to find heat
radiating from her skin, only to find the clammy flesh
of a woman who had just lost every bit of substance in
her stomach.

"Something didn't sit right, John. I just took a
good whiff of the bacon and it turned my stomach."
She stood erect now within his embrace, one hand
rising to dab the wet rag against her mouth once
more. "I'm all right now, I reckon. Just a spell of
some sort."

He felt his heartbeat slow with her assurance, knew
the relief of her safety assured by the strong tones of
her voice. "We talked about this the other night, Katie,
and I'm wondering if this isn't just what happens when
a woman gets in the family way."

His hand touched carefully a bit lower, in the cradle
formed by her hips, where the soft skin seemed just a
tad more firm to him. A thrill of anticipation shot
through him, and he held her upright against himself,
aware of her silence, of the steady heartbeat he felt vi-
brating from her slender body.

He turned her swiftly in his embrace, holding her
against himself, his arms banding her close and his
head bent to touch his forehead against her shoulder.
"I think Berta's right, sweetheart. We've made us a
baby, sure enough."

She tilted her head back, her hands touching his face
to lift him within her view, and a tear slid down her
cheek, even though the smile she offered belied sorrow.

"Well, if making a baby is what we've done together, John, I'll be so happy, I swear I'll just pop."

His grin widened. "Yeah, you will, sometime after the first of the year, I'll warrant."

She shivered, and he relished the excitement she radiated. That this lovely girl would want to carry his child, would yearn so to give him a son or daughter, was more than he could absorb. It would be the ultimate expression of their love and caring for each other, the evidence of their joining, of the acts of marriage that had cemented their relationship in this place.

He wanted to jump in the air, click his heels, shout the news to the world, and knew that Katie would not have that. That her modest soul would cringe from such a display, for she was womanly in the extreme, and if there was ever a girl prepared to be seemly and act the part a woman should during her months of waiting till a child should be born, Katie was the one to play the part. Part girl, part woman, she was the epitome of femininity to his narrow vision. For certainly he'd not spent an inordinate amount of time investigating the females of this world, his experiences were not wide, his hands had not touched more than a dozen other females until now, and his appetites were modest.

But there was within him the certain knowledge that after all his problems in the past, he had managed somehow to snag the one woman in the world who could complete him as a man, whose presence would provide fresh, new substance for each day of his living.

He would protect her and the children she gave him and be thankful for the rest of his life that in spite of his own faults and foibles, he'd been granted the rare joy of finding happiness.

IT WAS BUT A FEW DAYS later when John had pulled the wagon up before the general store and handed the list of supplies to Katie before he took his leave. "I'm going to the hardware, honey. Give your list to Shandy and he'll take care of you." Lifting her down from the wagon, he tossed her a quick grin and with a touch of his hand on her shoulder, he left her.

She went into the store, Jane wandering behind her, ever watchful, looking over her shoulder, as if she might see danger approaching at any moment. That Jacob or Agnes might be in town was a possibility, but it wasn't likely, Katie thought. Jacob usually made a solitary appearance in Eden once every month or so, but Agnes stayed back in the dingy farmhouse much of the time.

Aware of the facts, Jane had cringed when they left the Stanley ranch, speaking softly to Katie of her thoughts. "It's like someone's watching me," she'd said softly. And now she stood close to Katie's elbow, as if the shelter she found there would be enough to keep her safe. She assumed the pose of almost invisibility when they walked through the store, as if she feared to speak aloud. Katie frowned, urging her to enter into the shopping expedition.

"I was thinking maybe we could buy some paper and

pencils to use with our books," she told Jane in a low voice. "I'll bet there's something in that stuff Mr. Peterson got from back East."

"If not, maybe Mrs. Rice could find some supplies for us," Jane said thoughtfully. "I'll bet she can get things easy."

"Maybe that would be better, and then, too, we'll see if there's any chance of getting any more books. I'd like to find something special for John one day, a book maybe that he hasn't already read. I wouldn't know what to look for, but I'll warrant Mrs. Rice would."

She rubbed a finger against the wrinkle that had formed between her eyes. "I wish sometimes I was a whole lot smarter, Jane. I don't even know the names of the men who write the kind of books John has in his collection."

"We'll ask Mrs. Rice if she comes out on Saturday," Jane said soothingly. "You don't give yourself credit enough, Katie. You're learning fast, and John's proud of you."

Katie's eyes lit for a moment as she considered that idea. "I know more words than I ever did, and when I was reading to him last night, he said I was making real progress."

"Well, for now, we need to be thinking about the supply list," Jane said. "Did you give it to Mr. Peterson yet?"

Katie shook her head. "No, but I'm gonna let you take care of it. I want to walk over to the saloon and see

Molly. I've got a need to talk to her and maybe there's time while John's at the hardware."

Jane dug in her heels. "He might not like that, you know. He thinks you're going to be right here, and if he thought you were wandering around by yourself he'd be having a fit."

"I'll only be gone a few minutes. I've just got some things I want to talk to Molly about. And John won't care that I talked to her."

The list from her pocket was transferred to Jane's hand and Katie headed for the door. "I won't be but ten minutes or so. You just take care of getting the things John wrote down and I'll be right back."

Jane opened her mouth, as if to protest, but Katie was gone before she could draw a breath, the door closing behind her.

"This is something I have to do," she whispered aloud as she hurried to the alley. "I just hope John will understand."

CHAPTER SEVENTEEN

THE ALLEYWAY LEADING to the back door of the saloon was just a couple of doors from the general store, just past the barbershop and bank, and Katie made her way there quickly, careful to look around to be sure she wasn't being observed.

The back door to the saloon sat ajar, as if the woman who worked inside the room invited a cool breeze to enter her kitchen, and Katie pushed it open, rapping once on the surface as she did so.

"Come on in." The words were firm and welcoming, and Katie entered the warm kitchen with a sense of stepping into the past. Faint memories of this place rode the edges of her mind, and she recalled several women at the table, eating and talking together. A face rose before her, soft eyes and brown hair. A woman who seemed to remind her...

"Well, hello there, young'un." Molly's words were lilting, her accent familiar, and Katie walked toward her.

"I've been thinking about you, Molly," she said.

"Everything going along all right with that man of

yours?" Molly asked, her eye keen as she swept her gaze over Katie's form.

"Right as rain. He's good as he can be. And I've been learning how to be a wife."

Molly laughed aloud. "I'll just bet you have, young'un. You look like a happy girl." She poured a cup of coffee from the ever-present pot on the back of the stove and pushed it toward Katie. "Sit yourself down for a spell and talk to me."

Katie nodded her acquiescence and pulled a chair from before the table, settling into it and then looking around the room.

"This place seems familiar to me. I can almost see a couple of ladies here at the table, and I remember you at the stove."

"Do you now? And do you remember your mama?"

Katie stilled and shook her head. "I don't think so. But, there was one lady who was pretty, with dark hair and pretty eyes and I think she was someone I cared about."

"Sounds like your mama to me," Molly said firmly. "Claire was her name and she was just a youngster when you were born. She kept you upstairs in her room during the day, except when she took you for walks out in the countryside."

Molly joined her at the table then, folding her hands before her and slanting a long look at Katie. "You remember anything else about her?"

"No. Just that she was pretty and she used to brush my hair, I think. Seems like I remember her telling me stories, and there was one time we sat under a tree and she talked to me." As though memories streamed through her mind, she felt awash in thoughts that were new to her, and her heart stuttered within her breast.

"Claire? Her name was Claire?" Katie asked the question softly, as if not needing an answer and then she whispered another query that slipped from her without thought. "And who was my father, Molly? Do you know?"

"Claire never talked about your pa," Molly said, and Katie wondered if she were trying to steer their conversation from that information.

"Did she know who he was?" And if her mother had not known, if the knowledge of the man who had fathered her had been lost with Claire's death, Katie recognized that she would never know that truth, either. "Did she ever say anything about him?"

Molly nodded once. "I suspect she knew. We didn't talk about it, but your mama wasn't one to say much anyway. She cared about him, I know that, for she said more than once that she'd like for you to have a real family, and should she ever marry him, he'd be a good father to you.

"But mainly she wanted you to have a family, and I guess it didn't look like that was gonna happen here, with Claire and your pa. Maybe she let him know how she felt about you and having folks of your own. I guess that's why you got sent out to live with the Schrader family after she took sick and died. They said they were wanting a girl child to take in as their own. I guess

Agnes just couldn't have any young'uns, and when they put out the word that they were looking for a child to take in, you came to mind."

"Who gave me to them?" Katie spoke the words that had haunted her over the past, wondering who had cared so little for her that they would give her up to a family who didn't know how to treat a child.

Molly's lips tightened and she shook her head. "It was something that just happened," she said. "You were living in a saloon and it wasn't any place for a child. Anybody could see that. I suspect it seemed like a good idea at the time, to give you a real home and someone of your own to take care of you."

Katie laughed, a sound of derision, and her heart ached for the home she might have had, if someone had really wanted her. "They took care of me all right. Like you'd take care of a stray dog. And sometimes not even that."

Molly's eyes teared up and she reached for Katie's hand. "Well, you don't have to be looking for scraps of food nowadays, do you? I'll bet John Roper feeds you right well."

Katie's head lifted, her chin tilted and pride filled her voice. "I told you before. He treats me good, Molly. I can cook anything I want to, and—" She thought suddenly of her reason for coming here today. "And that's what I want to talk to you about."

"Eating? You want to talk about food?" Molly appeared puzzled and well she might, for Katie seemed to be well nourished and happy.

"No, not about eating, but about not feeling like eating." Katie swallowed, looking down at her coffee as if it were somehow not up to par. "I got up this morning and started in fixing breakfast and all of a sudden, I got sicker than a dead dog. I didn't have anything in my stomach to get rid of, but I sure enough tried to empty it out. John came in and found me in the bedroom, leaning over the slop jar, and he was all worried."

Molly grinned. "You feeling all right otherwise? Not ailing, are you?"

"No." Katie spoke the single word and then looked into Molly's eyes. "John thinks we're going to have a baby, Molly. I haven't had my woman's time but a couple of times since we got married, and he's figuring that we've made us a baby."

Molly rose and swept Katie from her chair. "Well, if that don't beat the band," she said with a laugh. "You ain't much more than a child yourself, girl, not even eighteen yet, are you?"

"Almost. I think my birthday is this month. If I recall, it's toward the end of July, but I'm not sure."

"You were born in midsummer, as I remember," Molly said. "It was warm, a nice day. Your mama had you all by herself. Didn't even tell us she was ready to deliver, just went upstairs all alone and when I went up to bed, I thought to check on her and she was holding you. You were still attached to her, must have just been born, and your mama was smiling and cuddling you up close."

"What did you do?"

"Went down and got a pair of scissors and some string. Then I cut the cord and took care of things, washed you up and found some things your mama had made for you to wear. Wrapped you up nice and snug in a piece of flannel and tucked you in beside her. She stayed right there in bed for a few days and I had the doctor come by and see to her. She thought she didn't need him, but I convinced her that she should be certain that everything was all right."

"And she named me Katie? Was I called that for anybody she knew, or was it just a name she liked?"

"It was her mama's name, she told me. She said it sounded old-fashioned and it was a good, solid name for a girl. She wanted you to amount to something, Katie. She was so proud of you, kept you so clean and nice. We made dresses for you and she bought you a bonnet from the general store one time, I remember."

"I wish I had all that in my mind." Katie felt frustration eating at her as she tried to recall memories that eluded her. "I wish she knew that I'm happy now."

Molly sat back down in her chair and folded her hands before her again, looking down at the work-worn fingers. "Maybe she does, girl. We don't know what happens when we die, do we? I mean, maybe somehow, your mama knows that you've found a good life. I'd like to think so anyway. She was a good woman, no matter that folks looked down their noses at her. She did the best she could, and that's all any of us can do."

"Who you talking to back here, Molly?" The voice of the newcomer was deep, friendly, and Katie felt no threat from his presence. He was a big man, tall, with dark hair and a nice smile. He cast her a measuring look and his eyes seemed to darken, as if he had something to say, but didn't want to spit it out.

"Hey there, Tom. It's just Katie, come to call. We've been talking about things out at the Stanley place. Her husband's the foreman there, you know."

"I know John Roper." Tom's words were careful, and he frowned at Katie, then offered a query in her direction. "You here to complain about him to Molly?"

Katie shook her head. "I got no reason to complain. My life's about as good as it gets. My sister is living with us now, and Mrs. Rice, the schoolteacher, has been coming out to work with both Jane and me on our learning."

"How far did you go in school, Katie?" he asked.

"I never went to regular school," she admitted, ducking her head, shame washing over her at the admission. "But Jane used to share her books with me. And John has a whole store of good books in his cabin. He lets me look at them."

"How does Jane happen to be with you?" Tom asked, his look inquiring.

"She ran off from the Schrader place, and came to us." It didn't seem wise to add much to the basic information, Katie thought. Nobody's business but Jane's anyway.

But apparently Tom thought differently. "Wasn't she happy there? Were there problems?"

Katie shifted uncomfortably on her chair. "It was kinda hard on her with me gone, and double the work for her to do."

"Doesn't old man Schrader have any hired hands to do the work? I can't imagine that a young girl would be—"

Katie blurted out the first words that came to mind. "You've got no idea what it's like out there. Jane and me did the work while I was there, all the milkin' and feedin' stock and such. And once I left, Jane was stuck with most of it herself. I feel bad that I left her to the whole mess, but I had to get away. And now that she's got all her nerve in one piece and hightailed it out of there, I suspect that Agnes and Jacob will be workin' up a sweat themselves."

She closed her mouth firmly and settled back in the chair. "Jane came to us without much to wear, just the clothes on her back and one change of drawers she brought, along with her schoolbooks. I'm gonna ask John to get her some things at the general store. I should have thought of it sooner, but she's been sharing my stuff so far."

"John's got his plate pretty well loaded, don't he?" Molly asked to no one in particular, as if the words were a statement of fact.

"Do you think we're expecting too much, me and Jane, living there and all?"

"I doubt that John thinks you're too much trouble, Katie," Tom said firmly. "And if Jane changes her mind, I can find her work here to do."

"This is no place for a young girl," Molly said sharply. "It's not even right that Katie's here now. She don't belong in a saloon."

"It's where I started from, Molly," Katie reminded her. "And if things had worked out different, I'd probably be here yet, maybe working here."

"Not on your life." Tom's tones were harsh as he spoke and his eyes fixed on Katie. "It was bad enough that you had a rough time growing up, but now things are different for you, girl. You've got a real future."

"More future than you know about, Tom." Molly sent him a look that he met with an inquiry of his own.

"What's that supposed to mean?"

"Katie's probably gonna be having a baby. It looks pretty certain anyway."

He grinned widely at that. "Is that so, girl? You're gonna be having John Roper's child? I'll bet he's tickled to death."

Katie felt a flush cover her cheeks, and wondered why Molly had so readily divulged her news. That Tom should know such a thing was beyond decency. He barely knew who she was and now he was privy to her most hidden secret. "I think maybe," she said quietly. "Time will tell."

Molly shot a look toward the back door. "John will be wondering where you are, I'll warrant, Katie. Did he know you were coming here?"

She rose, aware of the passing of time as she'd been talking to Molly. "No, he doesn't know where I am. I left Jane in the general store, getting the stuff on our list, and John is over at the hardware, picking up things for Mr. Stanley. I'd better get back, or he'll be wondering what's happened to me."

"I'll walk you to the end of the alley," Tom said. "There's fellas sometimes out back, and it's not a good place for a young girl."

He held the back door open and Katie moved toward it, turning to speak again to Molly, words of thanks for her hospitality. And then she was out the door, walking quickly the few steps to where the opening of the alleyway led to the sidewalk, and back to the general store.

Tom bade her farewell and stood watching as she left, her head turning once to see him there in the shadows. How strange, she thought, that he should be concerned about her safety. Perhaps he was a nicer man than she'd thought, being the owner of the saloon and all.

John stood in front of the general store, his hands on his hips, his hat pulled down, shielding his eyes from her scrutiny. "Where you been?" he asked shortly, holding the door open for her to enter the establishment before him.

"I went to see Molly for a few minutes, to let her know that I'm all right and that things are going well for me." And if John was upset over that, she'd have to bear the brunt of his anger, for she wasn't sorry for a minute that she'd gone for a quick visit.

But he seemed not to be angry, only concerned, for he took her arm and walked with her to the counter where Jane waited, foodstuffs piled high in front of her.

"You got everything we need?" John asked her, and her nod was answer enough, apparently, for he merely spoke quick words to Shandy Peterson, telling him he'd pay up at the end of the month, when Bill Stanley paid him his wages. To which Shandy seemed more than agreeable.

"John, could I talk to you for a minute?" Katie asked, touching his hand, drawing him to one side.

"What's wrong?" he asked, his frown showing concern.

"Nothing's really wrong, but I wondered if you could afford to let me buy a piece of material to make Jane a dress. She's only got the one she's wearing and another that's not fit for much but the ragbag. I thought maybe I could sew her up a nightgown out of my flannel pieces and if you'd let me pick out a nice piece of percale, I could make a dress for her."

His face cleared, and a smile replaced the frown he'd assumed. "Of course, you can, Katie. But you don't need to be using your flannel pieces for her nightgown. We'll buy a fresh piece of outing flannel for her or maybe something lighter, what with the warm weather these nights. And you'll need a new gown, too, for when the weather starts to get colder and your other things don't fit you anymore."

"I don't mind using the flannel I've already got, John," she said softly, not willing to cause more expense than necessary.

He bent and whispered against her ear. "I thought maybe those bits of flannel would sew up into diapers for the baby, Katie. Or maybe whatever babies wear, little dresses or whatever."

She looked up into his face, her heart light in her chest. "That would be good, John. I can practice on them a little bit. Never made anything so small, but I guess I could learn."

He laughed softly. "I think you could do most anything you set your hand to, sweetheart." Without another word, he led her to the counter where stacks of yard goods wrapped around cardboard bolts lay, luring ladies closer. And Katie was no exception, for the wealth of fabric was like a wonderland to her, various prints and plaids of all colors, striped material and solid pieces mixed.

"Jane, come look at this," she said, catching her sister's attention and drawing her close with a wave of her hand. "Do you like this flowered material or the striped one better?"

Jane stood back, clenching her hands by her sides, as if she would keep them from the temptation of touching the wealth of material on offer. "They're all pretty, Katie. Are you planning on getting something for a new dress?"

"She's gonna make a new dress for you, Jane," John said firmly. "And one for herself, too. She's going to need a different sort of dress before too long." And with that he shot Katie a look that spoke of the secret between them.

"John said you could pick out something, Jane. And we can buy stuff for a nightgown for you, too. Mine is too short for you. You'll be needing one of your own."

For indeed, Jane had worn Katie's old gown to bed, and being a few inches taller than her sister, the length was off. Even with the hem let down, it only reached midcalf.

"A new dress?" As if the offer was not to be believed, Jane's eyes widened and her mouth formed a soft O of surprise. "I don't mean to be any trouble, John," she said softly.

"You're no trouble at all, girl. You're Katie's sister and as such, you're my responsibility, too."

She stepped closer to where Katie stood, her eyes filling with tears as she reached out to touch a bolt of fabric. "This is right pretty," she said, her fingers seeming to treasure the simple cotton, rubbing back and forth as if it were the finest silk or satin.

"Do you think that four yards will be enough?" Katie asked. "You bought material before from the store, sometimes when I wasn't here with you. I'm thinking that it takes about five yards for a nightgown, but—"

"Get whatever you need, Katie. Just pick it out and Shandy can have his daughter cut it for you. Choose a couple of prints for Jane and something for yourself. And don't forget the thread or whatever else you'll need." John turned away after issuing orders and Shandy called to his girl in the back room, inviting her to come out and be of service.

Jessica Peterson came out from the storeroom, nodding at Jane and Katie alike and then joining in the fun of choosing what would make up well into dresses for the pair of them.

"If you'd rather, you can pick out something ready-made, Katie," he told her quietly. "I don't mind paying a little extra for you not to have to do all that sewing."

"Oh, John. It'll be fun. Me and Jane will have a good time." Her smile gave him assurance, and he seemed to be agreeable, for he nodded and waved at the piles on the counter.

"You got a couple of boxes I can put this stuff in, Shandy? I'll get it out to the wagon while the girls do their shopping."

In no time, the food was gathered together, John and Shandy carrying it easily to the wagon in front of the store, and Katie stood with Jane and Jessica, making the decisions that loomed before them. Jane hung back, not willing to take advantage and Katie laughed at her reticence.

"Come on, Jane. If John didn't want us to get all this stuff, he wouldn't have offered." And so they picked and chose, Jessica measuring and cutting fabric at their bidding, until four pieces lay before them, matching thread and a card of buttons in each color needed added to the pile.

"I've never felt so rich in my life," Jane said softly as Jessica added up the purchases.

"That's the way John makes me feel every day," Katie told her firmly. "It's like I'm living in a dream most of the time."

"I'll work hard to earn it out," Jane said. "Maybe I can do stuff in the house for Berta to help. I don't want John to think I'm taking advantage."

"He won't," Katie said blithely, more confident than ever now in her position as John's wife, his pleasure in the thought of a child being born to them buoying her self-assurance.

Jane carried the package by her side as they left the store, then held it on her lap once they were atop the wagon's seat.

"You can put it in the back if you want to," John said with a quick glance at the bulky bundle.

"No, I don't mind holding it," Jane said, exchanging a smile with Katie.

And so wrapped up in their happiness were they that the sight of a man on horseback in front of sheriff's office didn't register in their minds.

SATURDAY BROUGHT MRS. RICE to visit again and Katie and Jane were caught up for most of the afternoon with her books and papers. She brought them supplies to use for their schoolwork, and suggested to John firmly that Jane attend school more often in town, once the new school year began in a month or so.

"I'm not real fond of her traveling alone on the back roads," John said carefully.

"I think I have some idea of the girls' problems," Mrs. Rice said quietly. "But if it could be done, Jane needs to be in school this fall more than she was in the spring. She's entering her last year of school, and I've done all I can for her. If she can go on to the State Normal College next year it would ensure her a position in teaching. Perhaps not in this area, but certainly somewhere close by in the territory."

"We'll see what we can do," John said, leaving an opening for himself.

THE SUMMER REACHED AN END with a final display of tomatoes to be canned and put into the pantry for winter, the end of the green beans picked and awaiting Mason jars to be filled with their bounty. Beets were pickled and canned, carrots pulled from the ground and placed in piles in the fruit cellar under the big house, along with piles of potatoes that would provide nourishing meals all winter long.

Katie was weary at night when she crawled into her bed, for carrying a child was a task all of its own, and added to it now were the preparations for winter that were a housewife's due. She and Jane worked diligently at the duties that were implicit in running a household, cleaning a final time before winter should come and find them penned indoors. Under Berta's watchful eye, for she was much like a mother hen when it came to

Katie's well-being, they washed curtains and turned mattresses, hung the rugs over the line and used a carpet beater to clean them of dust before they laid them once more on the floors.

It was a satisfying time, a time of preparation for the long months of winter and Katie knew that soon Jane would not be there on a daily basis, but would be going to school as often as possible in order to complete her final year.

Their sewing was accomplished in the evenings, sitting near the fireplace, fabric in their laps, needles flashing as they sewed seams and hems for their new clothing. John deemed it necessary for Jane to have a new winter coat, and he helped her choose one in the general store. Determined to treat the two women in his household as they deserved, he bought boots for each of them, and a soft pair of house shoes to be worn once they came in the back door and removed their outdoor clothing.

Katie was filling out, her waist having lost the battle and growing at a rapid pace. She touched the rounded area beneath her apron frequently, rejoicing in the knowledge that she nurtured a small being within herself. It was a time of contemplation, of planning for the future, and she worked with Jane to sew small gowns for the child that would soon be in their midst, who would make his or her presence known in a mighty way before winter's end.

She spoke to Berta at length about her expanding

belly, about the timing of events and between them it was decided that the child would make an appearance in late January or early February. Berta's own sewing took on new life, for she was working diligently on hemming diapers and making small blankets that would enclose a tiny baby in their folds.

The movement of her child was a revelation to Katie, and she spent long moments with a hand against the rounding in her lap, feeling the movement inside, aware of small hands and feet that made their movements known to the woman who held such a treasure within her being.

It was a time of enlightenment, for she and John became closer than before, his big hand resting against her at night, waiting patiently for a sign of the child that made his presence noticed on a regular basis. For John was sure that she was to bear a boy, a son for him to rear and train and raise as his own father had done with him. Katie on the other hand was determined that her child should be a girl, that she would have the joy of braiding long hair, of dressing her child in skirts and sharing long hours with a girl child of her loins. Perhaps know the joy her own mother must have felt as she cared for her child.

Jane rode one of the horses to school almost daily, John escorting her some days when it was imperative that he go into town on errands for Bill Stanley. Other days, he simply rode beside her until they were within sight of the school, then he watched her until she had arrived safely before he headed for home and the chores that awaited him there. A long talk with the sheriff just outside of town one such day gave John reason to be fearful, for the lawman told him news of Jacob Schrader. The man had been asking around town for information on Jane, telling folks that she'd run off and he was certain she was with Katie out at the Stanley ranch.

The sheriff said that the man was angry, had made threats against John for his part in giving shelter to Jane, robbing Jacob of her much-needed help on the farm. All of which made John even more careful, more watchful over Jane in her trips back and forth to the school.

Winter was a quiet time on the ranch, but there was always the mending of tack, the repairing of stalls and the care and feeding of mares and heifers who would be bearing young in the spring. The men hauled hay to the fields for the cattle to eat when the snow covered the grassy areas, then brought the animals closer to the barns when the weather grew too cold and snowy for them to stay warm in the fields.

A load of lumber was brought from the mill in town one day, deposited near the cabin by the men who had hauled it to the ranch. Katie watched as they carried the long two-by-fours, the lengths of boards that would make up walls and the roof of an addition to the cabin, and rejoiced that their living space would soon be expanded. John said that they needed another bedroom for Jane's use, and their own room should be enlarged for a crib to hold the baby.

Bill Stanley hired on another man to help with the building project, an Indian from the Dakota tribe, a man who hailed from Holly Hill, twenty miles or so to the west. His name was Gray Wolf and he came well recommended, for he had worked with several carpenters building houses over the past five years or so. He was a tall man, stalwart and clean, and John took to him immediately, as if he'd known him for years.

Gray Wolf spoke of his sister and her husband, who farmed near Holly Hill, and told of his life on the reservation, but of late he'd been working on homes and businesses that were going up apace in the Territory. Men and women were moving from the East almost daily it seemed, and there was good money to be made in the building of homes for the newcomers.

Gray Wolf stayed in the bunkhouse with the men and made himself useful in several ways, riding out when an extra hand was needed and when the building was underway, he assumed leadership of the work being done. The men followed his lead without question, for he was obviously well trained in his work.

His help was invaluable, Bill Stanley said, and he praised the man to the skies, telling him he was welcome to stay on at the ranch for the winter, even after the building was completed.

The lumber for the addition lay in the weather for less than a week when the men gathered one morning to begin the work. Katie cooked all morning to feed them, for she felt compelled to bring them en masse into her kitchen for their noon meal. Berta came out to the small cabin to lend a hand and together they put beef and vegetables into a big kettle, then added dumplings on top to make a stew for the hearty appetites of the crew who spent the morning hard at work.

The kitchen bulged with men, the table crammed with their bodies around it, chairs brought from the big house to be used, for Katie and John did not have enough to hold all the crew. They ate rapidly, all of them anxious to get back to the work they had begun, for the framework was up and one wall almost completed. That the cabin would be almost doubled in size was apparent, and Katie reveled in the additional room she would have available for their use.

Gray Wolf's gaze seemed to settle on Jane often, his dark eyes watchful as she moved about the kitchen. Katie thought he was rather taken with Jane, for she noted him watching her sister on more than one occasion, his gaze ever respectful as he followed her progress about the ranch. And yet, Jane seemed to be oblivious to him, treating him in a reserved manner as she did all the other men.

Now that Katie and Jane were sewing and preparing for a child to be born, they had needed a new chest of drawers, and John purchased one from the catalog, having it sent to the general store and then brought home in a wagon. They filled the drawers rapidly with small items of clothing, blankets and diapers.

Christmas was a holiday for rejoicing this year, and

Katie welcomed it with open arms, for never had she found so much to be thankful for. The time of celebration was filled with happiness and the shirt she had sewn for John was welcomed with a grin and an immediate trial run, for he must put it on and be certain the buttons and buttonholes matched properly, he said.

As for Katie, she was the recipient of new mittens and a long scarf from Berta, Jane receiving the same items from Berta's knitting needles. John's scarf was brown, matching his eyes, and he wore it about his neck on a daily basis, pleasing Berta no end.

A baby's crib was brought into the house on Christmas eve, from the barn where the men had worked on it for the past weeks. Formed of oak, it boasted multiple bars that attached both top and bottom to the sides of the bed, with a mattress purchased from the catalog filling it neatly. Katie had made sheets to fit the small bed, tucking them in carefully, hemming a pillowcase for the feather pillow Berta said was to be used by the newborn.

They had a tree, a small spruce that filled one corner of the main room of the cabin, and decorated it with candles and a few choice ornaments that John had determined they should buy from the store. Made of blown glass and painted with sparkling gold and silver stripes, they were a delight to the two women who had never seen such a thing to be enjoyed at this time of the year.

The addition to the cabin was completed after the

first of the year, curtains made to fit the new windows and a braided rug put together from rags Berta found in the ragbag in the big house. Evenings found Jane and Katie braiding the strands of fabric together, sewing the ends of pieces to form long strips and then sewing the braid in a circular form to make a rug for the new rooms.

The excitement of readying a bedroom for Jane's use was a pleasure for Katie, for she knew that Jane would appreciate a room of her own in which to keep her things neat and tidy. She had made do with so little in her life, and now she found herself in possession of a small bedroom called her own, a bed made by the men in the barn for her use, a chest of drawers from the catalog, purchased by John and given to her with a flourish as a gift to his "sister." Jane had cried at the gesture and been the recipient of a hug and a kiss on the cheek from Katie's husband.

Now they awaited the birth of a child, Katie's body swollen almost beyond recognition, her belly enlarged until she thought it would surely burst. Her breasts were readying themselves for the child to come, and she looked forward to the time of nursing her baby and rocking in the chair John had purchased for her use.

It was late January when an aching in her back soon transmitted itself to a nagging pain that came and went with irregular timing. Katie was silent, not wanting John to be worried before time, and when Jane went to school one morning, she watched them leave the ranch and then returned to her work. Wanting to have the house as clean as it could be before she took to her bed, she scrubbed the floor and blacked the stove during the morning hours.

The pantry needed to be sorted out, she decided, and the afternoon was given over to that project, lifting jars of canned foods from one shelf to another until it met her standards. It was time and past for Jane to return from school and Katie watched the long lane to the main road for the sight of Jane astride the mare she rode. John had deemed it safe for her to come home on her own, after escorting her in the morning to the edge of town, and now Katie began to fidget, knowing that Jane was late, that it was beyond time for her to arrive.

John was out on the range, feeding the cattle from the hayloft, the men having loaded up the hay wagon after dinner and then made their way north to where the steers were penned. She watched for his return, impatient for him to arrive so that she could tell him of her fears for Jane. But he did not come and she began to fret overmuch about him. Perhaps the men had run into trouble, maybe the steers had needed to be brought closer to the barns and the men were herding them in a southerly direction.

She thought of all the reasons why John was late, dismissing them one after another, and then concentrated again on Jane's failure to come home. And in the midst of all of that, the aching of her back continued unabated, causing her to rub unconsciously at the lowest part of her spine where the drawing sensation began.

Supper was almost ready, and Katie slid the pan of beans and ham into the oven to finish cooking. The bread was sliced, applesauce poured into a bowl and pickles and beets dished up and waiting delivery to the table. She set out the plates and silverware, scurried around the kitchen to finalize preparations and then stood at the window and watched the lane for a sight of Jane's arrival.

An arrival that did not materialize.

CHAPTER EIGHTEEN

KATIE HAD WAITED LONG ENOUGH. John was not here to
send out looking for Jane and she was on her own.
Katie dressed warmly, donning a pair of John's long
warm drawers beneath her skirts, then wrapping herself
in a heavy shirt made of flannel before she put on her
winter coat and headed for the barn.

Shorty was tending the horses in their stalls, measuring oats into their feeding bins, lifting hay into the
mangers, and his surprise at seeing her invading his territory was apparent.

"What you doing out here, ma'am?" he asked, his
frown deep as he regarded the young woman who was
only days away from having a child.

"Jane's not home yet and I'm worried about her,"
Katie said. "I thought I'd take one of the mares and go
looking for her in case she's run into trouble between
here and town."

"Now, I don't think you riding off hunting her up is
a very good idea," Shorty said slowly.

"Well, I'd like you to saddle a horse for me," Katie
said firmly. "I used to ride bareback, and I'm sure I'll

do as well with a saddle under me, Shorty. And I can't be just sitting here waiting while Jane may be in trouble. I'll have to go find her."

"I surely don't like the idea, ma'am. Why don't you give it another half hour or so. The men should be back any minute now and John will take care of things."

Katie shook her head, determined now to do as she saw fit. "I'm going to go look for her, Shorty. If you won't saddle a horse for me, I'll walk."

Her jaw set and her mouth pouched out in a fashion that spoke volumes to the man who watched her. He seemed to recognize a stubborn woman when he saw one, and his sigh was loud and long as he went to the tack room to find a saddle that would be appropriate and a docile mare for her to ride.

"I'd be most happy if you'd wait till John shows up. He's gonna be madder'n hell at me for letting you go."

"I'll make it right with John," Katie assured him, leading the mare to a mounting block and climbing into the saddle.

She looked down at Shorty, hesitant that he might not do as she asked. But her courage won out and she pointed to his gun, secured at his hip.

"Will you let me take your gun with me, Shorty? I know how to shoot, but I don't intend to use it unless I have to protect myself."

Shorty peered up at her, as if he gauged her ability to do as she had said. "Where'd you learn to aim a gun, ma'am?" And Katie smiled smugly.

"John showed me a little, out in the orchard one day last summer. Just enough so's I'd know how to defend myself, he told me." With a smile, she held out her hand, waiting silently until Shorty took the weapon from its holster and with a last, worried look, handed it to her.

Much comforted by the weight of the weapon, she tucked it into the deep pocket of her coat and took the reins in hand, turning the horse through the barn door and then up the lane to where the town road curved off to the east. From the house, Berta called out to her, coming to the porch and waving in a frantic motion, but Katie ignored her, determined to complete the task she had begun.

The horse had an easy gait, and Katie rode well, so she felt confident that her trip would be short-lived and productive, once she located Jane. It was a ride of probably close to thirty minutes to town and she rode slowly, ever careful not to urge the horse on to a faster pace, but willing to take her time lest the animal slip on the snow and ice that covered the ground and rutted the road.

Ahead of her lay the schoolhouse, and it seemed to be abandoned, for there were no horses tied outside to the hitching rail, the door was closed and no light glowed from within the small building. Katie rode up to the door and bent to rap on it. There was no answer and then from around the side of the building came Mrs. Rice.

"Katie, what on earth are you doing here?" she

asked. "I just went to the outhouse and if I hadn't come in this direction, I'd have missed you."

"I'm looking for Jane. She didn't get home when she should have, and I'm worried about her."

"She left here over an hour ago, Katie. I can't imagine where she would have gone. I know she's always anxious to get home. Are you sure you didn't miss her on the way here?"

Katie frowned. "Of course not. I was looking for her every minute."

Mrs. Rice seemed worried, and her brow furrowed. "Perhaps we should go into town and see if she headed in that direction."

And so they traveled together, Mrs. Rice atop her own mare, which she kept in a shed behind the schoolhouse. It was a scant mile into town, and there they found the sheriff standing in front of his office. Katie told him about Jane.

"Old man Schrader hasn't been out to the ranch, has he?" the sheriff asked when she finished. "I know he's been upset over Jane leaving his farm, asking about her around town. She surely wouldn't head out there."

Katie felt a pang of fear shoot through her at his words. "I can't imagine such a thing. She wouldn't be caught dead within a mile of those people."

"Maybe she didn't have a choice," the sheriff said slowly. "Maybe old man Schrader got real brave and got hold of her when she left the school."

"Should we take a ride out to the Schrader farm and

find out if she's there?" Mrs. Rice asked Katie. "I'm willing to go with you if you want to."

Katie shivered. "It's not my first choice, but if I have to, I will. You know that. I wouldn't want to take the chance of Jane being kept there against her will. That fella's downright mean and Jane isn't strong enough to handle him."

"Is she afraid of him?" the sheriff asked and then as if he knew better he shook his head. "Well, of course she is. He treated her like dirt for a lot of years. Why wouldn't she fear him?"

"I think we'll take a ride out of town, Sheriff," Mrs. Rice said firmly.

"I'll follow you after I take care of a couple of things in my office, and then locate a deputy to bring along," he told her. "Just be real careful not to get within grabbing distance of that man, Katie. He'd like nothing better than to have you in his power and from the looks of you, you don't need anybody treating you rough these days." His gaze swept her form, the fullness of her pregnancy more than obvious.

"I'll look after her, Sheriff," Mrs. Rice told him stoutly. And they set off, their horses at a slow pace, careful not to hurry lest the animals slip on the uneven ground.

Their path took them past the school yard again and then to the west, following the road that led past several farms, where houses showed signs of occupancy, chimneys streaming smoke, lights glowing within their windows.

They had ridden for over thirty minutes, coming to
a hilly area where rocky cliffs stood sentry near the
road, and Mrs. Rice slowed her mare. "I wonder if we
shouldn't wait for help from the sheriff, Katie. It's
going to be full dark before long and we don't want to
be out in the weather once the sun goes down."

Katie nodded reluctantly. "I'm sure you're right,
ma'am. But I just can't go home without her. I just
know she's in trouble of some sort and I'm scared to
death it has something to do with Jacob Schrader."

"That may well be, but we'll be in the same mess if we
get caught on his land and he's in a nasty frame of mind."

Their horses were halted in the middle of the road,
snow blowing past them as the skies began to open up
again with another wintry blast. Katie's frown drew
her brows together and she peered through the falling
snow toward the west. "It's just a short ways down the
road to Schrader's place. Let's at least take a peek at the
barn, in case she's there. We might see her horse
anyway and we'd know where to look for her."

As if against her better judgment, Mrs. Rice nodded
her approval of the scheme and they continued on their
way. Katie worried that John would be frantic when he
arrived home to find her gone.

Surely he would follow her, probably head into town
to seek out her direction and if the sheriff saw him, he'd
let him know where they'd gone. John would have a fit,
sure enough, but she'd deal with him later on. For now,
Jane was her first concern.

The glow of a lantern showed from the barn where Jacob Schrader kept his livestock, and the bulky form of a man was seen making his way to the farmhouse, lantern in hand, barely visible in the blowing snow.

Katie shifted uncomfortably on her mare, aware more than ever of the aching of her back, the occasional pain that lanced through to her belly and seemed to surround the rounding of her child's form.

If she spoke of it to Mrs. Rice, that lady would no doubt turn back to the town road and head for the Stanley ranch, for she would consider it too great a risk for Katie to be caught out in the weather should she go into labor.

Drawing their horses to the side of the road, they watched, almost blinded by the falling snow, yet able to catch sight of a horse heading in their direction from the Schrader's farm.

Quickly, they turned their mounts and went deeper into the line of trees that lined the road, concealing themselves in the thick undergrowth, where tall pines were surrounded by bushes. Dismounting, Katie motioned to Mrs. Rice to leave her mare and follow her on foot.

In their dark clothing they blended into the surrounding thicket and found a shelter amid the heavy undergrowth. Behind them was a sloping hill and it was in that direction that Mrs. Rice pointed, catching Katie's attention. Carefully they crept upward, their movements slow, their attention torn between the sloping terrain before them and the man who rode ever closer behind.

Halfway up the hill, a small opening caught Katie's attention and she headed in that direction, Mrs. Rice at her heels. Shrubbery grew in a thick cover, but Katie pushed aside the branches and made her way within a small enclosure. Behind her, Mrs. Rice crowded close and her voice was a soft whisper.

"I don't think Mr. Schrader can see us in here, Katie. Sit very quietly against the wall and keep low. The branches out there should provide enough cover for us. Surely the sheriff can't be far behind us now."

JOHN RODE ACROSS THE pasture, urging his horse to a rapid pace, for he felt the need to be at home. Perhaps Katie needed him, maybe she was ready to have the baby. He didn't know what drove him on, but there was an urgency in his mind that would not let him be.

Shorty met him at the barn door, a frown on his face, his eyes dark with concern. And his words frightened John as nothing else could have.

The knowledge that Katie was gone, that she was riding astride a horse, even in her condition, was enough to make him angry, and more than that, fearful for her safety.

"Saddle me up a fresh horse, Shorty. I'll follow her to town. Maybe I can catch up with her."

"Doubt it, boss. She's been gone over an hour now. I tried to stop her but she wouldn't listen to me. Started off when it was still daylight and the sun's about at the horizon now. Why don't you hang on a minute, and I'll ride along with you? I should have let this work go and gone with her."

And so it was, with twilight falling around them, they rode out together. John felt a new surge of fear thinking of Katie alone on a horse, yet, more frightening was the consideration that she was not alone, that somehow someone might have found her and taken her with mischief in mind. And if that someone should be Jacob Schrader, it would be more than mere mischief, for the man was demented.

John saw Berta on the porch watching him, her face a mask of anxiety. "Where'd she go, John? Do you know which direction she headed? I saw her leave but she wouldn't stop when I called out to her." She leaned over the porch railing. "Here, take this with you. She'll be hungry when you find her."

John rode closer to her and Berta handed him a bundle wrapped in a dish towel. He stuck it in his pocket and nodded his thanks at the woman.

"I'll find her Berta. Don't worry."

She hurried back into the house, and he rode off toward town. Behind him he heard the sound of another horse and John turned to see Gray Wolf riding hard to catch up to them.

"I'll go with you if it's all right," he called out, as he caught up to ride beside John. "You may need another man with you, and perhaps even another gun if it comes to that."

John nodded briefly, knowing that the man would be

dependable should worst come to worst. Should they have to resort to violence if the girls were being threatened in any way.

They rode toward town and met the sheriff, who was already on his way. He hailed John with an uplifted hand and approached him.

"I saw your wife and the schoolteacher, John. They went out looking for Jane, your wife's sister. They left town a while ago, and I'm on their trail now."

"That's about what I figured happened," John said curtly. "If you want to ride along, the three of us are heading for Jacob Schrader's place. I have a notion that's where we'll find them."

"I'll go with you," the sheriff said quickly. And his horse turned in a half circle as he followed them, taking the road to the west.

THE TWILIGHT SURROUNDED HIM as Jacob drew his horse to a halt at the bottom of the hill and peered around, his figure barely visible to the two women who watched. Katie heard his voice, heard the curse he spewed aloud, and recognized his anger.

She curled even tighter against the wall of the enclosure they'd found, Mrs. Rice beside her as if she would offer her own body as a shield should danger come closer. And then they watched together as Jacob turned his horse and headed back toward the farm buildings that could barely be seen through the falling snow.

"Do you think he gave up on finding us?" Katie whispered, her heart seeming to be lodged in her throat, her voice sounding puny to her ears.

"There's a good chance he thinks we've ridden across the ridge. I'm just thankful our horses are quiet, and didn't give us away. If he'd known we were on foot, he might not have turned around."

Below their vantage point, the trees seemed to blend in with the snow, their branches covered now by the thickly falling white stuff, the world almost seeming a fairyland. How ironic, Katie thought, that such a place of beauty could contain so evil a man as Jacob Schrader.

"I'd think the sheriff should show up soon, don't you?" Katie asked her companion, hoping against hope that Jacob had not made a prisoner of her sister. And yet, she knew, with a deep inner conviction, that the man even now held Jane hostage somewhere on the farm. Probably in the barn. And in that case, the heat from the animals might be enough to keep Jane alive.

If only Jacob left her alone.

Mrs. Rice murmured words of encouragement, her voice soft as she spoke of John and his concern for Katie. "Surely your husband is on our trail already, Katie. When he found you gone from the ranch, you know he set off behind you. He'll have gone to the sheriff by now. I'd lay odds that they're on their way out here. John's a smart man, and he'd know the sort of thing Mr. Schrader would try to pull."

Her arm circled Katie's shoulder, her strength lending its power to the courage that was flagging within Katie's breast. The aching pressure in her back had not ceased but increased to a painful throbbing that seemed to grow in intensity and then ebb away for a few minutes before it once more wound its way through her body to center there at the base of her spine.

"Are you hurting badly, Katie?" Mrs. Rice asked, leaning to peer into her face as Katie stifled a low groan.

"My back's aching something fierce, ma'am. But not more than I can stand."

Mrs. Rice bit her lower lip, as if she held back words that might frighten Katie.

"I think the baby's gonna be making his appearance before the day's over," Katie said quietly, to which the teacher nodded agreement.

"I feared as much," she said with a sigh. "But I'm sure John and the sheriff will be here soon and get this whole thing straightened out. And in the meantime, I'm going to go down the hill to where we left our horses and lead them up here. So long as Jacob didn't find them, they should be over there to the left about a hundred yards or so.

"Will you be all right here alone for a few minutes, Katie? I hate to leave you alone, but if we decide to ride back toward town, it would be handier to have our mares here, close at hand."

"I'm fine," Katie assured her. "Just be careful that Jacob is truly gone back to the farm, and that he doesn't see you." She dug deeply into her pocket and drew forth the gun Shorty had given her. "I know how to shoot, ma'am, and if I have to, I'll use this gun. Don't worry. I'll keep a good eye on you, as much as I can, and watch for Jacob, lest he might have circled back and still be out there nearby."

Mrs. Rice looked stunned at the sight of Katie holding the weapon, but only nodded and crept from the opening in the hillside, making her way down the slope with care. Katie moved closer to the dim light outdoors, her gaze focused on the woman's figure as she worked her way toward where the horses were last seen.

A faint sound reached her then, a muffled thunder of hooves, as if riders were nearing the place where she was hidden, and Katie's breath caught in her throat. Perhaps Jacob had returned. What if Mrs. Rice were even now in danger?

And then she caught sight of five men below the tree line, there where the road led to the Schrader farm. Tall in their saddles, they were but a blur to her eyes, but something about the way the second man held himself made her heart pound harder. As if she recognized him, although it was highly improbable through the falling snow, she knew that John rode with four other men, there on the road a few hundred feet from where she watched.

And then she heard a muffled sound, recognized Mrs. Rice's voice and knew that she had also recognized the men. The five figures halted, turning in their saddles to look up the hillside and then one of them rode toward where Mrs. Rice surely must be.

In moments, the teacher appeared, leading the two mares, the figure of the deputy close behind her. His voice was crisp and his orders clear as he issued a command.

"You ladies stay right here and don't be exposing yourselves, you hear? The sheriff's down there with Shorty and Roper and that Indian friend of his. We're going on to the barn out behind that house and see if we can find the girl." He looked up to where Katie crouched just inside the small cave.

"Are you all right, Mrs. Roper? You haven't been hurt, have you? That husband of yours is havin' a fit, worrying about you."

Katie shook her head, uncertain if the deputy could see her, unsure whether or not he would understand her denial of John's worry. But he seemed to get the message, for he nodded and turned away, leaving Mrs. Rice to lead the two mares toward the cave where Katie sat.

Katie rose, unable to sit longer, hoping for respite from the backache should she stand upright. "I think we should go down the hill and watch from the road," she told Mrs. Rice.

"Katie, don't be so foolish. John and the others can handle things, and they'll feel a whole lot better about us if we're out of danger."

Katie's chin tilted upward as she stepped from the cave's opening. "I'd feel a whole lot better myself, if I knew that Jane was all right, and Jacob hasn't hurt her.

I'll bet he's thinking he's got her back home and he can keep her there."

Mrs. Rice wore a frown, her head shaking a denial to Katie's plan, but when the mare's reins were taken from her hand, she could only watch as Katie led the animal to a low piece of log and then proceeded to climb into the saddle. "Get on board, Mrs. Rice. We're about to watch a rescue."

Her mood bordered on mirth, and Katie felt a new lightness of spirit as she turned her mare, heading down the hill. Behind her, the teacher mounted her own mare, and followed at a slow pace. Fearful of the horse slipping in the snowy leaves beneath her hooves, Katie was careful to rein in the animal and ride carefully until they reached the side of the road.

Ahead of them the lane to the house and beyond it the barn, stretched for several hundred feet, the five horsemen who rode its length staying to one side of the fence line. A row of trees sheltered them somewhat and Katie uttered a silent prayer for their safety as she watched their progress. Abruptly, as if from some signal, they broke into a faster gait, heading for the barn, bending low over their horse's necks as though they would provide as small a target as possible.

Katie reined her horse closer to the lane, her gun held before her. For unbeknownst to the men who rode toward the barn, the door of the house had opened and Jacob Schrader stepped out onto the porch, a shotgun held before him.

The sheriff halted halfway between house and barn and called out stridently. "Jacob Schrader. Come on out here."

From the back porch, Jacob's nasal tones sounded a warning, and Katie shuddered, for John and the other three men were in the direct line of fire. "You're in my sights, Sheriff. I've got my eye on all five of you."

The sheriff spoke quietly to the men with him, and they slid from their mounts, holding the horses between themselves and the man on the porch. As Katie watched, they armed themselves, half crouched for shelter. Jacob laughed raucously from the porch, sounding as if he'd been drinking, and perhaps he had, Katie thought, for he was seldom far from his jug of rotgut.

His shotgun wavered a bit, and he leaned it on the porch railing, kneeling on the floor, the better to take aim at the men and horses before him. Even as she watched, John turned, looking at the barn, then with a quick movement, he ran to the wide doors that stood open and was inside the shadowed interior. A shot rang out from the porch and as she watched, the snow was scattered, blown about by buckshot, a few bits of the ammunition hitting the horses, sending them into a panic.

Katie felt a bolt of fury such as she had never known slice through her and she lifted her reins and kicked the mare into motion, riding quickly toward the house. From the barn a pistol sounded and Jacob jerked as a bullet apparently hit him.

"Katie, get back." It was John's voice and his command was clear, but Katie bent low over the mare's neck and rode to within twenty feet of the house. On the porch, Jacob pulled himself up on the railing, blood streaming from his shoulder, and gripped the shotgun, taking aim in Katie's direction. The weight of the weapon did not allow him to lift it far from the porch, but he managed to rest it on the railing once more and squatted behind it.

Katie pulled her mount to a halt and took aim, her pistol held firmly, her determination that Jacob not fire again at the men in the barn making her braver than she'd thought possible. Taking aim as John had shown her, she fired the gun, at the same time, hearing the sound of the shotgun's blast.

Jacob's body collapsed on the porch again, and beneath Katie, the mare shuddered and then fell to the ground. She crawled from the saddle, hiding behind the mare's bulky body, hearing the animal's snorts of fear and pain.

From the house, Agnes's wail could be heard, and then the door was jerked open and she came out onto the porch. "Damn you, Katie. Damn you. You've kilt him."

Katie's lips formed words she'd never thought to utter, and her whispered wish was fierce. "I hope he's dead. Oh, Lord Almighty, I hope the man is dead."

From the barn, John ran full tilt in her direction and he fell beside her, reaching for her, his hands harsh, his grip unmerciful as he pulled her beneath himself. "Don't fight me, Katie. Just lie still. Agnes has the shotgun now, and she's turning it in this direction."

But from the barn, the sheriff ran toward the house and his voice rang out, catching Agnes's attention. "Put that gun down, lady, or the next bullet fired is gonna have your name on it."

Agnes shrieked loudly, dropped the shotgun and slumped on the porch beside her husband. The sheriff and deputy sped quickly from the barn toward the house, and in seconds had pulled Agnes to one side and silenced her loud cries.

"You all right, Roper? That woman of yours still in one piece?" The sheriff's call was welcome, for Katie was uncertain of the outcome, hidden as she was by John's big body over her.

"We're fine, Sheriff, but I'm gonna get my wife out of here. Can you and your deputy handle things all right?"

John stood, helped Katie to her feet and together they walked toward the porch, Mrs. Rice, still perched on her mare, close at their heels.

"Old man Schrader ain't goin' nowhere," the deputy called out. "Leastwise not till we get him to town to the doctor. Your wife's got a good eye, Roper."

John's voice was low and menacing as he uttered words meant only for Katie's ears. "My wife's in big trouble."

"I want to see Jane," Katie said quietly. "I won't leave till I know she's all right, John. And then we can go home."

His sigh was long, but he nodded, as if he understood

her concern. Turning back to the barn, he shoved the big door open, holding Katie close and leaving Mrs. Rice to follow him inside. The teacher slid from her saddle and was behind them in seconds as they entered the dim interior of the building. From a stall to her right, Katie heard Jane's voice calling, and she went swiftly to where Jane huddled in a corner of a stall.

"She's tied up, John," Katie cried out. "Come turn her loose."

He brushed past Katie and knelt by Jane, bending to cut the bonds that held her hands behind her. The girl sat on the dirty straw, her coat rumpled around her and shivers seized her even as Katie watched.

"Katie, you shouldn't have come here. I was so worried. Jacob said if he caught sight of you he'd snatch you up and you'd be in the same fix as me. I didn't know how I'd get away, but I prayed that John would be taking care of you. And now here you are, with that baby comin' any time now." With a cry of anguish, Katie fell to the straw beside her sister, and her arms reached to encircle Jane's shoulders, even as she placed her fingers against Jane's lips, hushing the words she spoke. Even knowing her sister's concern was for the baby whose birth was imminent, Katie would not have her alarm John any more than necessary.

What Jacob had had in mind for Jane, and perhaps herself was a question she did not want to consider, and she could only be thankful that John had managed to find her and keep her safe.

Now his arms surrounded her and he lifted her from where she knelt beside her sister. "We're going home, Katie girl. Hang on tight, honey."

CHAPTER NINETEEN

MRS. RICE STOOD AT the wide doorway, watching as John carried Katie from the barn, Jane close on their heels. And it was to John that the teacher directed her words.

"You'd better get her home, John," she told him quickly, leaning toward him to look at Katie. Her arm was around his neck, her face buried in his throat and his clasp against her body was firm.

"I wonder if she isn't in labor," he said quietly, and felt Katie's body jerk at his words.

"I'm all right, John. I have a backache, but I just need to get home."

"And I need to get you there. In a hurry, I fear." His anger was subdued, had been quieted by the paleness of her skin, the trembling of her limbs. Yet there was within him a sense of fury that she had managed to elude both Shorty and Berta, the two people he had counted on to keep a close eye on her. He wanted to scold her, was tempted to shake her till her teeth rattled, and knew that he would do neither. For the woman he loved was in his arms, and he could no more hurt her in any way than he could fly to the moon.

For a moment he thought of the past, of the times when he had caused her pain, not physical so much as the pain of harsh words and actions. And he rued each circumstance that rose to his mind, knowing that she was more precious to him than his own life.

And yet, he could not help but speak his mind to her, make her aware of the worry that had filled his thoughts, of the pain he'd felt knowing that she might be at the mercy of Jacob Schrader.

"What were you thinking of, running off that way, Katie? I'd think *you'd* have known better, Mrs. Rice," he spouted, his words stern.

"I couldn't let her go alone," Mrs. Rice said calmly, "and I couldn't stop her from looking for Jane, once she'd decided that Jacob Schrader had her."

"I'm so sorry, John. It's all my fault," Jane sobbed, her head bowed, her clothing disheveled and her eyes red-rimmed. "He caught up with me right after I left the schoolhouse." She'd been brave up until now, John would be willing to warrant, but being rescued had allowed her to give in to her feelings. "I couldn't get away from him. He was holding a gun on me and he said if I gave him a hard time, he'd get Katie. And I couldn't let that happen. He said if I'd just come back to the farm, he'd leave Katie alone."

"We're all of us fine now," Katie said swiftly. She snuggled closer to his chest, her arms holding him tightly with a fierceness he hadn't expected of her. She held back tears, of that he was more than aware and as he held her close, he felt her body stiffen against his, knew a moment of panic as she groaned aloud.

"I think you're right, ma'am. Katie is having labor pains," he said to the teacher. "I don't know much about having babies, but I'd say she's well on her way."

And then he bent his head to peer into her face. "Katie?" John spoke her name. "You all right, honey?" She nodded.

From the back of the house two men called out, Gray Wolf and the deputy, leading horses and heading for the barn. "There's not much more to do here," the deputy told John. "We'll load up Schrader and take him to town in his wagon. His missus will have to go along, I suspect. And you'd better get these women home."

Gray Wolf stepped silently closer to where Jane stood, his dark eyes intent on her.

"Are you hurt?" he wanted to know, his hands touching her shoulders as he spoke, as if he would see for himself that she bore no injuries.

"He didn't have time to hurt me, really. Just tied me up and left me out here while he went in the house to talk to Agnes. They were planning on taking Katie, too, if they could get their hands on her, and leaving here tonight," Jane said simply. "Jacob was feeling pretty smart about having captured me. He knew that Katie would come looking for me, and he was just waiting for her to show up. I don't know what he thought he was going to do with us. He might know we wouldn't stick around any longer than it would take to walk out the door again."

"I don't even want to think what his ideas were, Jane. He's an evil man, and neither of you women need to ever lay eyes on him again. As to messing up his plans, he sure didn't bargain on the sheriff coming along right behind Katie," John said. "He's layin' there on the porch doin' his best to cover his patoot, and the sheriff ain't buyin' it, no way. Jacob told the sheriff that Jane needed a place to stay and she wanted to come back here."

Jane laughed, a taut sound that lacked humor. "Not even on my deathbed would I come here for help," she said firmly.

"Sheriff knows that," John told her. "He's not believing a word the old coot is saying in there. I'd say both the Schraders are going to spend the night in jail and when the judge comes to town they'll be up on charges of kidnaping. It won't go easy for them. Judge Henry wasn't much impressed with them the last time he saw them in his courtroom."

Katie's hold on John's neck tightened, and she stifled a sound that put him in mind of a kitten's cry. "I'm gonna have this baby before you know it, John," she said, and it seemed she swallowed a cry of pain, for her voice trembled. "I need to be getting home to Berta. She said she'd be with me when the baby came."

"I'll take her up on my horse, and make tracks for home," John said to the sheriff, who had approached, leading horses behind him. Katie's grip had crept up into his hair and he winced as her fingertips dug into his scalp. "Turn me loose, love," he said with a laugh. "You're about pullin' my hair out."

"I'm sorry, John. I'm just hurting pretty bad," she murmured, her teeth biting into her bottom lip as she leaned against him, sheltering in his arms.

"I'll take those two up at the house back to town and stick them in a cell," the sheriff said calmly. "I padded Jacob's wounds up good, and he ain't goin' nowhere but where I put him. I reckon Agnes will come along without any trouble. Shorty, why don't you tag along with me and my deputy, and drive their wagon into town. We'll put them in the back and tie your horse on. Katie's horse will need tending, what with that buckshot Jacob let loose at her. We'll take her along with us."

Shorty nodded his compliance, doing as the sheriff asked. Gray Wolf lifted Jane onto his own horse, mounting behind her and setting off. John held Katie before him, his arms enclosing her, riding carefully with Gray Wolf close by.

She clung tightly, and he felt her heart pounding against his wrist as he held her, ruing the need for leaving her alone today. He'd sensed that she was feeling edgy, that her body was not performing as was its usual, but the chores had beckoned and he'd thought that leaving her would be all right for the few hours he'd be gone. Shorty would be handy should she need help and Berta was in the house.

It hadn't turned out as he'd thought, for she'd been having labor pains for who knew how long already and her body was tense and stiff in his arms, growing taut every few minutes, soft sounds of distress coming from her lips.

He bent over her, kissing her forehead, speaking soft words of comfort, promising her to have her in her own bed in less than an hour. In those long minutes he thought of the calamity should she begin to have the baby out here in the open with the cold weather threatening to become even worse, with snow falling at a speed he hadn't counted on.

He rode carefully, lest his horse slip and toss both of them to the ground. His thoughts were upon the words she'd spoken months ago when she'd asked him if he thought there was someone in the heavens who cared for her, who would hear her if she prayed.

He'd glibly said he was sure of it, and now he put it to the test, for his thoughts were on the babe she carried, the tender female form of his wife who bore the responsibility of birthing his son or daughter. He even prayed that if Katie was set on a girl that God would send her one, that he'd do without a son, so long as Katie was happy, so long as she survived this night.

"John, I hurt so bad," she whispered softly. "I didn't know it would hurt this bad so early on in my labor. I thought just at the end it would be this painful." She stiffened against him as she spoke and he heard the tortured sound she could not contain.

"Ah, baby, we'll be there in no time. Just hang on, sweetheart. It will be all right."

And yet, he worried that it would not be all right, and though the words came to him easily, the torment of her pain filled him with despair. If something happened to Katie, he would not survive, for she meant more than the world to him, and he wondered suddenly if he'd ever let her know how much he cared for her.

He'd told her how lovely she was, how much he desired her, but he couldn't recall now if he'd declared his love for her, and with a cry from his heart, he knew that he must let her know right now how important she was to him.

"Katie, look up at me, baby. I need to tell you something and I want you to know that I mean it, honey. I love you, Katie. If I've never let you know before, I want you to know now that you're the most important thing in the world to me. I'm so sorry for all my meanness and ornery behavior and—"

She lifted her hand, placing her fingers over his lips as a smile curved her lips. "John, don't spoil what you just told me by trying to make amends for things that are in the past. If you love me, that's all that matters, for I can't live without you. I want to be a good wife to you and a good mother to your child, and if it's a boy, it'll be all right. We'll just have to have another in a couple of years." She frowned then as another pain seized her and she cried out, edging her bottom from his lap.

"Maybe I'll think about that," she said with a frown. And then she was quiet as they made their way to the ranch, John guiding his horse down the rutted road, careful to keep from the patches where snow had drifted in deeper billows of white stuff.

The lane appeared before him then, and he turned his gelding with a movement of the reins, the faithful horse obeying the silent command. "We're almost there, Katie," he whispered, looking down at her face that had become pale with the pain she endured. "If I could take the pain from you, I would, sweetheart."

It was the cry of his heart and he blessed her forehead and temple with his lips, needing, wanting to show her in some small way how he ached for what she suffered.

He knew that Katie had enjoyed being with child up to this moment, that she had faced each day eagerly, sewing small items for the baby to wear, no matter the pains in her back, the aching muscles beneath the load she bore. She had not complained, only thanked him fervently when he rubbed her back, purred when his hands massaged the firm rounding of her belly.

Berta came out on the porch as he neared the house and he shouted at her, bidding her come to the cabin. "Katie's having pains, Berta," he said, feeling helpless.

His horse stopped before the back porch and he eased Katie back to the saddle, then swung his leg over the horse's back and stood on the ground. With quick movements he lifted her, holding her in his arms as he stepped onto the porch. Before he could reach for the door, Berta was there, holding the door wide, helping with eager hands as he eased his burden over the threshold.

He carried her to the bedroom and she stood at the side of the wide bed. "Lie down, sweetheart," he said, attempting to make her sit on the side of the mattress. But she had other ideas and she shook her head with a determination he had to smile at.

"I want to undress first. My clothes are all dirty, John. I want to wash up and put my nightgown on before I get the sheets dirty."

"They'll be a mess by the time this is over anyway," Berta said with a wide grin. "Come on, sweetie. I'll help you get ready. You go on out and fetch her a cup of tea, John. She's gonna need it right soon. Once I get her lying down flat I'll go over to the house and get some dried herbs that'll help with her pains."

With Berta's help, Katie was tucked beneath a sheet and then the waiting began. She heard a horse outside the cabin, heard Jane's voice and knew that her sister had returned with Gray Wolf. And wasn't that an interesting development? It pleased her that the man seemed interested in Jane, for he was a fine, talented fella, John had said. Able to take orders and capable of giving them when the occasion arose.

And now he'd brought Jane home and Katie felt a wave of thanksgiving that her family was gathered once more beneath the same roof, that John and Jane would both be here for the birth of her baby.

And with that thought, she was seized once more by a wave of pain that threatened to bring not only tears to her eyes, but a moan from her lips. John came into the room, the cup of tea in his hands, his gaze sweeping over Katie's form on the bed, and he dropped to his knees beside her. The tea was settled on the table by the bed and John's hands reached for his wife.

"I don't know if I can stand seeing you in pain, Katie. This is all my fault, and I've already about pulled my hair out, what with you hurting so bad."

"I'm fine, John," she said, catching her breath as the pain eased, her belly softening as the waves receded and left her for a moment. "These pains are coming faster than I'd thought they would. Berta said I'm doing just fine, and she'll be back here in just a minute with something to help me."

"I think I'd better send someone to town for the doctor," John said. "I know Berta's got all the know-how, but it seems like it'd be a good idea to have Doc Benson come on out and see to things."

The front door opened and then closed behind her as Berta came back in the cabin. She stood in the doorway of the bedroom and her eyes darted to where John knelt by Katie's side. "Why don't you send Ben or one of the other men to town, John? I'd think this would be a good place for Doc Benson."

"That's what I just told Katie," he said, rising and

bending low to press his lips on Katie's forehead, patting her hand briefly as he headed for the kitchen and then on out onto the porch.

Katie heard his strong voice call out to Ben and in moments there was a hubbub of sorts in the yard as Ben called for a horse to be saddled and made ready. Jane came in the back door and called out to Katie, telling her she would get hot water ready for washing up and for the doctor to use when he got there.

"I think everything's under control, isn't it?" Katie asked Berta, her voice a whisper as she felt another surging pain grip her belly, causing it to contract and rise, the baby within her quiet for the first time in weeks. She'd had so much movement over the past months that it seemed strange now for her child to be so still.

She said as much to Berta, fearful that there might be something wrong that would cause the baby not to move about as it had done of late. Berta only laughed, explaining that it was just resting up for the big push and before they knew it, there'd be a young'un right there in the bed, squalling its head off.

Katie laughed softly at the explanation, thinking privately that it couldn't happen any too soon to suit her. It seemed that the pains were coming closer, one almost on top of the last, and she was perspiring and uncomfortable, her back aching to beat the band and the vise that seemed to enclose her belly was clamping down harder with each contraction that drew her whole body into a knot that radiated pain.

Berta sat beside her, instructing her to roll to her side, then rubbing the tender spot below her waist with a sturdy hand. It relieved the aching and Katie was grateful for her friend's understanding touch. "This would be a good job for John," Berta said. "I'll warrant he'll be back inside here in a few minutes and we'll put him to work, keeping you comfortable."

"I don't know if he'll want to be in here," Katie said softly, glancing at the doorway, remembering John's words about the pain she was enduring. "This is hard on him, Berta."

And then she was gripped by another gathering contraction, one that seemed to enclose the entire area where the babe lay, the pain holding her in its grip for long minutes. It seemed more like an hour to Katie, who shivered with a chill and found herself curling in a ball, her belly feeling as if it were too large for her skin to contain.

"I don't know if I can do this," she whispered to Berta, taking deep breaths as the pain eased, and then at Berta's encouraging smile, she watched as John came back in the room. "You don't have to be here, John," she said, worried that he would not be able to stand seeing the events to come.

Without pause, he came to the bedside, knelt beside her and tugged her to face him, his big hand circling her waist, pressing against the sore spot low on her back, and making circling motions with his wide palm. "I was here when we started that baby, Katie. I'll be here when it's born. There's nothing that could keep me away from you, sweetheart. I hate to see you hurting, but I'm not about to walk away and leave you to face this on your own."

Thanksgiving rushed through her as he spoke, and she attempted a smile even as another pain settled its grip on her. John's hand took up the circling movement again on her back and he bent low to whisper in her ear as she groaned aloud. "I'm here, Katie. I won't leave you, no matter what."

She'd begun to think that this task she'd taken on with such joy would never end when she heard the doctor's voice at the door. He came in the bedroom, shot her a quick look and then rolled up his shirtsleeves, heading for the bowl of hot water that Jane poured for his use. He scrubbed for long minutes, and when he'd finished, he dried off on the clean towel Berta handed him, turning to the bed.

"Well, young lady, let's see how far you've come. Looks to me like you won't be a whole lot longer at this."

And how he could tell that, Katie didn't know, but she surely hoped he was right. His hands were sure and comforting as he examined her and she held tightly to John's fingers during the ordeal, then smiled as she heard the words the doctor spoke.

"Another few pushes ought to do it, Katie. We'll have this baby born in no time at all."

He was right, for within fifteen minutes John was

called on to hold his son. Wrapped in a length of flannel, the dark-haired infant was crying up a storm, his eyes squinted tightly shut, his mouth wide as he protested the indignity of birth.

Katie inspected him quickly, kissed his damp head and then watched as Berta took him to the dry sink where she washed him and then found safety pins and a diaper to cover his bottom. A small gown, one Katie had made herself, was brought from the chest of drawers and tiny arms were slid in place, the buttons done up quickly and then another clean blanket put to use, swaddling the tiny creature into a bundle that Katie welcomed with a laugh of pure pleasure.

CHAPTER TWENTY

THE SHERIFF SENT WORD that he had wired to Judge Henry, and that man would appear in Eden as soon as he completed a trial he was involved in. Another messenger arrived just days later, announcing that Judge Henry was prepared to head a hearing involving Jacob and Agnes Schrader in the sheriff's office in Eden on Friday and asking that Katie, Jane and Mrs. Rice make an appearance.

John's concern was for Katie's health, for her days of lying in were not complete and Berta had been adamant that ten days was the shortest length of time for a woman to take to her bed after childbirth. Katie, on the other hand, was dead certain she was ready to go to town to testify at the hearing, no matter that it had been just a week since the birth of her son. And so, at the behest of the judge, John wrapped Katie in an enveloping quilt, after covering her with her cloak, and carried her to the buggy for the ride to Eden.

Jane and Mrs. Rice, who had arrived at the ranch early that morning, not wanting to attend the hearing alone, would follow on horseback, accompanied by

Bill Stanley, who seemed to have taken a shine to the schoolteacher.

Gray Wolf, who had been a silent shadow during the events, volunteered his services and accompanied the women along with Bill, and together they trailed behind the buggy, as soon as breakfast was over.

Katie held the small bundle containing her son beneath the folds of her cloak, rocking him in her arms and peeking beneath the blanket every few minutes to be certain that he was warm and well curtained from the wind. Berta had told her that catching a sudden waft of breeze could cause colic, and Katie was vigilant, not knowing what was involved in the disorder, but determined that her child would not fall prey to such a thing.

The sheriff's office was filled to overflowing, what with all the participants from the Stanley ranch, the two prisoners from the jail and the sheriff, who was determined that the couple would never again cause problems in his town.

Judge Henry bent a benevolent eye on Katie, making much of her child and offering a hand of congratulations to John. "I'm pleased that you got your marriage in order, Mr. Roper. Katie seems to be in good health and your son has a hearty set of lungs from what I've heard this morning."

Katie had gone into a back room to nurse the baby, his impatient cries making it a necessity for such a thing to take place, and accompanied by Berta, she fed young John and then returned to the makeshift court-room.

On one side of the room, Jacob and Agnes Schrader stood silently, enveloped in gloom, their eyes seemingly glued to the floor as the charges against them were read.

The judge was not kindly today, his wrath a frightful thing to Katie's eyes, for he charged both of the Schraders with kidnaping. For, even though Agnes had not participated in the actual event, her involvement made her an accessory, and as such she was as guilty as Jacob.

They moved to stand before the judge and Jacob swore that Jane had sought refuge with him, wanting to come back home to live. With a dubious look, the judge called Jane forward and her testimony rang clear and true as she told of the events of that day, when Jacob had taken her captive and dragged her into his barn, tying her in the stall to await nightfall when he and Agnes would load up their belongings in the wagon and leave town, taking Jane with them. Jacob had expressed his anger at Katie, long and loudly, and Jane said he'd groused that he'd not been able to get his hands on her, too. His need for revenge against the girls for running off seemed to have made him demented, for he rambled on to himself as Jane spoke to the judge.

The judge shook his head at such wickedness, his glare settling on Jacob as he decreed that the crime was punishable by imprisonment at the facility designated for those in the Dakota Territory who broke such laws.

Agnes was given a lesser sentence, but neither of them would be allowed within fifty miles of Eden or wherever Katie and Jane were living at the time of their release from prison.

Chastised severely for his grumbling at the sentencing, Jacob was led to a cell, Agnes admitted to the other empty space in the jail and then the judge stood behind the sheriff's desk and made his statement to Katie, Jane and Mrs. Rice.

"The law finds that you have all been victims of Jacob and Agnes Schrader and henceforth you will be under the protection of whatever judicial territory you reside within. If you remain here in Eden, you are under the protection of the sheriff here, and since you tell me that Jane will be going to the State Normal School next September, the authorities in that area will be notified to keep a keen eye on her in order to protect her."

Katie sat down in the chair behind her, the babe in her arms weighing her down, her body giving way to the ordeal of the day. John bent to her, whispering words of comfort, and Judge Henry spoke to them, as they looked up at his bidding.

"I can only say that I'm mighty pleased that the earlier hearing held in this office went as it did for you, Mr. Roper. You have a fine wife and child and your marriage seems to have been the best move we could have offered you. I congratulate you on your lovely wife and baby and offer my best regards to you all."

John shuffled his feet a bit, feeling embarrassed by

the words of praise, and Katie merely beamed her happiness as she heard the kindly judge offer his blessing on their marriage.

The office emptied out in minutes then, the hotel restaurant being the place of choice for their noontime meal. Before long, they were gathered around a group of hastily shoved-together tables, and white-aproned women flocked around them to take their orders for the meal.

"This is a celebration like we should have had when you got married, John." Bill Stanley stood and lifted his water glass in a salute to the young man who had fulfilled his duties so well at the ranch, and offered his congratulations on the couple's new son and their first anniversary of the wedding entered into here in town just a year since.

"I'd forgotten it was so close to our anniversary date," Katie whispered to John. "It's been a bit more than a year now, but we didn't even celebrate, did we?"

"I celebrate every day of our life together, Katie." His words were soft, unheard by any of the others who had gathered around the table, but to Katie they were like manna to her ears, an acknowledgment of his love and a promise for the future.

They rode home in a caravan, Jane beside Gray Wolf, Mrs. Rice having been left at the boardinghouse where she stayed during the school year. Jane was elated at the thought of completing the school year without fear of being accosted on her way to and from town.

Mrs. Rice had told her that letters had been written on her behalf by three of the local citizens who felt she was worthy of a scholarship and her own recommendation had accompanied them to the state board for consideration. She would know within weeks as to her financial help from the school and would have the whole summer to prepare for her entry examinations. A situation that pleased Jane immensely, for she would be able to help Katie with the baby during these early months of his life.

DURING THE LONG DAYS of summer, life began to resume its normal events. Gray Wolf did not allow his obvious feelings for Jane to become an issue between them, only watched her as might an older brother. He spoke one day at length with Bill Stanley and at the end of their conversation the two men shook hands and parted ways, Gray Wolf heading behind the barn to where his work with the young horses awaited him, Bill to the cabin where John had paused for his noontime meal.

With a single rap at the door, Bill entered, accepting the traditional cup of coffee offered to him by Katie, who was in the midst of putting the meal together. He settled at the table and his gaze shot to where Jane worked at the sink. And then he spoke to John.

"Gray Wolf will be here permanently, if that's all right with you, John. I told him before that he could stay on and work with the horses and help with roundup and branding—all the things that go on. But I wanted to clear it with you. We settled on a wage and he'll be living in the bunkhouse with the other men. Does that meet with your approval?"

John grinned widely. "All the men like Gray Wolf and he'll come in right handy with working on the new addition to the barn. We'll be needing more stalls and the only way to do it is to add on to the back, as far as I can see. What do you think?"

Bill nodded. "I've been considering the same thing, and we'll just put Gray Wolf in charge of the project. I'll ask him to draw up some plans and we can look them over next week."

John was in accord with Bill's suggestions, and when Katie and Jane put the meal on the table, Bill agreeably decided to stay for the soup and corn bread they offered. A quick message sent to Berta at the big house notified her of her boss's absence from her table, and things were settled.

They ate quickly, for much awaited their hands during the afternoon. New calves were being herded together for branding, the young bullocks being separated for the necessary task that was to be their destiny. One the men did not relish, but knew to be necessary on a ranch.

The newest of the foals were set loose in the pasture today, the weather being deemed warm enough to warrant their escape from the stalls inside. New birth was to be found everywhere on the ranch with the coming of spring, and Katie had announced it was time to open the windows and doors and let the warm air blow through the cabin.

The sun shone brightly, the breeze was gentle and Katie took young John outdoors to take his nap on a blanket beneath a tree. She settled beside him, covering him well from the prevailing westerly breeze and read a book while he slept. Before long, her own eyes were closing and she curled beside the babe, pulling him into the shelter of her embrace as she tucked his blanket around him and bent to press soft kisses on his head. The joys of mothering were many and sweet and she cherished each day and hour she spent with her child.

It was there that John found them as he finished up his chores and headed for the cabin to wash up. Jane came out onto the porch as he made his way from the barn and he pointed to where Katie slept and put a finger across his lips, motioning Jane to silence, lest Katie awaken and recognize that the afternoon had slipped away from her.

Jane went back into the cabin then and watched as John settled beside Katie on the quilt, his big body curled behind hers, his arms encircling her waist and the babe she held, holding them against himself.

He propped his head on his hand and watched his wife, enjoying the half smile she wore, wondering at the dreams that passed through her mind, simply enjoying the few moments of peace they shared beneath the apple tree.

And then Katie awoke, moved her hand to find John's

fingers and brought his callused palm to her lips, pressing her mouth against his toughened flesh. "Hey there, Mr. Roper. What are you doing out here in the shade?"

"Just enjoying my wife and son," John said easily, his hand brushing her cheek, then bending over her the better to catch a glimpse of the child she held against herself. "He's growing like a weed, isn't he?"

She laughed, turning her head to look into his eyes. "What a thing to say about your son. He's growing all right, but he's getting more like his father every day. Just look at those long fingers and the size of his feet. And that crop of black hair."

Katie preened as she listed the merits of her child, and John felt a thrill of appreciation for the gifts he'd been blessed with. A wife who loved him, a child to nurture and raise to manhood and a home filled with love and laughter.

"Katie, sweetheart…it just don't get no better than this, does it?" he asked quietly, his mouth touching her forehead and cheek with kisses that spoke of his love and commitment.

She turned her head a bit, the better to see him and her smile was a beacon that drew him. "John, I'm just so happy with you, with little John and all we have here together. I don't know how to tell you how much it all means to me."

"You don't need to, Katie girl. I can tell when I look at you just how happy you are, how much you enjoy your life."

He moved back a bit and rolled her to her back, the baby settling against her breast as he was shifted in tandem with his mother. Then he bent again, his lips touching hers, then moving to where his son lay, curling into a sleeping bundle of beauty that John could barely believe was their very own.

"I love you, Katie," he whispered, his kisses warm against her face, his long body warming the length of hers as he bent to her. "But we need to get up from here and get ourselves in the house, or I'm gonna be all over you like flies on honey, and that'll never do, right out here in the middle of the yard."

Katie blushed and lifted herself and her son to a sitting position, then handed the baby to John and rose from the quilt, gathering her book and folding the blanket to carry them to the cabin.

Jane was busy at the stove and her glance at the couple who joined her in the kitchen was filled with pleasure. "You two get that baby settled down and wash up. I'll have supper ready in about a half hour."

Settling the baby in his crib was easily done, and then they went to the kitchen, Katie helping with setting the table, Jane dishing up the food she'd prepared and John settling into his chair with a sigh. It had been a long day involving hours of hard work, and ending with a most satisfactory few moments beneath the tree outdoors with his wife and their son. Only more joy beckoned in the hours to come and he looked up to where Katie carried bowls to the table, then paused by his side.

His hand curved to cup her waist and he drew her closer as Jane turned back to the stove. Careful not to be intimate before others, he merely looked up with a wide grin, knowing that Katie read his thoughts, and was offered a saucy look in return.

And as he ate, he considered the weeks and months of the future that stretched before him, the happiness he would find here in this cabin with the woman he'd been smart enough to marry.

And when the night hours were upon them, he spoke those same thoughts into her ear, curled together in their bed, the starlight shining through their window, finding them entwined as was their wont, enjoying the final hours of their day.

"I love you, John."

It was the one truth he lived for, the joy of his life, and John Roper held his wife close as he offered up thanks for the joy he'd found with her.

EPILOGUE

THE SUMMER PASSED QUICKLY, and one of its surprises involved the arrival one day of Tom Loftin at the ranch. His visit was a time of awakening for the young woman who had thought that her paternity would forever be unknown to her.

He came to the porch where she sat, and dismounted from his horse, settling on the top step and watching her as she snapped fresh green beans from the garden.

"What can I do for you, Tom," she asked, curiosity winning out over her natural good manners, which would not have allowed her to ask his business in such a way.

"I think it's maybe more what I can do for you, Katie," he said, folding his hands over his knee and leaning back against the post behind him. "I've been putting this visit off for a while, but between Molly and me, we decided it was past time for you and me to have a talk."

Katie was perplexed at his meaning, but smiled and waited for him to continue. She'd rarely spoken to the man, only three times in her memory had he said words to her, and now, she could not understand his interest in having this conversation.

"I've got something to tell you, Katie. I probably should wait till your husband shows up this afternoon to spill this news, but maybe it'll be better with just the two of us here.

"You know that your mother and I were friends, years back when she worked in the saloon. She was a woman worthy of marriage and I was the fool who didn't offer my hand to her. Even when I knew she carried my child, I kept my silence and when you were born I didn't suggest that she put my name on your birth records."

Katie swallowed hard and her eyes filled with tears, unable to absorb the story Tom related to her, yet somehow unsurprised at his words. She'd felt a strange link between them, but thought it was because she had known him as a little girl. Now he'd told her facts that changed her perception of her life and left her with an emptiness within.

"Your mama gave birth to you and asked if she could keep you with her and I told her she could do as she pleased. I loved her, Katie. Claire was a special lady and if I'd been more of a man I'd have married her and given you a decent home. But when your mama died, I figured I couldn't provide for you and I made arrangements for you to go to a family I thought would love you and take care of you."

He lifted his gaze and it pinned her where she sat. "I was wrong, Katie. They were brutes and I didn't recognize it. I'd never heard gossip and they were respected folks. Didn't take the time to check on you and make sure you were taken care of as you should be. It wasn't till that night in the saloon when John Roper brought you back to the kitchen that I realized the life you'd led.

"I'm sorry, girl. I can't tell you any other way but that. I'm your father and I failed you. I should have taken better care of you, and I was wrong to do what I did. The only thing I can do now is ask you for your forgiveness and go on from here. I'd like to see the child you bore to John Roper. I understand I have a grandson, and it would give me great pleasure if I could be a small part of his life."

Katie was stunned by his words, her mind whirling at the news he'd brought to her. And as she tried to absorb the things he'd said, John walked from the barn, lifting a hand in greeting to Tom.

"I wondered how long it would take you to find your way out here," he said soberly. "I figured you'd be wanting to take a look at that baby inside the cabin before too long."

Tom stood and nodded at him. "You're right, John Roper. I've just asked Katie if I can be a part of my grandson's life."

"And what did she say?" John asked quietly.

"She hasn't said anything yet," Tom told him, casting an imploring glance at the woman who watched them both from her perch on the porch.

"Well," Katie began, sorting out her thoughts as she

went, "I'd say that baby in there can use all the relations he's got, and if his grandpa wants to meet him and make friends, I'd be the last one to put a stop to it."

Tom looked up at Katie, as if his best dream had come true and with two long steps he stood before her, grasping her hand, pulling her to her feet.

"I can't tell you how much that means to me, girl. I'd like to make up for a lot of things, beginning with the way I messed up your life. I want you to know that me and Miss Molly are getting hitched and setting up a place in town. I've sold the saloon and made enough money to keep that woman for the rest of her life. We're gonna have an extra bedroom ready for our grandson when he's old enough to come spend the night with his grandpa and grandma, if that's all right with you."

Katie's eyes filled again with tears and she sought John with an outstretched hand. He came to her, as he always had, readily and gladly, holding her in his embrace. "What do you think, John?"

He looked down into her face and his eyes were shiny with a trace of tears. "Our son sure can use a set of grandparents close by. It'll be a long time till he sees any of my family, and in the meantime, he'll be spoiled rotten by Tom and Molly, if I've got it figured out right."

Tom stepped onto the porch and his big hand held the screen doorknob. "Can I go in and see my grandson, Katie?"

"Sure, go on ahead. He's about ready to wake from

his nap and he'll need someone to hold him once I get his diaper changed and get him ready for his next meal."

"I've been waiting a lot of years to practice on just that thing," Tom said with a wide grin, opening the door and crossing the kitchen floor to where soft snuffling sounds were coming from the bedroom beyond.

On the porch, John held Katie close. "Are you happy, my Katie?"

And she only nodded and lifted her face for his kiss. "I've finally got a father, John. I didn't realize how important that was until I had little John. Knowing that he was a part of you and would forever be your son made me more aware of my own empty past. Tom has no idea how happy he's made me today."

"Oh, I think he'll figure it out right soon, girl. Let's you and me go on in there now and watch this family reunion. I think it's gonna be the finest time we've had since we got married. All but the moment when our son was born."

And in the next hour, Katie was tempted to agree, for she found that watching the three men in her life, her father, husband and son, was the greatest joy to have come to her in all the years she'd lived.

And when the day was done, and Tom had gone back to town, Jane had gone to her room to bed and the baby was settled in his crib, she spoke the words to John that had dwelled in her mind for the past months.

"I'm so glad that you rescued me, John, that you took me home and then married me. I can't tell you how wonderful my life is here with you. And now, we have even more to look forward to, with Tom and Molly in our lives."

"The best part of it all is that we've managed to build our own Eden right here in this place, Katie. Remember the night we talked about the Garden of Eden and how perfect it was for the man and woman who lived there? Well, I'm certain that we can be as happy in our own Eden as they could have been in theirs. What do you think?"

She laughed softly. "If this is Eden, then it's right next door to Heaven, John. For I don't know how much happier I could be than I am, right here with you."

His arms held her close then, his voice was a whisper in her ear and his hands moved against her flesh with knowing touches, coaxing her to a time of loving that would make this day complete.

It was late when the moon found them there, together in the big bed, their kisses and caresses seeming fresher and more splendid than ever before as their bodies blended in celebrating this day of new beginnings.

THE FIRST LADY OF THE WEST,
NEW YORK TIMES BESTSELLING AUTHOR

LINDA LAEL MILLER

BRINGS YOU A RIVETING NEW TRILOGY

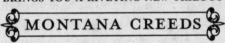

MONTANA CREEDS

Descendants of the legendary McKettrick family,
the Creed brothers couldn't wait to leave small-town
life behind. But now they're back, ready to raise
a little hell—and Stillwater Springs, Montana,
will never be the same.

February 2009   March 2009   April 2009

"Linda Lael Miller creates vibrant characters
and stories I defy you to forget."
—#1 *New York Times* bestselling author
Debbie Macomber

HQN™

We *are* romance™

www.HQNBooks.com

PHLLMT2009

REQUEST YOUR FREE BOOKS!

2 FREE NOVELS
FROM THE ROMANCE/SUSPENSE
COLLECTION PLUS 2 FREE GIFTS!

YES! Please send me 2 FREE novels from the Romance/Suspense Collection and my 2 FREE gifts (gifts are worth about $10). After receiving them, if I don't wish to receive any more books, I can return the shipping statement marked "cancel." If I don't cancel, I will receive 4 brand-new novels every month and be billed just $5.49 per book in the U.S. or $5.99 per book in Canada, plus 25¢ shipping and handling per book plus applicable taxes, if any*. That's a savings of at least 20% off the cover price! I understand that accepting the 2 free books and gifts places me under no obligation to buy anything. I can always return a shipment and cancel at any time. Even if I never buy another book from the Reader Service, the two free books and gifts are mine to keep forever.

185 MDN EF5Y 385 MDN EF6C

Name	(PLEASE PRINT)
Address	Apt. #
City	State/Prov.	Zip/Postal Code

Signature (if under 18, a parent or guardian must sign)

Mail to **The Reader Service:**
IN U.S.A.: P.O. Box 1867, Buffalo, NY 14240-1867
IN CANADA: P.O. Box 609, Fort Erie, Ontario L2A 5X3

Not valid to current subscribers to the Romance Collection,
the Suspense Collection or the Romance/Suspense Collection.

Want to try two free books from another line?
Call 1-800-873-8635 or visit www.morefreebooks.com.

* Terms and prices subject to change without notice. N.Y. residents add applicable sales tax. Canadian residents will be charged applicable provincial taxes and GST. Offer not valid in Quebec. This offer is limited to one order per household. All orders subject to approval. Credit or debit balances in a customer's account(s) may be offset by any other outstanding balance owed by or to the customer. Please allow 4 to 6 weeks for delivery. Offer available while quantities last.

Your Privacy: Harlequin is committed to protecting your privacy. Our Privacy Policy is available online at www.eHarlequin.com or upon request from the Reader Service. From time to time we make our lists of customers available to reputable third parties who may have a product or service of interest to you. If you would prefer we not share your name and address, please check here. ☐

BOB08R

HARLEQUIN® *Blaze*™

Make Me Yours

by *New York Times* bestselling author

BETINA KRAHN

Between a prince and a hot body...

The Prince of Wales chooses Mariah Eller for the "honor" of becoming his next mistress. However, she needs to be married in order for the affair to proceed, so he tasks his friend, Jack St. Lawrence, with finding Mariah a husband. But little does the prince know that Jack has found a husband for Mariah—*himself!*

Available in July wherever books are sold.

red-hot reads

CAROLYN DAVIDSON

77220	THE BRIDE	___ $6.99 U.S.	___ $8.50 CAN.
77285	NIGHTSONG	___ $6.99 U.S.	___ $8.50 CAN.
77179	HAVEN	___ $6.99 U.S.	___ $8.50 CAN.
77149	REDEMPTION	___ $5.99 U.S.	___ $6.99 CAN.

(limited quantities available)

TOTAL AMOUNT	$ _____
POSTAGE & HANDLING	$ _____
($1.00 FOR 1 BOOK, 50¢ for each additional)	
APPLICABLE TAXES*	$ _____
TOTAL PAYABLE	$ _____

(check or money order—please do not send cash)

To order, complete this form and send it, along with a check or money order for the total above, payable to HQN Books, to: **In the U.S.:** 3010 Walden Avenue, P.O. Box 9077, Buffalo, NY 14269-9077; **In Canada:** P.O. Box 636, Fort Erie, Ontario, L2A 5X3.

Name: _____
Address: _____ City: _____
State/Prov.: _____ Zip/Postal Code: _____
Account Number (if applicable): _____

075 CSAS

*New York residents remit applicable sales taxes.
*Canadian residents remit applicable GST and provincial taxes.

HQN™

We *are* romance™

www.HQNBooks.com

PHCD0309BL